DEATH
IN A
BYGONE
HUE

DEATH IN A BYGONE HUE

AN ART CENTER MYSTERY

SUSAN VAN KIRK

LEVEL
BEST BOOKS

First published by Level Best Books 2023

Copyright © 2023 by Susan Van Kirk

This novel is entirely a work of fiction. The names, characters and incidents portrayed in it are the work of the author's imagination. Any resemblance to actual persons, living or dead, events or localities is entirely coincidental.

Susan Van Kirk asserts the moral right to be identified as the author of this work.

Author Photo Credit: Kent Kriegshauser Photography

First edition

ISBN: 978-1-68512-336-9

This book was professionally typeset on Reedsy.
Find out more at reedsy.com

Praise for Death in a Bygone Hue

"Susan Van Kirk takes the cozy mystery into a new arena—an art gallery in a small midwestern city—and weaves fascinating information about the art world into a tale of murder, inheritance, Vietnam vets, and just a touch of romance. Fine reading as well as fine art."—Judy Alter, author of Irene in Chicago Culinary Mysteries

"A well-crafted mystery filled with twists and turns that keeps you guessing until the end. Van Kirk's page-turner effortlessly combines murder in the high-stakes world of art and art fraud with the heart of small-town life and family. Apple Grove is a place you won't want to leave."—Kait Carson, author of the Hayden Kent Mysteries

"This colorful cozy mystery has it all—textured characters, a well-sculpted plot, and a fascinating behind-the-scenes peek into the art world. A charming whodunit readers won't want to miss!"—Lori Roberts Herbst, author of the Callie Cassidy mystery series

"Judge Ron Spivey has been a great help to Jill Madison in opening her art center in the Midwest town of Apple Grove. But when Jill finds out that she, and neither of the judge's nasty children, will be executor of his estate, autumn feels a lot chillier. And much more dangerous. Is the image of the small, charming town ruined? A bright spot might turn out to be Dr. Sam Finch, an ER doctor with warm hands and an interest, it seems, in something more than being helpful. Toss in some shocking revelations judiciously scattered throughout the story, and the hues brighten up, but not in a good way."—Kaye George, author of Stroke, the fourth Imogene

Duckworthy mystery

"Susan Van Kirk's newest Art Center Mystery, *Death in a Bygone Hue*, is painted with a wide brush of intrigue starting with the suspicious death of Jill Madison's close friend, Judge Spivey. Van Kirk's artistic skill entangles the reader in a complex journey through the judge's professional life and personal secrets, and after the will is revealed, disgruntled children create a toxic situation targeting Jill. This, along with turmoil at the art center, an unscrupulous journalist, and a new doctor in town, makes for a "masterpiece" of engaging mystery, diverse relationships, and a strong, clever female lead: Jill Madison. It's a personal favorite no one should miss!"—Kathleen Costa, reviewer for *Kings River Life*

"In *Death in a Bygone Hue*, Susan Van Kirk shines a spotlight on greed, murder, and art fraud in an otherwise idyllic town. Don't miss this beautifully written and intriguing book."—Grace Topping, *USA Today* bestselling author of the Laura Bishop Mystery Series and Agatha Award finalist

"In *Death in a Bygone Hue*, Susan Van Kirk has created a delightful heroine, whom I sincerely want to hang out with, as well as a plot packed with so many twists, turns, and surprises that, at some point, I suspected *everyone*! Well written and highly entertaining, it kept me enthralled and guessing until the very end."—Annette Dashofy, *USA Today* bestselling author of the Zoe Chambers Mysteries

"From accusations of cover-ups and special interests to vividly described events that often impart a wry undercurrent of humor, Van Kirk creates many compelling twists and turns cemented by a sense of person, place, and ironic introspection...Libraries and readers seeking a stand-alone mystery that both supports the prior book and crafts new intrigue as Jill settles into her role and navigates the dangerous politics of her hometown will find *Death in a Bygone Hue* a delight."—D. Donovan, Senior Reviewer, *Midwest Book Review*

"I've loved all Susan Van Kirk's books, but *Death in a Bygone Hue* may be my new favorite. Jill Madison, director of Apple Grove's new art center, is planning her first national art exhibit when she finds the body of Judge Ron Spivey, her friend and mentor. Did he die of natural causes or is something more sinister at play? As Jill's police-detective brother heads up the official investigation, Jill learns she has been named executor of the judge's estate and his primary beneficiary. That doesn't sit well with the judge's greedy son and daughter. The mystery deepens when Jill begins going through the judge's papers and finds disturbing secrets from the past. Beautifully written and seamlessly plotted, *Death in a Bygone Hue* combines a smart and engaging heroine with an irresistible mystery and a pulse-pounding ending."—Connie Berry, *USA Today* bestselling author of the Kate Hamilton Mysteries and Edgar Award Nominee

Chapter One

L ife was filled with unpredictable people like my brother Andy. I liked that. Then I considered those others. Those terribly predictable hobgoblins who sported polka-dotted ties, had pointy heads, and never uttered an unexpected word in their lives.

That would be Ivan F. Truelove III, CPA.

I thought about him sporadically on my walk this morning.

Every other Saturday, I trekked down the brick sidewalk of my hometown, Apple Grove, where I was the executive director of an art center, to Judge Spivey's comfortable Cape Cod house for lunch. The judge was a friend and treasurer of my art center board. It was a brisk September morning—the tenth of the month, to be exact—the breeze fragrant with the familiar Midwest smell of leaves exploding in vibrant hues—saffron, amber, scarlet, Naples yellow, and vermilion—lovely names from my oil painting life. Amid this beauty, my phone pinged with a text. I knew that ping. I sighed, stopped, and pulled it from my tote. It was Ivan the Terrible, president of my art center board and nemesis supreme.

> Ms. Madison. If the weavers guild moves in on Monday, MAKE SURE they DON'T DAMAGE doorways with their brooms. Any scratch or scrape will come out of YOUR PAYCHECK.
> IVAN F. TRUELOVE III

He didn't understand autocorrect. "Looms," Ivan.

The man needed a life. And on a freakin' Saturday. Ivan "I have no life, so I text you" Truelove. I swore his name was a misnomer because I'd experienced no love there. He was the worst micromanager ever. Recently he'd learned to text, so he'd given up emailing me multiple times a day with advice and would now simply text whenever a random thought crossed his mind.

He was obsessed with capital letters. It wouldn't be a stretch to say he adored them, often hurling them at me in entire texts. I pushed his words across my phone screen and watched with satisfaction as they disappeared. At least it was easy to delete his text messages instantly. Which I did. Just now. Since he broke his leg on the treacherous basement stairs at the art center, he'd stopped his unsolicited appearances at my office door. Believe me, that was a blessing. I scrutinized my cell phone and thought, *Stick your pointy head in a bucket, Ivan.*

Dropping my phone into my tote, I hoisted the bag on my shoulder and marched cheerfully in the direction of the judge's brick house, a mere block up the street. These Saturday lunches with the judge—I couldn't bring myself to call him "Ron"—were the highlight of my week. Although Judge Spivey was retired from his law career, he engaged in volunteer work, and he'd become the treasurer of the Adele Marsden Center for the Arts. My nonprofit board. He contacted me occasionally on official business, but last night he'd left me a puzzling voicemail.

"Hi, Jill. Sorry I missed you. Tomorrow, when you come for lunch, could you please bring me a list of companies you'd recommend who do forensic art analysis? Thanks. I look forward to our get-together. Oh, and I've a surprise to show you. See you tomorrow."

The warmth of his voice always soothed me, but the message was puzzling. Companies that employed forensic analysts worked with collectors and galleries to make sure artwork was authentic. Well, I suppose sometimes collectors hired them to appraise their art collections too. Could that be his concern? The judge owned a valuable art collection. Perhaps he wanted one of his paintings appraised. Or could he be suspicious about the provenance of one of his paintings? The provenance was the history of ownership, proving a painting's authenticity.

2

Stopping short at the wooden steps of his front porch, I opened my tote, making sure the list of appraisers was inside. Yup. Sticking it back in my bag, I climbed the stairs and pulled open the door. It always felt weird to walk in because he had irreplaceable artwork in his house, but usually, if he were home and simply waiting for me, he'd leave the front door unlocked. He had a housekeeper, Tilda Swanson, who prepared a fabulous lunch for us, then left so we could talk.

"Judge?" I called out from the living room. Hmm. Maybe he had left on an errand. My nose caught a familiar fragrance. Fantastic! Tilda's famous brownies. I glanced around the walls, covered with oil paintings, many of them modern works. One, a Mark Rothko, and another, a Joan Mitchell. He had such an eye for collecting, honed by years in the New York City art scene. I was about to stroll over to examine the Rothko more closely when I noticed a photo album on the coffee table. Hmm. I perched on the edge of the mid-century modern sofa, its simple lines yet another indication of the judge's taste, and dropped my tote on the floor. Curiosity got the best of me. I opened the photo album and leafed through a few pages. Oh, my! Photos of my parents, the judge, and his wife, Laura. This must be the surprise he had alluded to in his phone message. I held back a sigh, reflecting on the thought that three out of four of them were now gone. The judge was the only one still alive.

Then I realized it was quiet. Too quiet. I closed the album.

Standing, I shouted a little louder. "Judge? I'm here." He might be in his office with the door closed, but I would think he'd have heard me.

Walking past the dining room to the sleek, modern kitchen, I observed two floral placemats on the table, our usual rendezvous spot, and headed for the kitchen. On the kitchen island rested a platter of Tilda's rich, dark chocolate brownies, and the mouth-watering smell of their baking still lingered in the air. Yum. All was assembled. No judge. Perhaps he'd left on an errand and was late getting back. He assumed I'd wait. It had happened before.

His home office was beyond the elegant dining room and the sleek, modern kitchen. I peeked in the office door, noting the mahogany shelves, which matched the rafters. He'd designed and filled it with only the best furnishings.

Since he'd retired, I had the impression he penned articles about topics that interested judges or lawyers—interpretations of laws, descriptions of famous barristers, or events in America's legal history. I always considered the judge a Renaissance man, interested in so many subjects besides the law. Because we shared a love of art, we had spirited conversations about our opinions of artwork and our thoughts of this period versus that. Of course, we also talked about memories of his wife and my parents. He was someone with whom I could share those memories, a thought I loved.

Where could he be?

I tiptoed through the office doorway, noting his massive desk. Papers, books, and ledgers covered its surface like my desk back at the art center. I smiled. Messy desks—we shared that characteristic. A colorful Tiffany lamp with geometrically shaped, stained glass graced one corner of the desk. Judge Spivey adored beautiful objects. He told me he allowed Tilda in his office only once a month to dust, admonishing her to be careful. I turned toward the wall where first editions of books lined multiple shelves, memorabilia from his law days occupied the top shelves, and framed photographs shared spaces between collections. This room had such a warm feeling, a lifetime of work in a milieu he loved. Light filtering in through the windows brought out the warm tones of the wood. I'd only seen this room from the doorway. This was my chance to snoop, so I ventured in.

Walking over to the bookshelves, I picked up a photo of Laura. How courageous she'd been. Cancer had taken her nine or ten years earlier. Next to her photo was another from his time in Vietnam. It was a group of young soldiers, one of those faded pictures with sepia tones. He was in the middle. Like a lot of veterans, he never talked about his time in the army. A silk rose lay on the shelf next to the photo, a symbol of remembrance. His two kids, John and Erika, were in another photo. Older than I, they were practically in college by the time the family moved here from New York City, so I hardly knew them. This picture looked like it was from their high school years. How old would they be now? I wasn't sure.

Suddenly, pangs of guilt crept up my chest. I was in his space. Or it could be the irrational fear he might walk in and demand an explanation. Even though I considered him a friend, I kept a respectful distance between us based on his life as a judge. Forty years separated our ages. He could arrive any moment and discover me here in his private office. I'd better wait in the living room until he returned. I could check out the photo album he'd left.

As I turned, I spied the toe of a man's brown shoe sticking out a tiny bit from behind the massive desk. A feeling of unease grabbed me. Moving closer, my body reacted before my brain—my eyes widened, my breath stopped. I froze. The judge. Only then did I notice a desk chair skewed at an odd angle, away from the judge's body, which lay supine on the floor. My eyes shot to his face. I gasped. He stared into nothingness.

Oh, my God! I scrambled down to the floor beside him, my shoulders shaking, my lips trembling, my chest aching with fear. Ow. I bit my lip. My breath caught in my throat. Reaching over his body, I patted his arm. "Judge?" Pat, pat, pat. Nothing. I put my finger on his neck. Searched for a pulse. Nothing. I moved my finger to the other side of his neck. Did I touch the wrong spot? It was tough to find the spot because my whole body shook. Backing away, I searched around him on the floor. No blood anywhere. What had happened? Heart attack? Stroke? After all, he was seventy-something. It's not every day you find someone you know staring into eternity.

It quickly dawned on me I should call nine-one-one. My phone. Where had I left my phone? I needed to get help. Now. I spied a landline on the desk. Then I remembered my brother Tom, the detective, and I knew I shouldn't touch objects on the desk in case it was a crime scene.

Standing, I felt a sob begin deep in my throat, and I scrambled to the living room in search of my bag. I grabbed my cell, punching in nine-one-one. Somehow, I managed, in fits and starts, to blurt out his name and address. It was impossible. I cried it into the phone screen again and again. The impersonal dispatcher at the other end replied she had it, told me to wait outside the house. The ambulance and police were on the way.

Dazed, I hit the end button, clutched my bag, and stumbled outside to the porch. It was what Tom would have told me to do. Leave the crime scene. The killer, if there was one, could still be nearby. Was it a crime scene? Dead.

No blood. I took a huge gulp of air as a more sobering thought hit me. Now the judge was gone too, like his wife and my parents. All gone. This was so wrong. I still had too much to ask him, too much to share. He was supposed to be like my dad. My chest heaved again, the sobs coming in waves. I sat on the porch swing, my fingers finding tissues in my bag, and wept because he'd always been kind to me. He'd understood second chances and had given me mine.

In the silence, I heard a siren approaching in the distance.

Chapter Two

I wiped my nose and took several deep breaths to stifle my sobs as Jake Singleton parked his squad car on the street, turning off the siren. Ned Fisher was riding shotgun. Short guy. Big ears. Ned had been in my high school graduating class twelve years earlier, but I guessed Jake was younger. I glanced across the street. The judge's neighbors crept out on their porches, curious about what was happening at the Spivey home. A few, their lips moving, pointed occasionally toward my spot on the porch. Cell phones appeared in some hands aimed in my direction. Others stood silently watching. I tried to ignore them.

"Jill," Jake said, nodding to me. "Judge Spivey?"

"In the office at the back of the first floor." I managed to blurt it out, my lips trembling.

"Got it."

A hasty retreat. Blubbering, red-eyed women were not Jake's thing.

I watched him enter the house as a green-and-white ambulance from Apple Grove Cottage Hospital parked in the driveway with two EMTs I didn't recognize. A man, maybe fifty years old, and a much younger woman with a blond ponytail jumped out the doors, each with a medical bag in hand. They glanced at me as I pointed them in the front door.

"In the back of the house."

"Thanks," the man said, passing me.

Directing traffic. My job for the moment. I could manage that.

My brother, Tom, the Apple Grove police detective, marched up the sidewalk, a grim look on his face. He'd driven up while I was watching the EMTs.

"Jill, are you alright?" He climbed the stairs, and I stood and hugged him. His broad shoulders and strong arms surrounded me, and I took deep breaths.

"It's awful. The judge. He didn't seem to be here when I came for our lunch. I found him on the floor in his office. Not sure what happened. He was just lying there. I tried to find a pulse, you know, like they do in the police shows."

At my remark, he looked at me like I was his kid sister again. I could see it in his face, along with the need to move on like Jake. I was a distraction.

"I'll check it out." He pulled the screen door open and disappeared inside.

I thought he'd tell me to stay on the porch, but when he didn't say anything else, I counted to ten and tiptoed into the house, quietly following him. Seeing no one, I figured they were all at the back, so I stationed myself in the hallway outside the office door and listened. Eavesdropping was not beneath me.

"The windows are locked, Sir. ACs on. Set at seventy-two. No lights when I came in." That voice was Jake Singleton's. A long pause ensued. I figured Tom was memorizing the scene, studying the judge's body, and taking in first impressions. I knew my brother. It was "by the book," and make sure you noticed all details of the scene and wrote everything down.

"Clothing looks normal…body position…don't see any signs of struggle. Ned, check the bathroom. See if there are prescription drugs. Bag up what you find."

"Yes, sir." I squeezed against the hallway wall as Ned walked toward the kitchen. He glanced at me but kept walking.

"Cleary, what's your take?"

I didn't recognize the name. I peeked through the crack around the doorframe and saw the male EMT rise from behind the desk.

"Maybe a heart attack. No signs otherwise. Victim's approximately seventy. Some bruising where he must'a hit the floor or the desk as he fell. No rigor mortis, so it's been less than three hours, although the ME can tell you more. The body temperature hasn't gone down much at all, and lividity along the back and shoulder blades looks like he died here. My best guess is he had a heart attack. Fell. Died almost instantly."

Stifling another sob, a bit of it escaping despite my efforts, I pulled back from the doorframe, imagining each of them glancing in my direction.

"Jill, go back out on the porch," Tom called, his stern, older-brother tone cutting through the silence.

As I walked, sulking, through the kitchen, I grabbed a brownie from Tilda's plate on the kitchen counter. Chocolate was always helpful, no matter what the situation. The rest of our lunch would be in the refrigerator, but chocolate would calm me down. Some people might say "suddenly" was a good way to die, so you didn't have to think about it. I knew the judge was sad after his wife's death years earlier, but he'd rebounded. He loved buying art pieces, being on the art center board, volunteering at the animal shelter or at his church. Judge Spivey enjoyed an amazing life, I had to grant him that. He always seemed in good health with a cheerful outlook about everything. I inhaled a deep breath. He sure had helped me keep my job several months earlier when the art center board wasn't so happy with me. Judge Spivey had given me a second chance. Loyalty was one of the qualities I loved about him. I guess this might be the best way to go, but it didn't help my sadness or the lump in my throat.

Sitting back on the porch swing, I figured I'd wait for Tom. I heard a weird sound like a beeper from the house. Moments later, the two EMTs came back out, glanced at me, and the woman said over her shoulder, "We're coming back."

They backed out and sped onto the street with the siren going full blast. Must be another emergency. Not sure what Tom was doing in the house. I called my art center manager, Louise Sandoval, and asked her to keep the lid on at the art center until I got back.

"Is all going smoothly?" I asked absentmindedly.

"No problem. Three more pieces for the upcoming exhibit arrived, the watercolor class Paige Lemon taught finished, and everyone left. Oh, a check for a million dollars came in."

"Sounds good."

"Aha. I knew you weren't listening to me."

"What?"

"We're fine. Get back whenever you can."

I watched a van pull in front of the house and park behind the police car. It was Abe Calipher, the coroner. I'd known him for years. He was the coroner when our parents were killed in a terrible car accident with a drunk driver six years earlier. Everybody in town knew Dr. Calipher. I thought the gold stud in his left ear was intriguing. He always sported a perfectly shaped moustache, classy clothing, and carried a paper cup of takeout coffee. He trudged up the sidewalk slowly, his medical bag in his left hand, coffee in his right hand, head down.

"Hi, Dr. Calipher."

He glanced at me. "Oh. Hi, Jill. How come you're here?"

"I was supposed to have my semimonthly lunch date with the judge." I paused and swallowed, thinking about what I should say. "I'm so sorry. I know you were close friends."

"For over a decade." He climbed the porch stairs, each foot moving hesitantly. "I hate calls like this." He leaned against the porch banister. An air of sadness surrounded him like a shroud, and he cast his eyes down, not able to look at mine.

I slowly shook my head. "I can't imagine how awful your job must be, living in a small town like this. Strangers dying are the exception rather than the rule."

He straightened up, set his bag on the floor, took a swig of his coffee, and sat next to me on the porch swing. Probably putting off the inevitable, I figured.

"Yes. Ron was a—a close friend." He paused, as if speaking were difficult. "We played cards in a men's group every other week and went fly-fishing a couple times a year. Shared a lot of meals because we were both alone." Abe set the coffee cup on the porch floor. "He was the closest friend I had after we both outlived our wives. Guess I know Ron better than most other folks in town."

I watched him pull a piece of gum out of his pocket, methodically taking off the paper and nudging the gum into his mouth. A hint of spearmint floated in the air. "He wasn't all that old. You find the body?"

"Yes. Seemed peaceful enough. The EMT thinks he had a heart attack."

Abe turned in my direction, caterpillar eyebrows lifting. "What?"

"Yeah. He was guessing, I suppose, but I didn't see anything out of place, no blood, nothing that would say otherwise. It wasn't like one of those murder scenes on a TV detective show."

He scratched his chin for a moment. "I'll bet it was the new guy, Cleary."

"I think I heard him called that."

"Hmm. He seems to have a lot of opinions." He nodded slowly, picked up his coffee and medical bag, and rose from the swing. "Guess I can't put it off any longer. Thanks for building my courage, kiddo."

I smiled. "I've never known you to need courage."

"Some days are better than others. This one's going downhill fast."

He walked in the door with his bag and coffee, and I could hear footsteps moving on toward the office. I considered what to do next. I could walk to the art center, but my curiosity was speeding like a mouse on steroids. The EMTs hadn't returned yet, so I decided to creep in once again and see what I could find out.

At first, it was quiet in the office. Assuming my usual spot, I stared through the crack between the door and the doorframe. I could see Tom's legs sticking out from behind the desk. He was on the floor, and so was Abe Calipher near the judge's head. His medical bag was nearby, just past the end of the desk, and every so often, a vinyl-gloved hand would reach back, feeling for something in his bag. Their voices murmured indistinctly, the volume too low for me to hear. Darn it. I pulled my head back, my back resting against the wall. By the time I silently counted to fifty, I could sense movement, and when I peeked in, both men were again on their feet.

Abe was the first to speak. "I'm ordering a presumptive test for drugs."

"Seriously?" Tom's voice. "Why?"

"I knew Ron well. We've told each other the details of our lives, from way back to now. He didn't have any heart problems that I knew of. Exercised regularly and ate healthy. He'd had a physical a month or two ago, and everything was fine. Least he said so."

Tom took a step over and studied the judge's body again. "I've known lots of folks who had a clean medical bill of health and then were dead a few days later. Why do you think this is anything other than a heart attack?"

"Call me suspicious."

"You think someone murdered him?"

Abe paused for a moment. "Ever known a judge who didn't make a few enemies during his time on the bench?"

"Well—"

"Not only that but look around you. This estate's gonna be huge, and where there's money, you'll find all kind of motives."

"You know something I don't know, Abe?"

"Let's just say the family history's not exactly *Father Knows Best*. You want to call the kids, or do you want me to?"

Tom cleared his throat. "I'll take care of it. I need to interview Tilda Swanson, the housekeeper, too."

"Tom, treat it as a crime scene. Get a crime scene unit in. Pick up fingerprints. Once those kids return, they'll want to charge in and settle everything. Believe me, you won't get much cooperation there. If it's a crime scene, you can keep it pristine for as long as possible."

"Yeah. I see what you mean."

"I've got what I need here. He hasn't been dead for long. A few hours. But I think I'll do those presumptive tests and see if anything turns up. Could be I'm worrying about nothing, but my suspicion light is blinking on and off, and I don't want to let any details slip away from us."

"Because you're too close to this case?"

"Could be, but I want to do him right. Ron was someone I admired very much. We need to watch out for him. Follow through on the details."

I sensed an end to this scene and hurried quietly down the hallway to a chair in the kitchen. In a few moments, Tom and Abe came into the room.

I couldn't help myself. "You really think this could be a murder?"

Tom gave me an exasperated look. "You, my dear sister, are going back to the art center. I have your fingerprints, so your work is done here. Now head out. Keep your mouth shut."

The corners of Abe's mouth were twitching as if to hold back a smile.

"All right, I'm leaving. But the judge was my friend too, and to think anyone could've killed him is horrifying. Bringing whoever murdered him to justice is important. To me."

"And you'll stay away from his house, the possible crime scene, and anything else that might have any connection with this. Right?"

I considered Tom's usual concern I be kept in the dark. He couldn't help but be eight years older than me and in charge of my life since our parents died. I was thirty, not a kid, and if the judge had been murdered, I wanted to know by whom and why. I owed him. Might be better if I worked quietly on this while Tom went about his business.

"Sure, Tom. Headed back to the art center. Your scene. I'm good."

It was déjà vu. I'd been at a crime scene a few months earlier. Tom had admonished me the same way, and while I loved my brother, I ignored him on that occasion. In fact, I'd actually been quite helpful. I stood in the frame of the front door and stared back at the judge's home. It felt so empty, devoid of his energy and enthusiasm. Through my mind ran a loop of memories from his house, laughing with the judge and gobbling up Tilda's lunches. It was hard to believe it was over. I decided right then I'd make good on the second chance he'd given me at the art center. I wouldn't let him down, with Tom's blessing or not.

Chapter Three

"Y ou're back!"

Louise glanced expectantly from my office door as I plunked my bag on my desk. Tall and willowy, she was a single mom, always hopeful she'd find her true love on some dating site. Her olive skin and reddish brunette hair were complemented by the earth-toned clothing she wore. The expression on her face said puzzlement.

"Everything OK? Lunch go well?"

I shook my head slowly and motioned her into my office. "No. Not at all. Judge Spivey's dead."

"What? *Our* Judge Spivey? I'll bet those were the sirens I heard. When? How?" Louise moved in and sat on my loveseat, leaning toward me, her face filled with shock.

Then I heard Tom's voice in my head saying to keep my mouth shut. "Oh, you must keep this under wraps. No one can know, although eventually, it'll be around town, I'm sure."

"I'm so sorry, Jill. Was it a heart attack?"

I pulled my phone out of my tote, dropping the bag lightly to the floor, and sat. "Oh, Louise. I don't know what's happening. One minute I was in his house and found his body on the floor behind the desk, and the next minute I was calling 9-1-1. That's why I'm late. They think it was a heart attack. I can't believe it. He was so full of life, such a mentor, and now I've lost him too." A tear trickled down my cheek, and I brushed it away.

Louise pressed her hands together, wrapping them around each other in a nervous ritual. "This is terrible. He's been so supportive of the art center.

Is there anything I can do that would be helpful?"

Shrugging my shoulders, I sat silently. This was a first because shocks usually made me faint. I heard a ping and pulled out my phone. Ivan. He had a scanner.

YOU'VE FOUND ANOTHER BODY? What is this with you and dead people? At least this time, it wasn't IN our art center.
IVAN F. TRUELOVE III

Then I realized Louise was waiting expectantly. I swiped Ivan's text across my cell screen to destroy it forever. "Uh, no. I'm alright, Louise. Go ahead. Take your lunch break. I need a little time to process it all."

She rose, stopping to give me a pat on the shoulder. "Nothing much happened this morning you need to know about, at least not here."

I suddenly remembered. "Oh, how did Paige Lemon's class go?"

"Mostly well."

"Mostly?" I raised one eyebrow.

"Paige is a born teacher. I can see why the elementary schools in town love her. She did such an amazing job."

"But?"

Louise crossed her arms. "All was going calmly, so I left to come back downstairs. The next thing I knew, the O'Connell twins decided to paint some modern murals on the walls of the elevator while riding up and down between floors. They splattered paint all over the walls and each other. It's watercolor, so it should come off without a problem."

"Where was Paige?"

"They sneaked out while she had her back to them helping another student."

"Did you talk to their mom?"

Louise rolled her eyes. "Of course. She laughed and thought they were cute."

"I suppose it hasn't hurt anything, but we might want to consider hiring a bouncer to watch over classes."

She chuckled. "It's an experiment in progress, isn't it?"

After Louise left, I sat for a while at my desk, thinking about the morning. I stared at the six photographs I'd taken and enlarged so they read like a journey of my life. My parent's studio photo was the only exception. My mother, Adele Marsden, was a world-famous sculptor whose works had won numerous awards. The art center was named after her. Her ebony coloring contrasted with the skin tones of my pale, white father, an insurance salesman, and eternal optimist. I liked to think they were looking down on my work, pleased I'd come home and was providing art education for our little town of fifteen thousand. At the same time, I'd recently found myself able to paint again after a long dry spell following their deaths.

I thumbed through the files on my desk. Now, where was that one about the program grant?

Sighing in defeat, I stared at the photos on my wall again. Joining the picture of my parents were ones of my home, the family, my siblings, the art center, and a famous sculpture by my mother called *Mother and Child*. I studied the one of my brothers and me. Tom looked most like our father—his skin color white—and he was following in the tradition of our dad when he became a detective. Dad might've been an insurance salesman, but everyone knew him and respected him; Tom was a detective with the same rep. He did his job with an eye for detail, and the consensus was that he was an exceptional detective. I loved him for his steady, rock-solid dependability, even though his overprotectiveness drove me nuts.

Then there was Andy. Our ages fell at thirty-eight, thirty-six, and thirty. Andy was the middle child and the wild one at that. He went to college, majoring in business and parties. There he'd met Lance Hughes, and they started a partnership in life as well as a gift store here in Apple Grove. Their rock band often played on the weekends at local bars, especially Priscilla's Pub, owned by my best friend Angie Emerson and her husband, Wiley. Andy's eyes were a deep brown and his skin tone honey, like mine. Yes, we were quite a "different" family growing up in Apple Grove, but I guess it made us special. The small, Midwest inhabitants grew used to us—diversity wasn't exactly a census factor in our town back then.

As if he knew I was thinking about him, Andy's ringtone sounded on my phone, making me jump. "Welcome to the Jungle" played, breaking the silence, and I let it continue for a few bars of thumping bass. Then I tapped the "accept" button.

"Yes, Andy."

"Ah, my sis. Heard you had quite a morning. You should hire yourself out to find bodies, kind of like those people who are diviners of water sources. You know, they hold out those forked sticks."

"Andy, please. This isn't anything to joke about."

"Who's joking? It could be a second income. At least the new body wasn't in your art center."

"Stop it. You knew the judge too. How can you make jokes at a time like this?"

"Better than crying."

I put the speaker on so I wouldn't have to keep holding my cell against my ear and moved over to the loveseat. "It sounds like he had a heart attack."

"I have to tell you it isn't keeping people from repeating creative theories."

"About what?"

"You know. Judge. Dealing with jailbirds. Lots of money. Crazy children."

"I'm putting my money on heart attack. Abe Calipher is shaken up."

"I'd guess so. You know what I think about when I remember the judge?"

"I can't imagine. Juvenile court?"

"Oh, come on. I was never in court."

"Sheer luck."

"Remember when I was in basketball in fifth grade, and the judge was a referee at the Y?"

"Sure. We used to go to your games on Saturday mornings. As I remember, it was mostly a bunch of uncoordinated boys scrambling around on the floor, trying to hang onto the basketball. Unsuccessfully. Few baskets."

"Yeah, well, OK. We could've used some talent."

"...and self-discipline, practice, and focus."

"That too. Anyway, remember the Cramer family? You know, the ones who were in town for a couple years and thought they had an athletic dynasty with their five kids?"

"Yes, especially the mother." I sat back, picturing Allison Cramer, the scary mother of the brood.

"She was on Spivey the whole first half of this Saturday game, screaming instructions about his refereeing, complaining when he called a penalty on her son, and causing everyone else to shake their heads as she ranted on, full blast. You could hear her throughout the gym. The woman had a set of lungs."

I pictured the scene as if it were yesterday. I was only nine, but I'd never seen a mom act like that.

"After the second half started, remember what the judge did?"

"No. I hope he threw her out of the gym."

"He blew his referee whistle loudly, stopped the action, bounded up the bleachers, and handed her the whistle. The whole gym was watching. Said if she wanted to call the rest of the game, it was fine with him. Never heard another word out of her."

"Now you mention it, I do seem to remember that. Judge Spivey understood people and was usually well-liked, like Dad, but he could sure state the facts with certainty. He didn't suffer fools." I paused. "I think they're doing an autopsy, so I guess we'll see what comes out of that."

"His kids been called?

"Tom or Abe planned to deal with contacting them."

"That should be interesting." Now Andy paused for a few seconds. "I don't remember them well, but I have a gut feeling I didn't like them much."

"We're all grown up now, Andy, so I imagine they'll be sad the judge has passed, along with their mother. Like us, they're orphans."

"Could be. Got to go. Hang in there. Seriously, think about a body-finding business."

And he was off like a wisp of silliness.

I loved my brother, but it was so easy to follow him. Unlike Andy, I hadn't taken the car out at age thirteen, hit an ATM machine, broken the side mirrors off three parked cars, and ended up in a pond in Bentley Park. And Dad, the insurance broker, had to deal with the claim and the police. He had insured the car, of course. Andy lost his allowance for several years over that one. I think he was still paying Dad off when he got his driver's license. See? Angel Jill.

I found the file I was searching for under a stack of others on my desk. The national, juried exhibit would run from September 30 to November 25. Entries had to be in by September 23, and the date was fast approaching. The gallery opening would be on September 30, and I'd made numerous calls and appointments to raise the money for the opening, the awards, and the promotion. I'd found the juror, Anthony Arteaga from the Philadelphia Museum of Art, through the Americans for the Arts Conference. I'd nervously approached him, but he was generous and interested. The theme of the exhibit was *Harvest Time*. Anthony had made his selections of entries online, and already we had artwork in the storage area that had been shipped to us from all over the country. It was exciting. Our first national exhibit.

A knock on my office doorframe stirred me from my reverie. When I turned around, Chad McKenna, recently hired to be our janitor and odd-jobs person, was standing there. His name was Charles, but he went by "Chad."

"Reporting for work, General."

I laughed. "Like a breath of fresh air."

"Oh." He scratched his head. "Not such a good day?"

"Could've been better."

"Ready to work as ordered, ma'am." He saluted me. He had on carpenter's jeans, a faded sweatshirt with the Grateful Dead on the front, and a red St. Louis Cardinals cap turned backward on his head. It had seen better days. A well-trimmed reddish beard with lots of white patches covered his narrow chin. About five foot ten, he moved with the grace of a much younger man than his sixty-six years. When I interviewed him, I learned he was retired and looking for part-time work. He'd been in the army during the Vietnam era.

"Jill. Call me Jill."

"Right. I checked the doors, Jill. The key works perfectly, as does the security system. I'm good."

"Oh, you might check the elevator and classroom upstairs. Evidently, we had a major skirmish between a set of twins armed with watercolor paints.

"Will do. I'll start mopping the second floor. Got a couple grandkids of my own, so I know how that goes. Anything else? Other than the usual?"

"No. But thanks for being here, Chad. I've spent a lot of time doing every possible chore in this center, and I'm thankful to have help."

"I'm glad to have the work. Retirement's fine but boring. Only so many times I can go with my wife to flea markets. I'll start upstairs." With that, he turned and left my office.

I was so pleased to finally have a janitor. The months of getting the place together and making huge changes in the nineteenth-century Lowry Building had worn me out, not to mention frazzled my nerves. But now it was all coming together, and I was sad to see the judge miss all the excitement. He used to tell me, "Patience."

Ping! A familiar sound. It was Ivan. Blast the man. For weeks we'd argued about a handrail on the basement stairs. He was a tight-fisted miser when it came to spending a nickel. To his regret, he'd fallen down the stairs, breaking a leg as well as injuring his pride. I held myself back from saying, "I told you so." Once he was in the hospital, I had a carpenter install a handrail at the disaster scene. What was he texting about this time?

MS MADISON. YOU FOUND YET ANOTHER POTTY? AM I CORRECT IT WAS JUDGE RONALD SPIVEY? OUR JUDGE SPIVEY?
IVAN F. TRUELOVE III

I assumed his "another potty" meant "another body." Ivan Truelove. Someone should not only bury his scanner but also destroy the shift key on his computer and cell.

As I changed the screen on my phone to make a call, I received another call from an unknown number. It was local. My ringtone for generic calls was the Disney classic, "Somewhere Out There." Perhaps I should take a chance it wasn't an offer to sell me an extended warranty on my Austin Mini.

"Adele Marsden Center for the Arts. This is Jill Madison."

"Ms. Madison. Ken Winters, of Sampson, Keckley, and Winters."

"Ah, yes. I remember you, Ken. We've met a few times at Chamber of Commerce events and, if I recall, you came to our *Home in the Heartland* exhibit."

"Yes, you remember well." He paused. "Your brother Tom called me about the judge's passing. I was sorry to hear the news."

"Me too. He was a valued friend, watching over the art center. I'll miss him because he also gave me wonderful advice." I caught the start of a break in my voice. I took a deep breath and centered myself. "What can I do for you, Ken?"

"I was hoping you'd be able to come to my office on Monday morning around nine. I'm the judge's attorney, and I need to speak with you about some details he added a few years ago to his will."

"Not sure what I can help you with, but I'll be glad to stop in. Monday at nine. Right?"

"Yes. I'll see you then."

I tapped the end button on my phone, set it down, and leaned back in my chair. What was this about? Had Judge Spivey left me a painting in his will? That would be exciting. He had an amazing modern art collection. I imagined by now his son and daughter were coming back to town. The funeral would probably occur sometime next week. Tom would know the details because he'd have spoken with John and Erika.

I was about to gather my things and leave for the day when my phone pinged again. I knew that ping. Sorry, Ivan. Not now. I'm busy saving the world.

Chapter Four

We were sitting around the table on Tom and Mary's backyard deck, drinking coffee and gazing with reluctance at all the dirty dishes we would have to trundle in the house. It was Sunday morning, and Andy and Lance were involved in bookwork at the gift store. Their absence negated a huge entertainment factor for this meal.

"Mary, I don't know when I've eaten so much food." My best friend, Angie Emerson, was patting her stomach, smiling at Mary. Blond, with her hair pulled back in a ponytail, Angie sported gold hoop earrings, a pink, long-sleeved T-shirt, and ripped jeans. Best buds since early grade school, Angie and I got into bits of trouble together over the years, but no matter what, we had each other's back. She was a friend for life and often spent time with my family. In fact, she might as well have been family because we'd shared most episodes in our lives so far.

The cook and baker in the family, Tom's wife, Mary, worked as a receptionist at a doctor's office. As I watched, she pushed her blond hair away from her tortoiseshell glasses and stared at the dishes on the table. The thing I always remembered about her was that she was the calm person in the family, much calmer than Tom, the police detective. She handled emergencies so much better than he did when it came to the family. I thought about the time Emily, their daughter, sprained her ankle in a softball game a few months ago. He was literally jumping the fence to go check on her, while Mary calmly waited and became the cleanup batter at the hospital.

Tom came out on the deck and dropped the morning newspaper onto the center of the table, where I quickly snatched it. "At least Jezbhel Gushman can do a decent news story without her incessant editorializing."

"So that's how you pronounce her name. I've always wondered if it's like Jezebel."

"It's like Jezebel, but from what I understand from one of the stringers, it's an old family name."

"Oh." I opened the front page and read the brief story about the judge out loud to Angie and Mary. "Judge Ronald Spivey, retired, was found dead in his home on Saturday. While no cause of death has been ascertained by this newspaper, inquiries at the police department or the coroner's office have been met with stony silence." Wait a minute. That sounded like editorializing to me. It was those words, *stony silence*. "It appears there is an ongoing investigation. More information, plus an obituary, will be forthcoming."

Tom sat and regarded each of us. "I take it back. She can't even do a four-sentence news story without adding her two cents. Don't know where she came from, but it's obvious she doesn't have any journalistic integrity. That's the least number of words she's written in a news story since she got here. I should be happy she only had two words of opinion."

"Does this mean you're not talking, and you have your department zipped up?" Angie said.

"Exactly." Tom leaned over the table and grabbed the coffeepot, pouring a few dribbles in his cup. "End of the coffee, my dear." He handed Mary the coffeepot. She smiled and set it back on the table. Tom shook his head, smiling at Angie and me. "This is her way of saying I've had enough caffeine for the day."

"Oh, what's this?" I folded the newspaper better so I could read it. "A police blotter?"

"Editor Gushman's met her match," Tom said, chuckling. "The newspaper owner's niece, Alberta, is writing a social page, and she's decided to add a police blotter. She stops at the station to check on our calls from the public, calls that are a matter of public record. Hilarious. Now the public knows the insanity we deal with every day. I suppose it's in the spirit of transparency and freedom of information."

Angie laid her napkin on the table. "Does this mean Gushman can't do anything about this?"

Tom laughed. "Not if she wants to keep her job. It's funny."

"Oh, my. Listen to this," I said, laughing. "At 10:32 a.m., a caller on Route 320 at Haber's Corner complained that he had an ongoing problem with a neighbor's pigs coming onto his property. If it continued, he threatened to have lots of bacon and ham for his freezer."

"That's pretty good," Angie said. "Read another one."

"At 2:14 p.m., a caller on Robin's Egg Lane reported her mother had attacked her and driven off in her wheelchair. She couldn't decide whether to let her go or ask for assistance."

I dropped the newspaper on the table, watching it soak up a few drops of cranberry juice I'd spilled. "Have you talked to the judge's kids yet?"

"Erika and John. Yes. They're both in the Chicago area, so I imagine they'll drive back here at the speed of light."

Angie glanced up. "Why do you say it like that?"

Tom pursed his lips, thinking about whether he should walk it back. "I shouldn't have put it that way."

"Come on. The words are out of your mouth now. What's with his kids? I can't remember how old they are. What would you guess?" I sat straighter in my chair, took my napkin off my lap, and set it on the table.

Tom was quiet as if counting in his head. "If I remember correctly, Erika is a year or two older than me. Thirty-nine or forty. John is older than her by a few years. I said they'd make a speedy trip because, over the years, they've been at odds with the judge, often needing money. After Laura died, he cut them off. Not sure why. I imagine Tilda, the housekeeper, knows about it. Wouldn't guess it's a pretty story. When I told them about their father's death, I was met with what the newspaper editor called "stony silence." Anyway, the lawyer, Ken Winters, told me they aren't allowed in the Spivey house. The judge left express orders. I predict a huge explosion soon."

I set my coffee down, considering that. "Must be a story there. He never talked to me about his kids. I guess they're adults now. Why wouldn't he want them in his house?"

"I think Winters, the attorney, knows more about it." Tom saw the question on my face and asked, "Yes?"

"I'm supposed to see this Winters on Monday morning. Something about the will. Did he say anything to you about it?"

"No. Lawyers are notoriously tight-lipped in situations with wills."

"And that's because…"

"Oh, wills are curious things. I'm glad I'm not in his shoes right now. People tend to get crazy over wills. Feelings are hurt. People are left out. Anger ensues. Fights occur. Lawsuits are threatened. It's a situation I'm glad I don't have to deal with as a detective. Leave it to those guys who make the big bucks."

Mary started piling dishes. "How long do you expect to be in Peoria, Tom?"

"Peoria?" I asked.

He turned to Angie and me. "I'll go to the autopsy this afternoon. Abe Calipher said he'd go, but I vetoed his suggestion. He was too close to the judge. As it is, he's called in favors from the state lab, and we should have test results soon."

"Test results? What kind of tests?" I asked.

"Oh, nothing you need to worry about."

And there it was—those words saying I was too young; I shouldn't worry about it. I needed to butt out of this investigation of my friend. I was about to protest when a woman came tromping around the lilac bushes from the front of the house. She had bright red hair worn in a complicated hairdo and a stylishly cut dress above spindly high heels. I studied her face. Her complexion had that painted cement look, and her lips pursed tightly. She was walking at a brisk pace, her arms swinging as if she were on a mission. Our eyes followed her, and Tom rose as she came around the side of the deck.

She glanced at him, smiling. "Oh, Tom. Good to find you here. We talked on the phone yesterday."

He stood and motioned her over to the deck stairs, saying, "This is Erika Spivey-Prather." He introduced each of us. Mary started to pull another chair from a corner of the deck to the table, but the woman motioned her not to bother.

"I won't be here but a few minutes," she said to Mary. "Nice to meet you all. It's been a long time since I've seen you, Jill. You're all grown up."

Before I could say a word, Tom said, "So what can I do for you, Erika?"

I was surprised he was abrupt. I could tell he wasn't happy being hunted down at home on a Sunday.

"Ah, right to the point, Tom. I like that. I need to get into Dad's house, and John should be here this afternoon, so we'll want to go over Dad's papers so we can start getting his financial records in order."

"I'm so sorry about your father's death," I said. "He's been a real mentor to me, and I will miss him terribly."

"Well, yes. We need to get the *I'm sorry's* out of the way so we can get on with this matter. We're sorry about it too." She turned to Tom. "Do you have a key to the house?"

I almost gasped, then shut my mouth. Why would she feel that way? He was her father.

Tom scratched his head a moment, considering his answer. "Erika, we've a bit of a problem."

"Problem? What problem? It's John's and my house now. I can't imagine a problem. This estate will take a huge effort to put together. The sooner we can get started, the better. John and I have jobs to go back to in Chicago. Do you have a key?"

"Not that I can give you. Did you notice a police officer at the house?" Tom's voice was quiet, measured.

"Yes. As I drove by, I was thankful you were guarding his artwork. But he wasn't there for John or me. We're the new owners."

Now Tom leaned over the table and spoke directly to the woman. "I'm afraid no one will be going in the house for a while, Erika. It's officially a crime scene until we have lab results back. The police are there to keep it closed to everyone until we finish our investigation."

Now I noticed her eyes narrow and focus directly on Tom, while her feet moved to a combative stance and her hands sat on her hips.

"What are you talking about? Investigation? Crime scene? Dad just died. Heart attack? Stroke? Why would there even be any question? If this is a plan to somehow cut John and me out of his estate, you'll be dealing with our lawyer."

I could feel my body slinking down farther in my chair. Angie and I exchanged glances.

Tom put his hands out, palms forward, as if pushing back. "I've nothing to do with your father's estate, Erika. That's his lawyer's purview. The police have a few questions about his manner of death. Abe Calipher, the coroner, has ordered an autopsy. Until those questions are answered, the house stays out of bounds to everyone but the department. We should have answers today or tomorrow. It won't take long to get lab tests back."

"Lab tests? An autopsy? Why? Why would you do an autopsy? I'll find a way to stop that, just see if I don't."

"I'm afraid you can't stop an autopsy when there is a question about whether this was a natural death or a murder."

"Murder? That's ridiculous. There's no way John or I would let anyone do an autopsy on our father. Why all this delay when he obviously died a natural death? And what should we do while you put us in a holding pattern? Where are we supposed to stay? This is beyond contempt. We came here to deal with his estate, but we're told to back off. This is ridiculous. We can't get into our own house. We'll see what John has to say when he shows up. Believe me, you'll be hearing from our lawyer."

"And your lawyer would be...?"

"Soon." With that, she turned, stomped down the deck steps, and marched through the grass around the house in the direction she'd come from.

"That went well. So much for diplomacy," I said. "Somehow, you didn't get the tactfulness gene from Dad."

Tom chuckled. "I expected her reaction. Over the years, civil war's ensued between John, Erika, and their father. I've only heard bits and pieces, but I gather it's all about money. Where they spend it...how they spend it. Anyway, it's a topic I plan to ask the housekeeper about. Figured I'd give her a day to pull herself together. Tilda Swanson is a deep repository of knowledge about the house and the judge's family. The Spiveys assume the house, the art, and the entire estate will fall into their laps. I knew Ron, and

I've a feeling they may be in for a surprise. He was also a philanthropist. Part of Ron's estate is undoubtedly earmarked for his pet causes. Another opportunity for me to be happy I'm not in Ken Winters' shoes."

"Interesting talk, big brother. She was pleasant while she was getting her way. I was shocked by her cavalier remark about getting the 'I'm sorry' part of the conversation over. She doesn't seem too sad her father's died."

Tom pulled his cell phone out of his pocket. "I think I'd better call the department and put another guy over at the house. Can't imagine she or John would try to push their way in, but I'd rather be proactive. I'll check to see if either of them owns firearms."

Angie stirred. "Seriously, Tom? You think it might come to that?"

He nodded, saying, "You never know what you're dealing with when it comes to police situations. You always want to think ahead. Ron's told me an occasional story over the years about his son and daughter, usually with sadness in his eyes. They've been disappointments. I imagine I only know about ten percent, so I'm anticipating fireworks in the next few days."

"What kind of fireworks?" I asked.

"The kind I don't like to deal with, which ends up wreaking havoc in town."

Chapter Five

Ken Winters started the conversation with, "How are things going at the Marsden Center?"

"Quite well. We're getting ready for a national exhibit, classes are full to bursting, and the weavers guild moves their equipment in today. So much excitement." I sat back in the leather chair in front of his desk on Monday morning, waiting to find out why I was there. It was an impressive office, very lawyerly. Leather furniture, walnut desk, plush carpet, and framed law degree on the wall. A photo of his blond wife and two children sat on a shelf behind him, and rows of law books adorned the shelves to my left. File cabinets stood at attention while a laptop sat on the desk with a printer off to the side. Exactly what you'd expect. Clean lines. Modern. Quite efficient. Expensive.

He was as I remembered him. Dark hair peppered with a bit of silver on the sides over the ears, a summer suit with a conservative, dark tie, a Rotary pin on his lapel, and an air of total competence. I'd met him once or twice at community functions and found him pleasantly charming.

"When I heard an art center was going into the Lowry Building, I wondered how you would bring the venue in compliance with safety regulations. Looks like you did it. Fascinating story about how you raised the floors and made sure the building was up to code. You impress me, Jill."

I crossed my leg, relaxing more as I sat back and waited for whatever he planned to spring on me. Sweet talk often preceded requests. I was getting cynical. "Yes. Huge project, but we came through it well, and now that it's over, we can concentrate on our next exhibit. However, I'm sure you didn't call to discuss my art center agenda. What's up?"

Winters pulled several files to the middle of the desk from a slender pile on the side. "Since we both know about Judge Spivey's passing, I can skip the preliminaries. I've been his lawyer for the past fifteen years. It's my job to deal with the judge's will and estate."

"I understand. His death has been a terrible shock. I feel like I only had a few months with him as my mentor and friend, and now he's gone." I looked down. If I studied my hands in my lap, I'd keep my feelings in check. A deep breath kept me steady. No tears in front of this guy. "One time at lunch, I said something about missing my parents. It was stupid because I'd momentarily forgotten he'd lost Laura too. Why would I be so stupid as to bring up such sad memories? But he told me it was all right. We had to live in the moment and appreciate the people we loved because we didn't know how long we'd have them in our lives. And now he's gone too."

He nodded. "We all feel the shock. He was a huge force in this community. I know he loved the art center and cared about its executive director." He smiled. "My impression was you brought energy and happiness back into his life. He spoke of you many times."

I leaned forward, considering how to reply to this compliment. "He and Laura were friends of my parents, and we shared lots of dinners at their home and at ours when I was young. But I didn't realize until I came back here from Chicago recently that he felt an obligation to keep an eye on me because my parents had both passed away by then. I valued his friendship as an adult. We often talked about our memories of them. I'll miss those conversations."

"That's why I asked you to come in today. I don't know if you were aware the judge and his two children had a falling out in recent years."

"I had an inkling of it, but we never discussed his family, other than Laura. I hardly knew Erika and John. They were older than me and didn't live here."

He opened a file on his desk, glancing over the first page. Then he looked at me. "In normal circumstances, John would probably be the executor of the judge's estate, with Erika as a backup. But because of their estrangement, he named you as executor."

"Wh—what?" I think I must have stammered, my breath held in limbo.

"You are the named executor," he said slowly. He hesitated as he saw the surprise on my face. "He didn't mention this to you?"

I scooted to the edge of my chair. "No. Why?"

"He felt you would do an efficient job, making sure his wishes were conducted as he wanted. Much of the estate involves artwork, and you would be an expert on that."

"This is crazy. I'm not related to him like John and Erika are."

"I understand. But he has the right to name whomever he wishes, and he wanted to bypass the children. It's a big job, but after seeing the way you've reinvented the Lowry Building and launched the art center, I believe you're up to it."

I sat a moment in silence, my mind flailing in multiple directions. Then I took a deep breath and let it out. "What would this being an executor involve?" I was thinking about the long hours I put in at the art center.

"You'd have lots of details to pull together, but I'd collaborate with you as his attorney and help you cut through any red tape. If you agree to become the executor, I'll file a petition with the circuit clerk to open the estate, and another petition called Letters of Office, which asks that you be named the executor. The filing would begin a six-month probate period, which is required in Illinois with an estate of this size."

Was it warm in his office? I felt a trickle of moisture behind my knees and down the center of my back. I leaned forward. Seeing a blank piece of paper on the desk, I grabbed it and began to fan myself. I watched him chuckle. This was crazy. This sounded terribly official and complicated. "Then what happens?"

"You would take charge of his estate and pay off funeral expenses, taxes, and debts owed to places where he did business. As you did those jobs, you'd keep track of your hours and be paid a generous stipend per hour for your work. We'd get a tax ID for the estate so you could open a checking account to pay creditors. Once probate ends in six months, you'd distribute legacies or items he left to specific legatees. Then you'd close the estate and give the court your records. They will make sure it was done correctly. As I said, I'll help."

Panic rose in my chest. It started around my waist and moved up. It was anxiety, pure and simple. How could I do all this and manage my job at the art center? It sounded so complicated. If the judge had been a pauper, I wouldn't have much to do at all, but my guess was his estate was worth millions in artwork alone.

Ken Winters sat quietly, waiting for me to say something.

"I—I guess I could do it if you were around to answer questions and make sure I didn't screw it up. I'd have to balance it somehow with my job at the art center."

I watched his face relax.

"I hoped you'd say that. I'll do whatever I can to help you, and I'll make sure you don't make any mistakes. I've been through probate situations many, many times, although this estate is certainly larger than I'm used to." He picked up a fountain pen on his desk and pushed a paper in my direction. "You'll need to sign here. It's a paper that says you're fine with being the executor, and I'll prepare the accompanying papers to file with the court."

My hand was shaky as I scribbled my name on the line at the bottom of the paper. I handed it to him, and he placed another set of papers in my hands.

"This is the judge's will. You should read it because it's your roadmap for the probate period. Would you like a cup of coffee?"

"Sure," I said. I sat back and stared at the cover. Last Will and Testament of Ronald L. Spivey. It made everything real—his death. I felt a tear trickle down my cheek but wiped it away.

Ken had gone for coffee and wasn't in the room when I began the first of several gasps. Maybe he'd left on purpose. OMG, the judge had left his children out of the will completely, except to name them at the start. Disinherited them. Feeling like I couldn't get a deep breath in, I set the paper on my lap and did several breathing exercises I'd learned to calm my anxiety. I shifted in my chair, trying to get comfortable. What time was it? Two minutes from the last time I checked.

Taking a deep breath, I imagined Erika's face when she heard about the will. She had planned to camp out at what she considered her house once she returned to town. This would be a total explosion. I read about bequests to various charities I knew the judge supported, and a few specific items he wanted to give Tilda Swanson, his housekeeper. There were a few other bequests for Abe Caligher and another person I didn't know. But the bulk of the estate went to the Adele Marsden Center for the Arts. What? If I thought I was in shock after the judge's death, his will left me speechless. Deep breath in, push small breaths out. Also, me. Money. A substantial salary to manage his collection and his house. Why would he leave the art center and me so much? He'd left the house to me to manage and also had put me in charge of the money left to the art center. I was sure his children would have something to say about this.

I reread the paragraph about leaving control of his artwork to me. "To Jill Madison, who has demonstrated with deep devotion, her love and passion for art, I leave the handling of my collection of artwork. I know she will care for them with expertise and follow my directions to share them with art galleries. She has my faith and my confidence. As executor, she has the right to buy and sell artwork in the collection and dispense proceeds with the Adele Marsden Center for the Arts. I know she will be a trustworthy caretaker of my collection and will share it, as I have shared, with the world."

I was wiping more tears from my eyes after reading that when Winters walked in with two cups of coffee, followed by his secretary, Doris Weaver, who carried a tray of creamer and sugar. One look at my pale face and he knew I had made it to the end of the document. He waited for Doris to turn and leave, then shut the door again.

"How can this be? I'm not related to the judge. Why would he cut the children out of his will and give me so much? This is insane." I laid the papers on the edge of the desk. "I don't understand."

He pushed the coffee cup over to my side of the desk, added sugar, and said, "Drink this. It'll make you feel better."

I took a couple of large gulps. Then, closing my eyes and blowing out a deep breath, I sat back and opened them again. Nope. Not a dream. Ken

Winters still sat there, and the papers were in my lap.

"First, the judge can leave his estate to whomever he pleases. I know he regarded you as a surrogate daughter. He admired your arduous work ethic, your knowledge of art, and your gutsiness, and especially your steadiness in dealing with the art center building. Frankly, all the traits he wished his children had. As a friend of your parents, I'm sure he felt he wanted to provide for you in their absence. He made some changes recently once you returned to manage the art center."

"Provide? That's quite a word for what's in this document."

Winters pulled open a drawer in his desk, bringing out a set of shiny keys. "The police aren't done with the house yet. I'm sure your brother will tell you when it has been cleared. I took the liberty of changing the locks because I don't know who else has keys. He was adamant John and Erika stay out of the house because, just between you and me, in the past, a few valuable items went missing when they came home on visits. Once he clears the death scene, Detective Madison will let you know. You can go in the house any time after that. Keep it locked like Fort Knox. Tilda Swanson also has a new set of keys. Another decision for you to make—how long to keep Tilda on. Once the court finalizes your position, you'll have to do an inventory of the judge's possessions. You'll need to have the artwork appraised, which is another reason the judge trusted you. You'd know how to make that happen."

I rubbed my eyes and considered how much work this would be. On the other hand, the judge was counting on me. I couldn't let him down. "Alright. I can do this, Ken, if I have you to call on when I have questions."

"Absolutely."

"What about his adult children?"

"What about them?"

"Do they know what the will says?"

"I doubt it. They aren't entitled to a copy until the will is placed in probate. Then they can petition the court for copies because they're family members."

"I've met Erika. She was already planning to move into the house."

"That won't happen."

I bit my lip gently. "I don't have to tell John and Erika the contents, right?"

"No. Let them find out once the probate period begins. I'll file it later today. We may as well get the shock over with."

I pursed my lips. Once the explosion was over, the Spiveys would calm down. Who was I kidding? I might have to camp out at my friend Angie's house for a few days or get a watchdog. Once the town heard about this, they'd think I had persuaded the judge to leave me his money. Couldn't the judge's children sue me, saying I had undue influence on him? Oh, this wasn't a good position he'd put me in. It might be good to get advice from Tom.

As if he'd heard me, Tom's name came up on the lawyer's cell phone, which lay on the desk near me. "Go ahead," I told him.

He picked up the phone, pushed on a spot on the face, and said, "Hi, Tom."

I sat there, scanned the top page of the will, but listened to the long silences on Ken Winters' end of the conversation.

"Yes...What?" Long silence while he listened to my brother. "You must be kidding...Yes, she's still here. All right. I'll tell her. Thanks, Tom."

I sighed. "I suppose he's checking on his little sister again."

Ken laid his cell down and sat in silence for a moment. His face wore a grim expression while his eyes glanced at the desktop. In the silence, I could tell he was considering what to say next. Did he have bad news to break to me?

"Well." He shook his head. "Yes, that was Tom. He wasn't checking on you. He was calling me as the judge's lawyer to tell me the house would be under wraps a bit longer."

"How come?"

"The coroner's tests showed the judge's death wasn't a heart attack after all."

"What? I don't understand."

He had been fiddling with a fountain pen. Frowning, he set the pen down carefully, sat back in his chair, and said, "He was poisoned."

Chapter Six

Ken had given me a plastic zippered pouch for my copy of the judge's will, so I carried it with me to the art center, stuffing it in my top desk drawer. Through my mind charged *poison, poison, poison.* Who would do such a terrible thing? The judge had been kind to me, but I realized he was a judge. I was sure he had enemies among people whose sentences he'd pronounced. Snapping out of my dark thoughts, I could tell the art center was a bit chaotic when I walked in the door because the weavers guild was moving into what used to be our first-floor classroom.

Chad's voice drifted up to the main floor, his drill sergeant background barking orders. A door slammed, a woman's voice yelled, "Wait, the corner's stuck!" I needed to drop my tote in my office, and then I'd go check out the clamor. I pushed poison and wills into a back corner of my mind.

The judge's bequest would surely help in six months, after the probate period ended. Our classes met on the lower level at the back, past the hallway with mine and Louise's offices. But now we'd moved the classes to the second-floor classrooms, and the weavers guild would take over the classroom just off the first floor on a lower level. I figured here at our center they could offer weaving classes, and we would sell their lovely scarves, hats, and other creative endeavors in our gift shop. They'd make beautiful displays.

After I unlocked my office, I walked down the hallway and stood at the top of four steps, studying the scene below in the former classroom. Sharon Green, who owned a sewing shop in town, directed traffic. Sharon was in her sixties, had strawberry blond hair thanks to her hairdresser, and an air of leadership that translated into action. She was the efficient president of the weavers guild. Louise held one end of a floor loom, with Chad on the other end, halfway through the back door. They'd already moved two other table looms in, along with assorted baskets of yarn, fabric, and scissors. I stepped down the stairs and turned toward my left where we had a small kitchen. I brought out multiple bottles of chilled water from the refrigerator and set them on a table for the workers.

When I glanced back at the looms, the EMT guy they called Cleary was moving in the corner of a loom. Why was he here? It was an unseasonably warm day for September, so I walked over and handed him a bottle of water once they'd moved the loom in and positioned it.

"Mr. Cleary? Thanks for coming to help. You EMTs have all kind of talents."

He accepted the water bottle and held it up to his glistening forehead. "It's Chance. Chance Cleary. You're welcome. Chad told me you might need more guys to move these heavy looms, and I had a day off, so it sounded like a volunteer job I could do. I haven't been here long and don't know a lot of folks in town. Met Chad at one of the bars the other night. Struck up a conversation and, well, here I am."

I nodded. "Thanks again. Glad to have your help." I hadn't noticed his face much when he'd come to the judge's house. Now, I examined him. He wore a ball cap, but he'd taken it off to rub his arm across his forehead, and I noticed his hair was sparse and half gray. It had been blond at one point. I'd guess he was in his fifties. His eyebrows and lashes were so light you could hardly see them, but his complexion was smooth, with only a few wrinkles around the eyes and mouth. He had a small chin, tiny and slightly crooked teeth, and his T-shirt was wet from the exertion of moving the heavy looms. Altogether, a calm and ordinary face.

He turned, downing about half the water in the bottle, then set it on a table and walked over to help Chad move another huge floor loom into place. The boat shuttle used with it fell to the floor with a clatter, and he picked it up with one graceful swoop.

I surveyed the situation and realized Louise had figured out where every loom would fit. They didn't need me, so I went back upstairs to keep an eye on the gallery. I walked to the front door and stared out at the public square. It was such a beautiful—if warm—fall day, and my artist's eyes studied the various colors of the leaves now displayed in their gorgeous fall hues—Burnt Sienna, Alizarin Crimson, and Cadmium Yellow Light. Couldn't help it if I always saw the hues through my painter's eyes.

Thoughts about the judge's death crept into my head. Why would someone want to kill him? Were Tom and Abe right when they thought it could involve a person he'd sentenced or greedy family members? But the only people who gained from his death were me and the art center. Several charities too, but they didn't know about his will. I certainly didn't before his death, and his lawyer, Winters, wouldn't open his mouth. Did this mean someone who hated him had murdered him? The word "murdered" stuck in my brain. I turned to go back to my office. On my way down the hallway, I straightened a couple of photographs on the wall. I had to admit I was OCD about out-of-balance artwork.

As always, my office was messy. I'd left on Saturday in a hurry after the unexpected tragedy at the judge's house. Straightening the grant papers I'd been working on, I stuffed them in a folder. I glanced at the wall in front of me, smiling at the three whiteboards. After the first exhibit went spectacularly, the judge told me I could have as many whiteboards as I wanted, despite the huffing and puffing of Ivan the Terrible, Curmudgeon Supreme, Keeper of the Funds. Now I had three whiteboards, and they listed current and future jobs. They kept my life and job organized. I read the lists: grant writing, social media, exhibit schedule 2016-2017, partnerships for sponsors, reception details. In the long term, I'd written membership drive, check in with juror, newsletter, and volunteers. My office might be messy, but I had a firm grip on the jobs I needed to finish.

My cell phone sang from my tote bag. *Anytime You Need a Friend*, a song from our high school days. Angie had been married shortly after high school to Wiley Emerson. He was perfect for her, and they owned a bar business they began together. They called it Priscilla's Pub, named for their pet dog Priscilla, an Akita. I hadn't talked with Angie alone since all this craziness with the judge's will. I walked over and closed my office door, then punched the accept button on my cell phone.

"Hi, Angie."

"Hey. What's up?"

"You have no idea how that question is fraught with scary implications."

"What? Talk English."

I sat back in my desk chair. "I think I should stop by the bar tonight. I could use a beer and girl talk. Woman to woman."

Silence on Angie's end of the phone. Then, "The gossip line is humming, and the judge's death has been the topic of conversation every night at the bar."

"Great. I'm afraid it'll get worse before this is all over. We may have another investigation on our hands." I only mentioned "another" because several months earlier, one of our friends was found murdered, and we helped Tom investigate. Angie and I helped solve the murder, much to Tom's annoyance.

"What? Why? I heard he had a heart attack. That EMT was here at the bar with Chad McKenna, and I caught a few words about it."

"Yes. So was I. But not a heart attack. I'll fill you in this evening. I need to get work done at my real job today. Ivan Truelove has been suspiciously quiet, and that generally means the universe is somewhat off balance. I don't know what he's up to."

"Alright. See you tonight. I'll have the beer cold."

"Good. Till then." I punched the screen to end the call.

I needed to get to work on this grant. I opened the folder and spent an hour researching information to fill in the paperwork. I could hear voices and noises in the lower room as people arranged the looms, talking and laughing. Weavers would be a terrific addition to our art center.

My next search was for a file in the stack on my desk. Our first national juried exhibit. I had named it *Harvest Time*, and it could refer to the fall season, the changes in life, the end of a project, and, I figured, many other possibilities I hadn't dreamed of yet.

The Call to Artists went out months ago. It listed all the information and deadlines the artists would need. The possible entries had been photographed and placed online, where Arteaga could see them and decide which entries would make the cut. Unlike our earlier regional exhibit, where artists had to have lived in the area at some point, this exhibit was national. The regional exhibit had accepted every piece of artwork submitted. However, the *Harvest Time* juror would select fifty to sixty pieces from the online portfolio of more than six hundred entries.

I was much more confident in the process this time because Louise and I had organized the earlier regional exhibit. I'd made calls and scheduled appointments to raise money for the reception, the awards, and the promotion. Once I found the juror, it was all systems go. Smiling, I remembered how nervous I'd been when I first started this job. I had grown into the position.

The bell on the side door jingled, indicating someone familiar approached. Everyone but Louise and I used the front door. We also had a side door on an alley that separated our building from an insurance business to our south. My brother Tom was walking in. He noticed me and smiled through the window of my office.

I moved to my office door and ushered him in, removing several items from the loveseat just inside the door. "Morning, brother."

He glanced at his watch. "It's almost noon." He sat on the loveseat with a deep sigh. "Long morning for both of us."

"Yes. Weavers Guild is moving in, but I think they're about done. What brings you here?"

"I spoke with Ken Williams, so I'm aware I have a celebrity sister who'll be managing a lot of money for the art center and a bit for herself."

"I thought he had to keep the details of the will confidential. Isn't there privilege attached? Lawyer-client?"

"Yes. But once I checked on Ron's tox report, I felt I should discuss the will with him. After all, who gains financially makes a difference in terms of the investigation."

I thought about that for a moment, anxiety rising in my chest. "Did you come to arrest me?"

Tom laughed. "No. But now it's a murder investigation, and whether the inheritance has to do with motive is a big question mark. Ken opened the file with the court today for probate, so I could have found out the contents anyway."

"I talked to him this morning."

"Erika and John don't have a clue what's in the will, and Ken corroborated that. They must have thought they'd get his money, a classic motive. Especially true because the judge and his children haven't spoken to each other for a long time. I plan to interview both kids today about alibis. But they won't know what's in the will until they get a lawyer and file with the court to see its contents. That's a few days until all hell will break loose, and I want to make sure you're protected."

"What? You think they might harm me?" My chest, as usual, registered anxiety. I took a deep breath, trying to quell it.

"It's one of the reasons I wanted to talk with Ken. Legally, if anything happens to you—"

I giggled. "Like my unexpected demise?"

"Yes. There is something called residual legacies. After the executor distributes bequests to charities and a few named people, the rest reverts to the family if you're dead, even if they weren't named as legatees. Oh, and if you're found guilty of killing the judge, the slayer law goes into effect, and you can't inherit even so much as a blank canvas. The Spiveys are mentioned at the beginning of the will because they're related to him by blood, but not as legatees. Probate goes on for six months. I'd rather keep you around during that period."

I laughed. "Only six months?"

He smiled. "Well, you know what I mean. After the probate period is over, the bequests are dispersed, and then you're home free."

"You're kidding, right? I can't imagine the judge's kids would come after me."

"It's happened before. Lots of money. Once I have information about the whole situation, I can stand back and reconsider my concerns. I also need to go through his last cases before he retired. Could be some motives there."

I rubbed my mouth, a simmering tension in my fingers. "Guess I shouldn't have signed the executor paper, huh?"

He shook his head. "Well, I don't know John and Erika as adults. They've not been around in recent years, but I need to get a feeling for what they're capable of."

"But you won't tell them about the will?"

"Are you serious? Of course not. That will come later when they find out themselves."

I thought over what he'd said. "Is there anything I can help you with? I worshipped the judge. He was a real friend, mentor, kind of like Dad. I am so angry someone did this. How? How did they do this?" I could hear my words, their heightened volume betraying my irritability, but I shouldn't take it out on Tom. I relaxed my shoulders and calmed myself.

"Digitalis."

"I thought that helped heart attacks."

"It does in a small amount. In a larger amount, it's a fast killer. Someone loaded him up with Digitalis, giving him an injection in the inside of his elbow. The coroner found the injection mark during the autopsy."

I swirled the thought around in my head. "Oh, my gosh. They gave him a shot? I wouldn't even know how to do that." I thought about that briefly. "So, I repeat, how can I help?"

Tom stood. "I had a thought. You and Tilda can go in the house by Wednesday. Only you two. I don't know much about the art business or what his paintings are worth. You know all about artwork. You'll have a key to his house, and you'll need to inventory everything, including the papers in his desk, files, and office. Ken said you do that as his executor. I want you to keep an eye open for anything that looks strange or out of order. But that's it. No playing detective or coming up with theories about criminals. It's your art knowledge I need."

My face beamed, and my legs moved back and forth, almost in a dance. I had to carefully consider my words so he wouldn't realize how excited I was. "Sure. He left a voice mail for me Friday night asking about the names of companies who analyze art works for fraud or appraisal."

"Is that usual?"

"Not really. If he wanted appraisals, he might have been concerned about fraud. But he never got to tell me what worried him. I know he had a partner who acquired artwork for him. Peter Angelini. He's mentioned him before. You'll want to talk to him. I'll see what I can find about their business together. Anything else?" I was excited. My art expertise meant I could give information to Tom. For once, I knew more than he did about the art side of this investigation. Ha!

"Yes," Tom said, opening the door slightly to leave. He turned back and pointed his finger at me. "While you're at his house—you or Tilda—make sure you keep all the doors locked. I'm deadly serious about that."

Chapter Seven

Tom's concern for my safety echoed in my brain as I drove to Priscilla's Pub around six thirty that evening. I parked in the nearly empty lot—Mondays were slow—and walked through the heavy metal and glass doors of Angie and Wiley's bar. They'd built their business successfully over the last seven years.

Once inside, I let my eyes adjust to the bar lighting, a soft glow accompanied by the buzz of conversation. Not too loud, because only a few patrons sat at the long, polished cherrywood bar. Starting on Thursday nights and going through the weekend, millennials and thirty-somethings packed this place. Unlike small towns with alcoholic dives, Apple Grove could be proud of Priscilla's Pub. As usual, all was polished to perfection—glass stemware hanging from a rack behind the bar, garnish trays, crystal glasses, and sinks all lovingly cared for. Wiley had five beers on tap in the center of the bar and several flat-screen televisions on the walls tuned to various sports channels. Framed photos of current local teams and sports memorabilia accompanied the television screens as decorations. This was a town proud of its teams, from Little League through the Apple Grove College teams.

Wiley caught my eye. He walked over to my end of the bar carrying my favorite beer, Bent River Uncommon Stout. Angie had made a few questionable decisions in her life—don't even ask me about the pink, poofy maid-of-honor dress I had to wear at her wedding—but Wiley wasn't one of them. He loved her with all his heart, and you could see it on his face and in his gestures. A deep sense of humor punctuated his every word. She'd met him after high school when she worked at the *Apple Grove Ledger* office.

They'd been together ever since. He reminded me of a young Sam Elliott, a movie star my mother used to point out in Westerns. Handsome.

"Hi, Jill. Angie's in the back room grabbing some extra towels, but she told me to keep an eye out for you. How's tricks?"

"Tricks? If you mean, how am I after finding yet a third dead body in my life, then tricks are only making me tougher."

"Heard about the judge. Shocking news always travels fast. Sorry. I never knew him, but Angie says he was a standup guy." He leaned over and polished the already shining cherrywood bar, lowering his voice. "Please tell me you're not taking my darling girl breaking and entering again. I can't stand the thought of buckshot in her backside."

His reference was to a house where Angie and I had sneaked in. The parents of our best friend owned it. Her evil stepfather came to the window with a gun full of buckshot as we tore through the backyards to Angie's car. So, all right. We did do some things best not mentioned to my brother Tom, but no harm, no foul. Right?

"No, Wiley. I will not lead her into temptation again, but I must say the decisions we make are usually Angie's too. In fact, sometimes they're all hers."

He chuckled. "Figured." He glanced down the bar. "Ah, here she comes, the B&E expert."

And there she was. My best bud, her blond hair tied back in a ponytail, hoop earrings dazzling in the light, her bar apron tugged close around her slender body. A big smile broke across her face when she saw Wiley and me shooting the breeze.

"I didn't know if you'd make it after the day you've had. This is great. Lots of time on Monday nights to talk. Wiley will take up the slack. Right, honey?"

"Absolutely. Go have your beer." He paused and turned back. "Oh, and don't rustle up any plans that call for bail money, OK? I'm short on cash."

I saluted him. "Gotcha, Wiley."

Angie grabbed a beer, and we wandered over to a booth at the back of the bar, glancing around to see if anyone else was in the area. No. We had it all to ourselves. She plopped on the seat across from me, both of us taking long chugs of our beers. Setting hers down, she grabbed one of my hands. "How are you? I still can't imagine how awful it must have been to find the judge."

I stared right into her blue eyes, shaking my head. "It was awful. I think I have a curse. First, our high school friend and now the judge. Oh, let's not forget the body I stumbled over with a knife in its back. Perhaps Ivan Truelove, the micromanager, is right about me finding dead people." I shook my head, releasing a long sigh. "What is it about me and murders?"

"Timing. You didn't have anything to do with those murders."

"Tell that to Ivan F. Truelove the Third."

She laughed. "He still texts?"

"Several times a day. The wrong person has been murdered."

"He's only a little gnat. An irritation."

"So true," I said, wondering why I hadn't had a text from him in the last hour. "I have no idea what's with the judge. Between you and me, Tom said he was poisoned. A shot of digitalis in his arm near the inner elbow. When I went to his house, the front door was unlocked, as it usually is on Saturday when we have lunch, so anyone could have walked right in."

"Poisoned? Oh, my. What about his kids?"

"What about them?"

"They were here at the bar this afternoon together."

"What did you make of them? Other than Erika showing up at Tom's house yesterday, I haven't seen either of them in years. Her brother's here too?"

"Yeah. At least, I assume it's who she was with."

"She has a different name after Spivey. Maybe it was her husband."

"Didn't see a wedding ring."

"Oh." I sipped my beer and thought about that. "Divorced? Widowed? Do you suppose she murdered him?" We both chuckled.

Angie studied her own ring, turning it around on her finger. "What's Tom think?"

I tilted my head slightly. "He doesn't say much other than to mention John and Erika—they were on the outs with their father. It could have been someone the judge had sentenced in recent years. It simply seems strange because he's been retired for a while."

Angie grimaced. "But people do get out of prison. This could be a person who had a grudge."

"Could be. I haven't told you the biggest part of it."

"What?" Her eyes were laser-focused on me like an artist as she dabbed one more spot on a canvas.

"I'm his executor."

"What? His what?"

"Yeah. And his children don't know it, but they'll find out soon. Also, he left me in charge of his art collection and the art center a lot of valuable paintings plus cash, stipulating I should make decisions about it."

She sat back in her seat, her mouth open, as if she'd heard me say I'd found a boyfriend. "Oh, my. Did you know about this?"

"No. Not a word."

"Correct me if I'm wrong, but doesn't this give you a prime motive to kill him, and you found the body?"

"I should be thankful Tom's my brother. He realizes that besides pranks I've played on Andy, I don't have a mean bone in my body. And I know nothing about poisons, I can't give injections, and I didn't know about his will."

Now she leaned forward again, nodded, and glanced around. "Thank goodness. I must tell you the bars buzzed with the news, especially on Saturday night when word got out about the judge's death. But all the gossipers thought he'd had a heart attack."

"Unfortunately, they'll find out differently. That's what Tom said. I don't know how or why, but Abe ordered tests because he was suspicious. Now it's a murder."

Someone put money in the jukebox, and a twangy country song began playing. Not exactly my favorite kind of music. The bar had a live band on the weekend, and often it was my brother Andy's band. Over the sounds of the country notes, Angie put her hands on her mouth and stared at me with worried eyes.

"What?"

She took her hands down. "Now I know what happened late this afternoon."

"What are you talking about?"

"The Spivey sibs were not alone. Their heads were together in a sneaky-looking collaboration as if they were part of John Wilkes Booth's gang."

"We all know how that ended. Did you hear their conversation?"

"No," she said, her voice quiet beneath the musical interlude. "But they were here with Jezbhel Gushman, that weaselly newspaper editor. It appeared they were cooking up a plot. She was writing items on a pad of paper as they talked to her. Every so often, they'd glance around as if they were worried someone would hear them."

I thought about it for a moment. "Hmm. You're right. Not good."

"She's such a weasel. I'm not even a journalist, but I know the difference between a fact and an opinion. She always mixes the two and makes innuendoes about situations. I think she must do it to try to sell more papers. Believe me, this is a story ripe for innuendo."

"I can't become the target of a story about this. It would be terrible for the art center. It was bad enough when we dug up a body in the basement." I paused. My chest tightened, and I could hear my heartbeat throbbing in my ears. I almost lost my job a few months ago because of bad publicity. This time there would be no one to give me a second chance. No Judge Spivey to calm Ivan down and take my side with the art center board.

Angie grabbed my hand. "Don't let it throw you. Once the truth came out, your art center flourished. No one blamed you. It'll happen again."

"But the newspaper didn't have a sleazy editor back then."

"Nothing you can do about it for now. Will Tom let us help?"

I inspected my hands in my lap for a moment. "He says I can help with what I know about artwork." I sighed. "Guess that's a start."

She sat back, dejected. "I was hoping we could follow the Spiveys. You know, see if they had poison in their bags in their hotel rooms. I know where to get hotel maid costumes."

I admired, as always, her enthusiasm and didn't ask her why she might have a hotel maid costume. "Let's wait till we see what happens once they find out about the will. Well," I said, "I need to go home. One beer's it for tonight. I had a long day, and tomorrow will come soon enough."

Looking over my shoulder, Angie added, "Oh, oh. He's walked in the door."

I turned around, checking the bar area. Chance Cleary walked in with someone trailing behind him.

"Let me describe," Angie said. "Sparkling blue eyes, wavy brown hair with a hint of highlights from the summer sun, and a gorgeous smile with perfect white teeth. Remember the description that rolled off your lips a few weeks ago?"

It took a minute for my brain to register. "The doctor at the emergency room. Dr. Finch." He had taken care of me in the ER when I was a huge mess, having run from a murderer intent on killing me. Covered in sweat, vomit, and dirt, I had puked several times, and he checked me out when Andy took me in to get medical help. I didn't exactly look like great date material. Most embarrassing moment of my recent life. Finch. No wonder I'd never heard from him again.

Angie leaned over, a conspiracy of her own playing out. "They just sat at the bar. This is what you do. Trust me. Walk past them to the door, and I'll follow you. After you leave, I'll go back behind the bar. If he's interested, he'll ask me who you are, and I'll mention you run the art center. And are SINGLE. Plan?"

"Plan. Not sure if he'll be interested in someone whose name is all over the newspaper as a suspected killer."

"A little celebrity never hurt anyone."

"Now you sound like Andy. All right. Let's do this."

I was halfway home in my little Austin Mini when I got a text. Was it Ivan on a Monday night with nothing else to do? Pulling to the side of the road, I opened my texts. There it was. Not Ivan. Angie. "Oh, he's interested. Wanted the story of your life. My lips were sealed. You're a lady of mystery. WHOO HOO!"

Chapter Eight

L ate Tuesday afternoon, I organized paints, brushes, and a canvas in the small art studio in my backyard. It had been my mother's sculpture studio, located behind our family house where I now lived. The sun was still above the horizon, and light filtered in through the windows on either side of me. It was a miniature house, connected to our house by a brick sidewalk my dad had laid. Before I started painting, I sat back and considered how the day had gone at the art center. Lots of traffic I hadn't expected.

First, Tom called. Darn! I had hoped it was the ER doctor, so each time the phone rang, I jumped a bit with expectation. But no. Could be the doctor was working all day.

"Adele Marsden Center for the Arts," I said into the desk phone. "Jill speaking."

"Thought I'd call and let you know I should be done at the judge's house later today, so tomorrow you can go in." It was Tom. "I'll let Tilda Swanson know too. If you find anything unusual, let me know."

"Perfect. I have time off tomorrow, so I'll head over there in the morning." I paused momentarily. "By find 'anything unusual,' you mean...?"

"Oh, a clue that might implicate a possible suspect in the judge's death. Any improprieties in his finances. Unusual situations with his artwork. Of course, his desk and files have lots of papers, many of them pertaining to art, so I will count on you to watch for suspicious possibilities when you inventory it all."

"I'm your woman. All right. I'll check it out tomorrow. Anything else?"

Tom hesitated a moment. "Jezbhel Gushman stopped in today to get information for a story in the *Ledger*. There wasn't much to give her, only the few facts we know. She did get an autopsy report, so she knows about the poison. Whether she's filed with the court to find out about the will, I don't know. I'd guess yes."

"Oh, great." I told him about the sinister meeting at Priscilla's Pub. That could only lead to more community gossip. Imagining Tom's head shaking through the phone line, I figured the nefarious team was plotting against me and the art center. "Don't worry. I'll keep my eyes open and the doors to the judge's house locked. Just like you said. Try to be careful."

"Perfect. I plan to chase leads and alibis today. Take care of yourself."

"Don't worry, Tom. I'm thirty, not fifteen."

He chuckled. "What's the difference?" he said and punched off.

I'll show him. Why does he always think I'm incompetent because he's eight years older than me? Michelangelo finished *David* at age twenty-nine. I'll show him.

After his call, Louise and I had a lengthy list of jobs to do for the national exhibit. I'd already checked out several of the digital copies of pieces. I gasped, admired, and smiled at the creativity of the artists.

We'd divided the jobs in half, but as I always reminded Louise, she needed to know my jobs and vice versa. That decision worked out well in our early summer exhibit, *Home in the Heartland*. I was unfortunately delayed for the opening, but Louise and our intern knew exactly what to do because we had cross-planned.

I was about to leave for lunch when I glanced out the window of my office. A middle-aged man opened the front door and began to walk slowly around the photography exhibit on the walls. He was a stranger. I guessed him to be in his forties, dressed quite elegantly for Apple Grove, with brown hair gone silver in places—the aging change that made women look older but men appear more handsome. Now that was unfair. His clothes screamed urban dweller. He stopped in front of an eight-by-ten photo of a barn set back against a landscape of long prairie grasses. Examining it, he turned his head slightly, as if to memorize it or try to figure out if he knew the location.

As I stared at him, I wondered if he had walked into the gallery by accident or if he had a reason to check out our exhibit. Standing, I pushed my chair in and headed out the door.

"Hi. May I help you?"

He noticed me, seemed to know me, and smiled in a charming way. I tried to remember where I'd seen him before, but my memory disappointed me. He seemed vaguely familiar.

Reaching out his hand to shake mine, he said, "John Bradford Spivey. I imagine you are Jill Madison."

"Oh." I took a step backward, my body reacting before I even thought about it. Hints of the judge's features were obvious in the line of his jaw and the arch of his eyebrows. Recovering, I forced a smile. "Right. It's been years, John, so forgive me if I didn't recognize you. Lots of years." I examined his face closer now. There were lines I hadn't seen at a distance and a puffiness to his face. He looked older than his age, as if life hadn't done him any favors.

He nodded at my assessment of time. "Yes. I didn't live here long."

"How can I help you? Are you interested in artwork?"

He appeared to think about my question. "Well, no. Actually, I hoped to speak with you."

I blinked, thinking about what to say next. Nervously, I mumbled, "You found me."

He moved forward a bit into my space while I automatically inched back again. "I hope you can clear up an obvious bit of false gossip my sister Erika brought to me. She said she'd gone to your brother's house the other morning."

"Yes. I was there when Erika stopped by."

"Is it true we're not allowed into our own house? I find this rather inconvenient, to say the least."

I noticed a slight edge to his voice as if he were trying to be pleasant yet indicating his frustration. "You are correct about what Tom said. It's a crime scene, and until he clears it, no one can go into the house."

"Ah." He nodded as if all was crystal clear. "I would suppose once the police release the scene, Erika and I will be able to deal with Dad's papers.

His financial bits and pieces. It won't be an easy estate to understand or organize, but I believe my sister and I are aware of our father's affairs. We'll make short shrift of it."

Now my brain raced around, trying to figure out what I should say or not say. He stared at me in an uncomfortable way, as if the silence was a demand that I tell him all I knew. I sure didn't plan to do that. I took a deep breath. *Delay, delay…*

"My understanding is Illinois has a probate law. You know, my brothers and I had to deal with our parents' estate, so we've been through the process. I believe your father's estate will stay in probate for six months."

He studied the ceiling. Were there probate answers written there? Then John Spivey touched his chin as if mulling over the legal situation. "Are you saying we won't be able to liquidate any of his estate for six months? Why?" His voice began to sound churlish and slightly angry, but unlike Erika, he kept his cool.

"I'm not a lawyer, John." Thinking fast, I reinforced the parent story. "I remember from our own experience with my parents. I believe his lawyer is Ken Winters."

He considered this. His charming smile once again appeared, and his voice moderated. "Thank you so much, Jill. You've been an immense help. I'll check on the legal situation. Then I'll stop in and see if your brother can tell me when the house will be open again. Both of us have jobs in the Chicago area. We can't be gone from them forever. We hope to get this situation sorted out quickly. Right now, we're planning his funeral, and once it's over, we hope to deal with the legal aspects of his estate. Again, I appreciate your help. I'm sure we'll meet again."

You have no idea how true that is.

He turned and walked out before I could say anything, and I briefly wondered if he and his sister played good cop, bad cop. No matter which, he wouldn't be happy when he discovered I was the executor while he was the disinherited dupe. Why, oh why, didn't I tell him the truth? Because I hated confrontation. I was a chicken. It was hard enough to come home last year after my career as an artist in Chicago had fizzled to a dead halt.

Returning to Apple Grove seemed like the final defeat. But miraculously, it brought me back to my painting. My emotional balance set in, allowing me to paint once again. However, I still didn't like to confront people on unpleasant subjects. This executor's job I'd agreed to was sure to back me right into that corner.

Now it was late afternoon. I still had time in the light to work on my latest painting. As I checked to see if the gesso had dried on my canvas, I thought about my mom and all the hours she'd spent in this little studio, wrestling images from clay. She had been a famous sculptor who had won many prizes—including the prestigious Brookington Award—and taught art at the local college. At times when I sat here in her chair applying paint to canvas, I could sense her encouragement, her loving spirit wrapping itself around me. Silly, I know, but this place was so imbued with her. My father often teased her about the hours she spent here, but I understood her passion. Feeling her presence inspired me.

My thoughts traveled back to this morning at the art center. Something kept niggling in my brain. What was it I couldn't remember? I began with broad strokes of raw sienna on the canvas, concentrating on the placement of the color with confident strokes. Pulling my brush back, I remembered. The judge had asked me to check on forensic analysts. I still didn't know why. Tomorrow, if Tilda was at his house, I'd ask her if she knew about his concern. I also needed to find out about his children. What had caused such a rift that they'd stayed away for years? Why did he leave them out of his will? The judge I knew was such a kind, compassionate person I couldn't imagine what had caused such a long estrangement.

My parents had died six years earlier when I was twenty-four. Prior to their deaths, I'd spent three years in the city, coming home only occasionally. Now I wish I'd been home more often. Who knew they would die together so young? I took a deep breath, dabbing more ultramarine blue on the canvas. The real question in my mind was what my parents might have said about the Spiveys and their children if I'd been an adult back then. As close as the two couples were, I figured my mom and dad knew a lot of details about the Spivey family's life they never shared with me. Sometimes being the youngest helped you get away with things, but other times you missed out.

I nearly jumped out of my chair when a faint knocking came from behind me on my studio door. Fortunately, I hadn't had my brush near the canvas. Turning, brush in midair, I almost gasped. The ER doctor was standing in the doorway. OMG. I set down my brush, turned again, and said, "Oh, hi." In my head, I counted to five, trying to remember if I'd touched up my hair or makeup when I got home from the art center. No. But I couldn't possibly look as bad as I did the first time I met him in the ER. I almost sighed at that unhappy mental picture.

He smiled. "I tried the front door to the house but figured you didn't hear me." He took in the studio. "This is a great spot for painting." That smile again.

I pulled off my paint smock and laid it over the back of my chair. "It is. It was my mother's studio, but I've commandeered it. It's nice to see you again. At least I'm not a mess after running away from a killer."

He stood where he was and chuckled. "Why do I get the feeling you lead quite an exciting life? First, running from a murderer, and now stealing away an inheritance from the two rightful owners, according to the local newspaper. I'm sure the whole town is expressing their indignation." He shook his head. "I work in the ER, but I don't see half as much trauma as you appear to deal with."

Great. He must think I'm a hot mess. I put my hands up and motioned him back from the doorway and out into the yard. I wouldn't mind being a little closer to him, but my studio was claustrophobic, and I hardly knew the man—a problem I'd love to fix. "Dr. Finch—"

"Sam, please."

"Sam. And by the way, how did you find me?"

"Your very helpful manager at the art center. Louise, I believe. She said to try your house because you'd left early to paint. Made me a map to walk the two blocks. Suggested you might be in your studio painting. Seemed eager to give me your cell number and address. A helpful woman indeed. The art center is quite an amazing place for a town of this size. I heard you were getting ready to install a national juried exhibit. I'm impressed."

Thinking about Louise, who never found a dating site she didn't like, I reminded myself to reward her. Admiring Sam Finch, I considered my firstborn child as an apt reward. I lifted my eyebrows, vaguely remembering my flirty days. "You're interested in art?" Wide smile, interested expression, moving my foot a step closer to him.

"Sure. When I was in medical school, I often spent my lunch hours—when I had them—checking out art galleries a few blocks from the hospital. In fact, I was surprised when I saw the name of your art center. Adele Marsden. I used to see her sculptures in exhibits. What an amazing artist."

"My mother."

The expression on his face was priceless. "What? I knew she was from here, but I guess the name didn't connect to you because they're different. How wonderful. You must have that creativity running through your DNA."

My face was toasty warm, an annoying reaction that occurred when I least wanted to blush. I should change the subject. "How did you find your way to Apple Grove? I know you didn't grow up here. I'd remember you from school." What a dumb thing that was to say. I was so stupid. I could tell I was losing my touch, out of sync with my dormant flirting techniques.

He leaned toward me, reached out, and touched my cheek, producing not an entirely unpleasant reaction on my part.

"What?"

"You have a bit of red paint there on your cheek." Now he raised his eyebrows.

I put my finger on the spot he'd touched. "Oh. That. Sometimes I get a little too careless with my brushstrokes." Geesh. I didn't know what to say. I stuck my finger in my mouth, pushed it around on my cheek, and probably made it much worse. Raw sienna rubbed all over one side of my face.

The sides of his mouth quivered as if he was trying to hide a reaction to my raw sienna makeup.

"What can I do for you now that you've looked me up and discovered I hide back here and paint?"

He tilted his head and gave a slight smile. What perfect, white teeth he had. How could one man be so gorgeous? Oh, yeah. He's a doctor. Probably eats healthy and works out. Sooo unlike Angie and me, who often polished off two bottles of Savvy B in record time.

"I wondered if you might like to have lunch with me Wednesday. I don't get a lot of time off, but Wednesday's the next day I'm able to get away. Lunch?"

"Are you sure you want to be seen with me? I am, as you say, rather notorious." I reminded myself to keep it light.

"Absolutely. I'm an excitement junky. I work in an emergency room. I'd like to take a chance. How about you?"

"Sure. Want to come by the art center and pick me up, or would you like to meet somewhere?"

"Happy to drop in. Say, eleven-thirty?"

"Perfect."

"All right, then. See you Wednesday." Then he turned and headed back around our house, waving once with his hand in the air.

I simply stood there in shock. Next Wednesday. Lunch. More importantly, what did I have to wear?

Chapter Nine

On Wednesday morning, I trekked up the five steps to the front porch of 724 Winslow Avenue. I would put in several hours at the art center in the evening to make up for mornings like today. Sam Finch was coming by to take me to lunch at 11:30, and I felt a lightness in my step. Nothing seemed different since I'd sat on the swing last week—same swing, same steps, same burgundy front door, same numbers next to the mailbox. Everything was still here, waiting, except for the judge. It was hard to believe I'd never see him again, have lunch in his exquisite dining room while we laughed about a story from the art community, or discuss financial numbers before board meetings. I swallowed hard, said hello to the policeman by the door, Dominic Aubrey, and felt through my tote bag.

Pulling a set of keys from my bag, I inserted the shiny new one, turned it, and heard the lock click. I was in. Tom told me he'd asked the post office to hold the mail until I could get it. I guess he'd forgotten the newspapers. I picked up several that had accumulated in the area under the swing. Clutching them to my chest, I pushed open the door and wondered what I'd find. No life. The closed drapes made the living room dark, but the air conditioning hummed. The air had a stale feeling and smell of a house closed for several days. I took a deep breath and stood totally still in the middle of the room. Nothing. No feeling of human habitation. Dropping the newspapers on the coffee table, I walked to the windows and opened the drapes. At least I could get sunshine in the place. Black powder covering the surfaces of the coffee table and end tables. I guessed Tom's crew didn't clean after trashing. Tilda could take care of that. I'd let her know I'd be at the judge's house this morning.

Oh, gee. I'd almost forgotten Tom's warning to lock the door behind me, so I did. I thought it was overkill, especially because Aubrey stood outside the door. If the judge had been poisoned, someone out there was the culprit, and even though I doubted I was a target, I figured it was better to follow Tom's instructions. After all, the Spiveys were in town, and I stood between them and millions. Although Tom was far more conservative than I was, in this situation, his cautionary thoughts were wise. Erika was scary. John could be a quiet ticking bomb.

Fifteen minutes later, I'd opened all the curtains throughout the first floor and felt much less nervous with the sunshine streaming through the windows. It was just a house, right? The brownies still sat under cellophane on the island in the kitchen, a memory of what might have been last Saturday. Sighing at that thought, I opened the doors under the sink, and there were the cleaning supplies. I should check the office and clean the fingerprint dust because I'd work in that room most of the time.

What a strange feeling. Saturday, I was so nervous about coming into his office, but today I knew no one would be sitting at his desk. I flipped on the light switch. Fingerprint powder covered most surfaces. It was an invasion of his inner sanctum. The desk chair, which had been at an odd angle, sat alone and forlorn in the middle of the room. I set my tote on the chair, took a deep breath, and walked around to the back of the desk. What had I expected? The judge's body was no longer there, and the various indentations in the carpet revealed where feet had moved him out to the coroner's van. Sadness crept into my heart. For a moment, my shoulders drooped, and my chin quivered. Then I pulled my shoulders back, and a surge of determination filled my body. I would work hard to find his killer. The secret might be in his records. And he had believed in me.

I was considering where to start when I heard a noise from the living room or kitchen. I tiptoed down the hallway and realized it was the lock in the front door. The door swung open, and Tilda Swanson walked through, pulling out the key and closing the door behind her. Tom must have talked with her because she locked the door once she was in. I coughed politely so she wouldn't be surprised. Still, she jumped as she turned and saw me.

"Oh, my." Tilda put her hand over her heart. "You startled me."

"Sorry."

A tall, spare woman with a no-nonsense air about her, Tilda had been with the judge since before his wife died. Her face had settled into lines around the corners of her mouth and eyes, and her hair had grayed over the past decade, pulled back in a chignon held into place by a hair clip. She glanced at the furniture. "Black snow?" Folding her arms across her chest, I watched as she glanced around the room and shook her head. "Tom will hear about this."

I chuckled. "He's heard worse."

She laid a large bag on the sofa and asked, "Is the rest of the house this bad?"

"Lots of fingerprint powder. I was about to clean the office."

She nodded briskly. "Out to the kitchen." She pointed and sped off. I followed.

Pulling buckets, sponges, and canisters of dusting spray, she handed me my marching orders. "You do the office; I'll do these other rooms. Fifteen minutes we meet in the kitchen for a cup of coffee and confab about where we go from here."

"Perfect. I haven't checked the basement room. After we talk, we should check the artwork."

She stared into my eyes. I was relieved to see an expression of respect on her face. "Agreed."

I cleaned black fingerprint powder away from the surfaces—the desk, chair, shelves, and light switches. His desk was still covered with papers, and I gently laid them on a window seat, shaking the powder from them into a wastebasket, sneezing twice. Once all surfaces were clean again, I pulled the desk chair over and sat behind the massive walnut desk, looking out at the room. What a wonderful place to work.

A yellow corner of a sticky note stuck out of the middle drawer. I opened the drawer and discovered paper clips, pencils, pens, and other office supplies. I carefully opened the crinkled sticky note. On it were two words: Ted Bender. Who was Ted Bender? I had no idea. I smoothed out the note and laid it carefully in the drawer. Shutting it, I moved to the three drawers on the left.

I stared at those drawers and sat for a moment. This would be quite a job, and I hadn't even gone to the basement's temperature-controlled room I'd seen on a few occasions. Turning to the right side of the desk, I opened the top drawer and gasped. Then I slammed it shut. Then I opened it cautiously. A gun. The judge had a small handgun—I didn't know anything about guns—and I closed the drawer, not touching it. I wondered why he had this in his office. And if someone came after him, why didn't he use it? Maybe Tilda would know why he had a gun.

The second drawer held files organized in a vertical way. Their corners contained tiny, wire grips that hugged round, metal arms on either side of the drawer. They had different labels, and I recognized the name of a big auction house on one. Perhaps they were business papers from his art acquisitions. Enough time to study those later.

Toward the back of the files were more files with personal topics on them. One had Laura's name. I pulled it out and leafed through the various papers. Bills from her cancer days, her funeral, and a few miscellaneous papers. At the back was a copy of her will. I laid it on the desk and examined the pages. She'd left each of her children $100,000. I'd call it a substantial sum, so why were they always out of money? I knew it took more money to live in a large city like Chicago or New York, but both had stable jobs and no children to support. Where, in heaven's name, could all that money be going?

I closed the document, replaced it, and put the file back in the drawer. Another file with John's name on it was right behind Laura's. It contained only a few letters, but they all were from collection agencies. Replacing it, I closed the drawer and rubbed my eyes. In one sense, I hated finding out these personal things about the judge and his family. People were entitled to their privacy. On the other hand, at least it gave me a sense of what I would deal with as his executor. Now I understood why he hated to leave them the money of a lifetime of work if it ran through their fingers like water.

I went to pull the bottom drawer open but found it wouldn't budge. There was a keyhole, though. Hmm. How could I get in? I pulled the keyring out of my pocket and found a tiny key that might fit. Pushing it in, I heard it click, and the drawer opened smoothly.

Inside were several legal papers and a copy of his will. I didn't rifle through them because I figured there would be time later. Today, I wanted to know where everything was, and I had to work at the art center this afternoon after my lunch with Sam Finch. Now I had a glance at what the drawers held. I'd have to devise a method of examination and recording information I'd need for his estate.

There was still a large closet behind me to the left, and I stood, opened the door, and took in the contents. They appeared to be mundane house items—wrapping paper for presents, shelves holding objects that were stuffed in there to get them out of the way, and several old scrapbooks pushed to the back. Time for those later too. I glanced at my watch and left for the kitchen.

I smelled coffee before I even made it down the hallway. It was a bonus Tilda was around. I figured she might make more brownies.

She poured a cup of coffee for me, then found creamer and sugar in the refrigerator and in a cupboard. Out of the microwave came a plate with two brownies. "That's strange."

"What?"

Tilda walked back to the cupboard. "I always have a method for putting the cups and saucers away. I trained Ron, so he would too. This cup and saucer are not the way I left them when I walked out of the house on Saturday morning. Nor are these." She pointed to two saucers on the cupboard shelf.

"Don't touch them. In fact, give Tom a call and let him know. He told me to watch for anything unusual."

"I will." She closed the cabinet door. "There," she said. "Warm brownies are God's creation to show we are loved." Setting the plate on the table, she grabbed two small plates from a different cupboard and two paper napkins. We were ready.

"You're an angel, Tilda."

Then I remembered what I wanted to ask her. "Tilda, have you ever heard the name Ted Bender?"

She thought for a moment, then shook her head. "No. Doesn't ring a bell."

"Did the judge ever mention it?"

"Not to me." Before she even took a bite of her brownie, she said, "I still can't believe he's gone. This is terrible. I thought he'd had a heart attack even though he's always been healthy. He plays—played—racquetball and swam. Tom spoke to me. Why would anyone want to kill him? It's senseless."

I'd taken a huge bite of brownie. I glanced at Tilda and saw tears in her eyes. I didn't know what to say. I could change the subject. Holding my hand in front of my face to somehow excuse my talking with food in my mouth, I said, "Someday, you must tell me what you put in these brownies."

"Ah, a Swanson family secret." She wiped her eyes and smiled.

I swallowed the bite in my mouth. "Did the judge give you any indication he was worried about someone or something? Anxious? Nervous?"

She shook her head. "It was business as usual. I know he looked forward to your lunch on Saturday. Told me to make those brownies because he knew you liked them."

"Tilda, he has a gun in his top desk drawer."

"He mentioned that to me. Hasn't had it long, but I can't tell you exactly when I was aware of it."

I wiped my mouth. "You don't know why he got it?"

"No clue."

"Erika stopped at Tom's house on Sunday. I had a tough time connecting her to the woman I'd met once or twice earlier in our lives. She seemed abrupt and not at all compassionate about her father's death. My guess is she and her brother figured they'd sell the house, liquidate the artwork, and be done with Apple Grove."

"Do they get the house? I had a feeling there might be some glitches in Ron's plan from Tom's few words. You're so right—if they're in charge of his estate, they'll strip the house of all valuables and take off for the bright lights."

I paused for a moment, thinking about how much I should say. "When did you start work for the Spiveys?" I watched Tilda take her plate to the sink, brush off the crumbs, and set it in the dishwasher.

"Shortly after they moved here. Around 1995." She sat again. "The kids were in college by then, so I didn't see much of them except on holidays for a while. Eventually, they tended to travel or stay at their schools. Don't think they cared much for Apple Grove."

"Why?"

"Erika went to one of those fancy colleges on the East Coast, and for her graduation, Laura took her on a three-month tour of Europe. After college and that trip, she had a bunch of jobs as time went by. Last I heard, she had a job as a receptionist at a pharmaceutical company."

"Maybe this means she was earning her own way."

"Sometimes. I had the feeling from what the judge said she did a lot of 'clubbing,' whatever that is, in New York City, where she lived for a while. At least when her mother got sick with the cancer, she came back several times to see her. I figured she felt guilty for all the wild stuff she'd gotten into."

"Wild stuff?"

"The judge had to bail her out financially on several occasions. The never-repaid loans were her mother's doing. Laura was a soft touch where those kids were concerned. Would give them the world."

"Where did all her money go?"

"Beats me. I have my suspicions."

When the phone rang in the judge's study, we both stared at each other like, 'who should answer that?' Tilda stood and walked to the study. I could hear her end of the conversation.

"Spivey residence. Yes, Tom. We're both here and have the doors locked as you requested. Uh-huh….Oh, Jill said to tell you a couple of cups and saucers were put back in the cupboard by unknown hands. Might want to check them. I've been meaning to ask you about my job. How long should I stay on? I 'spect I should start a search? Oh. Jill? All right. Thanks. Bye."

I heard her footsteps echo through the hallway toward me.

"Strange. I figured Erika or John would tell me not to let the door hit my butt on the way out. Tom says I should ask you about my job. Why?"

The secret was out. I'd have to tell Tilda to be circumspect. "The judge named me his executor, Tilda. This means I make the decisions, not the Spivey children."

Her face broke into a huge smile. "Perfect."

Chapter Ten

Obviously, I had Tilda on my side. "Don't tell anyone else. The will has to go through a six-month probate period before his estate is dispersed, so it will be a while before it's settled. Frankly, Tilda, I'm a little nervous about all this. I've never been an executor before, and his estate has a lot of artwork worth millions."

"Nonsense. The judge wouldn't have put you in charge if he thought you couldn't do it."

I turned my head and pursed my lips. "He has—had—a lot of faith in me, I guess. Here's what I think. I'll need you here to occasionally answer questions for me and help me find items. I'm also not sure what will happen to the house. If I decide to sell it, someone will have to keep it up while it's on the market. Think you could do that?"

"Sure, I'd be glad to help. He was always kind to me, and Laura even kinder."

I was curious. "How did you happen to get a job as housekeeper for the family? I just wondered."

Tilda pushed the dishwasher door closed after she added soap and turned it on. "I came to work for the family in 1995, before Laura was diagnosed with cancer. I stayed on after her death, poor thing. Been here now for almost twenty years."

"You must have gotten to know the Spiveys quite well."

She nodded. "Oh, yes. Of course, the children weren't here most of the time, and when they were, I could figure on loud fireworks. My husband died in an accident on the job, and the judge helped me invest the money I received from the settlement. Don't know what I would have done without his help. He's always been fair to me." Now, she paused and looked down. "It's hard for me to realize he's gone. I still feel him in this house, a place he cared for with such love."

I glanced at my cell. "I hope to keep his estate intact, so his memory lives on. I haven't figured out what to do with the house, but time will tell. At least I have time to think about it. All right. Consider yourself hired under the same terms as the Spiveys hired you. I'll feel better knowing you're around sometimes when I'm not. I must leave to go work at the art center in about forty-five minutes, and we still need to check out the artwork downstairs. Can you answer more questions for me about the Spiveys?"

"Sure." She took the coffeepot from the counter and refilled our cups. "What do you want to know?"

"I've heard the judge make references to Erika's husband. Where is he?"

"Owen Prather. They're separated, I think. She met him in college, but the judge and Laura weren't impressed. It was a whirlwind courtship, a fast marriage. He came here a couple of times, and for Laura's funeral. I didn't like him much—one of those arrogant types— there was something else I didn't like about him. Couldn't quite put my finger on it. After Laura died, Erika came from New York with Owen, and I heard a huge argument. Not sure what it was about, but the judge sent them packing. In fact, he told them never to come back here again."

"Did they?"

"A few days before the judge's death, only Erika was back. She could always twist her dad around her little finger. She wanted him to give her money to get a divorce. I guess the separation had cleared her mind about that. He didn't. He'd been a soft touch while Laura was alive because each time those kids crawled back begging for money, she'd talked the judge into giving it to them. But something happened after her funeral. Don't know what. He made up his mind not to give either of them money ever again."

"Did he say anything to you about it?" I'd finished my coffee and glanced at the time on my phone again.

"Only once. Some quotation from Shakespeare about children and teeth."

"Oh." I laughed. "Yes. *King Lear*. 'How sharper than a serpent's tooth it is to have a thankless child.'"

She pointed at me. "That's it!"

"Hmm. What about his son? John?"

"He's also been a problem over the years. My guess is he has a love for the bottle. He works for an insurance company in Chicago, but earlier, he worked in New York City as a loan officer at a big bank. The judge got the job for him. But he kept losing jobs. Then he'd come home, tail between his legs, hoping the judge could help him again. He didn't like me much because he couldn't sweet-talk me."

"Was he ever married, or does he have kids?"

"Long ago. She left him, probably because he couldn't keep off the alcohol. They divorced, no kids. But he's another one: always wanted the judge to give him money or help him out of a jam. The gravy train finally stopped when his mother died. Laura couldn't understand his weakness for the bottle. She'd always forgive him no matter what he did."

I thought about Tilda's description. "So, you believe after Laura's death, the judge stopped coddling both of them and told them not to darken his doorway again?"

"That's the story."

"I noticed in the judge's papers they inherited quite a bit of money from Laura."

"Oh, yes. Each of them. But it was like water through their fingers."

"Where do you suppose they spent all that money? They don't have children to support."

Tilda's head shook. "Not a clue."

"What a sad story. Why were they both so weak?"

"You want my theory?"

"Sure."

"From the day they were born, they were given anything. If they'd grown up here in a small town, they'd have more character, less money. But neither of them has ever been content with what they have."

"Do you think John was also involved in the big blow-up after Laura's funeral?"

"Definitely. It happened after the funeral group had cleared out of the house. People—a small group—came here for a drink after the funeral reception—mostly family, friends. We'd cleared all the glasses and dishes from the living room. I was in the kitchen loading the dishwasher. The swinging door was closed"—she pointed at the door behind me into the living room—"and I heard their voices get louder. I figured it was money again and on the day of Laura's funeral." She shook her head and made a derisive sound. "At least if the will is in probate now, they'll get nothing for another six months. That should frustrate the hell out of them."

I didn't tell Tilda they'd get nothing, period. Figured she'd find it out soon enough. My cell phone sounded. "Excuse me, Tilda." I walked to the living room and tapped "accept." It was Sam, apologizing that they'd had an emergency and he'd been called in. He promised to reschedule. I was disappointed, but it still meant I'd see him again. After hanging up, I went back to the kitchen, walking a bit slower, my shoulders drooping. I had looked forward to lunch.

Tilda said, "We should inspect the rooms with all the paintings. I have the key. I checked Saturday to make sure the thermostat was where it should be."

"Perfect." It had been a long time since I'd been down there. Millions of dollars in paintings with their own security system. The judge liked to sit in a swivel chair and contemplate his artwork.

On the way down the stairs, myriad thoughts went through my head about the Spivey children. Could they have killed their father for his money? Were they that desperate? Erika sure thought they should be in the house immediately to "work on his legal papers." Greed can be a strong incentive, and he had sent them out of his life when something happened. What was it? I always knew Ron to be a kind, compassionate person. What could his children have done to cause him to disinherit them?

I knew Tom had investigator friends in both Chicago and New York City. Maybe he'd find clues about their whereabouts last Saturday. Greed was one of the biggest motives for an act of passion like murder. There were others, too—jealousy, hatred, protection of someone or a secret, revenge, robbery, lust or passion, and envy. Tom had filled me in on all of them. Right now, greed was a good motive in my mind. If Tilda had described the Spivey children and their past accurately, they would be at the top of my list for the judge's murder. I reminded myself to keep the Spivey house locked while I was here.

We walked down the stairs to the lower level. I'd been there before but wasn't around when the judge designed this special set of rooms.

I turned off the alarm temporarily, unlocked the double set of doors, and we entered Judge Spivey's special kingdom. I was in awe of the paintings on the walls, mostly modern, and quietly stared for the first few minutes.

"What do you know, Tilda, about how this specific area works? I wasn't here when the judge did all the renovation for this art gallery."

She dropped her own keys in her pocket. "The judge talked to me about this on several occasions. He had the foundation lined and prepared so not a hint of mold or mildew could invade this area. No windows, so no destructive sunlight, and the air vents didn't blow on the artwork. The entire collection had been photographed for his inventory folder. I'd expect you'll find something about that in his files."

"I haven't dug deep enough yet, but I'm sure you're right."

"He keeps the humidity between forty and fifty percent. Over there, you can see the thermostat with the humidity gauge. The temperature is always a steady seventy degrees."

"What happens if the electricity goes off?"

"Oh, he has a backup generator. Every few months, someone from the heating and cooling company comes to check it. I imagine you'll see the name of that company in his receipts in the office."

I nodded, making a mental note to check on it.

"Each time he bought a new painting, he had a professional art handler come in and make sure it was installed correctly. Also, he'd often rearrange the artwork so they could inspect for any damage."

"Sounds like he took care of his collection correctly." I glanced up at the ceiling. "Tell me about the sprinkler system."

"There are smoke detectors in each of the three rooms, and the sprinkler system isn't water. It's, well, what he called a 'gaseous agent.' I had the impression he meant a powder. But I'm not a hundred percent certain I understand. Anyway, it doesn't hurt the paintings if there is a disaster."

"Makes sense to me. We have something similar at the art center. I'll walk around a bit and examine each of the paintings, so I have an accurate memory of the collection. Did the judge say anything to you about a possible worry he had with any of this artwork?"

"No. Do you think it has anything to do with his gun purchase?"

I shook my head. "I'm not sure. He asked me to find a forensic art appraiser, so I thought he might have been worried about fraud. But I could be wrong."

"That would be Peter Angelini you'd need to talk to."

I thought about Peter for a moment. "Were the two of them getting along recently?"

"Far as I know. He never said anything to me about Angelini or the paintings."

I'd have to check the provenance papers of his artwork in his office. While I didn't have time now, I'd put the job at the top of my list. The most recent work the judge had mentioned to me was an oil painting called *Death in a Bygone Hue.*

After the luxury of enjoying his artwork, I told Tilda I needed to go to the art center. My job called. We locked the rooms, set the security system, and headed upstairs once again. Before I could get out the door, Tilda handed me a box of her brownies to take back to work. Louise and I would love these.

On the coffee table were the rolled-up newspapers I'd brought in. I grabbed each one and dropped them in my tote. I'd dump them at home after I read them, then cancel the judge's subscription. That was one of the many details I needed to remember. The list was growing exponentially.

Chapter Eleven

L ater that day, I unlocked the front door of my house, kicked off my shoes, and dropped my tote on the sofa. Long day. Every muscle in my body hurt. Shuffling out to the kitchen, I took a wineglass from the cupboard next to the refrigerator and filled it with a Pinot Grigio from an already-opened bottle in the fridge. A slab of Monterey Jack cheese would complete my restoration from tired art curator, so I grabbed it along with a cheese cutter, crackers, and cheeseboard and headed back to the living room, where I plopped onto the sofa.

Yawning, I cut a few slices of cheese, added a cracker, and popped it in my mouth, washing it down with the wine. I decided to examine the judge's copy of the *Apple Grove Ledger* from this morning—the copies I'd brought home in my tote bag. Spreading the most recent issue out next to me, I chewed away on the cheese slices and opened the paper to the obituaries. Cracker crumbs dropped to the sofa cushion, but I'd clean them up later. Too tired now. I took a deep breath. The judge's photograph was at the top of the page. Silently, I read his obituary.

Judge Ronald L. Spivey, 71, of Apple Grove, Illinois, died suddenly on September 10 at home. He was born in New Haven, Connecticut, to the Honorable J. Allister Spivey and Ruth Lawton Spivey on February 16, 1945. His early years were spent in New Haven, where he loved to sail in the summers and ski in the winters. His appreciation for art, especially modern art and artists, began at the All-Saints Preparatory Academy. Later, he graduated magna cum laude from Yale University with an ROTC commission. He served a tour of duty as a second lieutenant in Vietnam, earning a Vietnam Service Medal, a Republic of Vietnam Campaign medal, and two Bronze Stars.

Enrolling in Columbia University Law School, he graduated with honors in 1971. While at law school, he met the love of his life, Laura Ann Singleton. They married on March 23, 1972. He spent decades working at Withers, Slater, and Conklin, a law firm in New York City. The couple shared a love of food, wine, and music, and a passion for art. While living in New York, the Spiveys supported several art galleries in the city and began their own collection of artwork. They were a fixture in the New York City art scene, often attending openings, and became well known within art circles for their modern art collection.

In 1995, the Spiveys moved to Apple Grove, Illinois, where Mr. Spivey began a private law practice. He was appointed to a judgeship in 2003, retiring in 2015. Judge Spivey was a member of St. Patrick's Catholic Church and served faithfully on its various boards. He also became the treasurer of the Adele Marsden Center for the Arts, a trustee of the Second National Bank of Apple Grove, and a member of the Midwest Animal Shelter. He spent countless volunteer hours in these endeavors. He took up bridge in his retirement years.

He was preceded in death by his parents and wife, Laura Ann Singleton Spivey. He is survived by his son, John Bradford Spivey, of Chicago, Illinois, and daughter, Erika (Owen) Spivey-Prather, of Chicago, Illinois.

Mass will be celebrated at St. Patrick's Catholic Church at ten o'clock Thursday, September 15, and burial will be in St. Mary's Catholic Cemetery with Father Ryan Cather officiating. A luncheon will follow at the Apple Grove Country Club. Online condolences may be left for the family on the Anderson and Packworth Funeral Home website. Donations may be made to St.

Patrick's Catholic Church, or the Midwest Animal Shelter.

Boy, an obituary never completely claimed the essence of a person. I stared up from the newspaper and squelched a sob in my throat. Anyone who reads this obituary would probably wonder why such a powerful New York City lawyer would move to a tiny town like Apple Grove. But I knew. His mother-in-law had been extremely ill, and Ron and Laura moved here to take care of her. People who read obituaries saw only the facts. They'd never know how kind the judge was and how he took me under his wing, making sure I was cared for after my parents died. Unlike my brother Tom, he didn't smother me, but kept an eye out from a respectful distance.

Sighing, I turned back to the second page of the front section. There was the new column we'd talked about at breakfast, a police blotter written by Alberta Canary, the niece of the newspaper's owner, Jefferson Canary. Oh, my gosh. It was hilarious. I scanned the stories, laughing out loud.

Sunday, September 12. The following reports were gathered from calls made to the Apple Grove Police Department.

At 5:16 a.m., a caller reported he saw a cow running loose on Highway 74 West near Anderson's Corner.

At 8:32 a.m., a resident of Ninth Avenue reported a strange man wandering through the neighborhood, talking to himself and playing a harmonica. A cow was following him.

At 11:45 a.m., a caller reported his estranged wife had been accosted by a man wanting her to pose in revealing lingerie.

At 2:30 p.m., a resident of Flatiron Street reported her jewelry was missing.

At 4:17 p.m., a caller stated three teenagers walked through Apple Grove Park, making obscene suggestions to women with small children.

At 6:32 p.m., a caller reported a man lying next to Highway 1405 near Sturgis Point with a bottle in his hand, possibly passed out. A dog licked his face.

"This is insane," I said aloud. "But it's quite entertaining. I must remember to ask Tom about it. Journalism at its best! Who knew I lived in such a colorful town?"

I took several sips of wine, sat back on the sofa, and thumbed through the rest of the newspaper. Summer sports were over for my niece and nephew, Tom's kids, so I glanced through the sports pages in a few seconds. Then I returned to the front section. Hmm. What might Editor Gushman have found to write about? I pulled open the editorial page and gasped at the headline: "Cover-Up is Alive and Well in Murder Investigation." It reminded me I despised the woman. I folded the page back and read her editorial. Dread came over me.

It has been brought to our attention that a heinous crime was committed in our normally safe hamlet. A good and just man has been tragically struck down for no reason. On top of that, the motive of interested parties is being covered up by a relative who is paid by the public tax monies. Having tried to get information from the police chief, we would venture a guess about what happened and why the facts of this case are being unlawfully (in our opinion) withheld from the public.

Judge Ronald Spivey, a noted lawyer and revered judge, was brutally murdered in his home last Saturday. Judge Spivey was a prominent member of our community, and his death is a terrible blow to justice in our area. Then there are his children. They have been deprived of the company and love of their father in the later years of his life. John Spivey and Erika Spivey-Prather rushed here from the Chicago area upon learning of the unexpected demise of their father, only to be told they could not go near their own family home. Unbelievable. Their...own...home!

No, instead, they were told to keep out by our police department.

The police are treating their family house as a crime scene. Imagine rushing down here to deal with a terrible injustice only to be told there's no room at the inn.

We have made numerous calls and trips to the Apple Grove Police Department only to be turned away. When we asked to be apprised of the facts of this case, we were simply told, "No comment." This appears to be sheer arrogance on the part of a public body paid with taxpayer money. We will have to resort to weapons of journalistic power to pry the facts from the police department. There is such a thing as freedom of information.

In the opinion of this editor, there's more than one way to skin a skunk. In the interests of our readers and their desire for justice, we filed with the court here in Apple Grove and discovered the legatee of the judge's estate—which may run into the millions of dollars, or even billions—is not his legitimate children, as we might imagine, but someone related to the principal detective in the Apple Grove Police Department in charge of the investigation. We don't know about you, but we would quote the Bard on this and say something's rotten in the hamlet of Apple Grove. There is a legal term called "undue influence."

The *Apple Grove Ledger* has purposely withheld the name of this "party of interest" because we would not want to hold anyone up to ridicule or scorn. After all, this is America, where the accused are innocent until proven guilty. But we have been drawn into the fray with this injustice. We will see it through to the end. NO ONE WILL TELL OUR READERS, "NO COMMENT." Watch this space for further developments.

Jezbhel Gushman, Executive Editor

I threw the newspaper on the floor and yelled, "You idiot!" What a horrible journalist she was. Seriously? The royal "we" will make a guess because "we" have no facts? Why *wouldn't* Tom do an investigation that needs to be kept quiet? He never announces what he's doing in the newspaper. I picked up the paper again and reread the middle paragraphs of what Gushman thought passed for ethical journalism. So many passive verbs. Even I knew not to use passive verbs. She called herself a journalist! The Spivey children.

They were up to their necks in this crusade of hers. Unbelievable. The poor, grieving Spivey children who rushed here from Chicago because they couldn't wait to get their hands on their father's estate. I finally understood why the judge had decided to cut them out of his will.

I was so mad I could spit! I closed my eyes, took five deep breaths, and blew them out slowly. Didn't help. Such an idiot. Jezbhel Gushman. She's making me sound like the killer, mentioning I was the "party of interest" related to Tom, since he's the only detective on the police force. Saying I was greedy and must have known the contents of the judge's will. She doesn't name me by my name—I'd sue her for libel—or defamation—if she did.

As I was about to scream and tear up the newspaper, my phone went off in my tote. "Welcome to the Jungle." Andy. I turned and moved to the sofa as the muffled song played from my tote bag. Feeling through all the items in my bag, I finally located my phone. I must have hit the cancel button because it stopped. Turning the phone over, I redialed Andy's number.

"Hello, this is Andy, who is innocent until proven guilty. Most likely related to a possible killer. What can I do for you, Jill? Need a bodyguard?"

"Funny, bro. I am so angry. I can't believe she could write such horrible things, hinting at my identity as a killer, and get away with it. Can't I sue her or something?"

"Let me think. Did she come out and name you?"

"No."

"Did she say Tom's sister Jill, because otherwise, it could be me related to the Apple Grove police detective. Right?"

"Oh." I brightened. "I could blame it on you, couldn't I?"

He paused a moment, thinking. "Am I named in the will? If so, it would work."

I snorted. "No."

"She doesn't have any evidence. Only conjecture. People will see through her fiction."

"Only if they've been hiding under a rock. This is the third dead body I've found, Andy."

"You have a point there. How do you do that?"

I picked up the newspaper from the sofa, walked with it to the kitchen, retrieved a pair of scissors from the drawer, and proceeded to put my phone on speaker so I could use both hands to cut the editorial into shreds. "I have no idea. Sheer talent."

"You must admit she's created a well-balanced newspaper. The judge's obituary is somber and factual, the new police blotter is hilarious, and the editorials are ill-conceived and filled with opinions with no evidence. Truly a reflection of the world we live in. Kind of genius, actually."

"Andy! Must you take her side? What about me? Your sister? Shouldn't you be taking my side?"

I could hear him yawn through the phone. A long pause. Then, "True. The family bond thing. What would you like me to do? Egg her house? Her car? Flatten her tires? You know this will die down."

"Until it does, people will look at me like I'm a killer."

"There is that."

The front doorbell rang. I walked down the hallway to the living room, balancing my phone in the crook of my neck and holding my scissors and the newspaper. I could see Tom in the window.

"I have to go. Tom's here. Finally, the cavalry has come to rescue me."

"Sounds good. Call if you need anything. I'll send Lance."

I punched off the phone call and unlocked the front door. "Tom. Thank goodness."

He read my face and walked into the living room. "Yes, I saw the editorial. It's just Gushman."

I took a deep breath. Tom was like the John Wayne of my life. Always responsible, always doing the right thing, always conservative, and always bending too far to protect me. Then I noticed Jake Singleton right behind him.

I considered Jake for a moment, then moved my gaze back to Tom. "What's going on?" Anxiety began to creep into my chest. My breath suddenly grew shallow. I took a step back from Tom and Jake.

"Nothing that's a big deal. It occurred to me I hadn't taken a formal statement from you. Because the powers who apply pressure are doing just that, perhaps we should make it official. Let's go to the station, and I'll take your statement. Make it official."

I hesitated. "You're not arresting me, are you?"

"Absolutely not. A formality. This way, when the police chief reads the newspaper, I can say we have dotted our i's and crossed our t's."

"Oh." Now I breathed easier because this was the Tom I knew, the phone number with the "Theme from Law and Order" on my cell phone. Always-go-by-the-rules Tom. I went back to the kitchen, grabbed my tote, and followed them out to the unmarked car. At least he didn't bring a police car with the lights flashing or the siren blaring, nor did he put handcuffs on me. There had to be a few perks for being related to the local police detective.

Chapter Twelve

The music at the judge's funeral was classical. Thank goodness for that bit of class because his two children spoke and created an imaginary world where they had a close-knit, loving relationship with their father. When we walked into St. Patrick's Catholic Church on Thursday morning, a string quartet played Bach's "Sheep May Safely Graze." It was lovely, and as my entire family moved into a pew, along with Angie and Wiley, I took a deep breath and tried not to cry. It was so final, this last rite we observed for a kind and considerate man who had now joined my parents and his wife. I tried to ignore the stares I got as I walked down the aisle, undoubtedly from people who had read the words of Jezbhel Gushman. I must have had a target on my back that said, "This is the woman who is inheriting money from a man who was murdered. Stealing the estate from his children." It made my stomach feel rocky.

Halfway through the service, the string quartet once again took up their instruments and played Dvorak's "New World Symphony, Second Movement." I had learned a simple version of it when I'd taken piano lessons long ago. The melody was certainly funereal and haunting. At one point, I glanced sideways at Tom and caught his eye during the Spivey children's eulogies. The expression on his face was the same as mine, skeptical, if not disgusted.

When we all arrived at the country club for the reception, the wine flowed, and the string quartet had set up once again, playing "Jesu, Joy of Man's Desiring." The judge was a classy man, and I was sure his children did not pick this music. He must have left instructions with Ken Winters. People stood around in small groups as they awaited the arrival of the family from the private interment at the cemetery. I knew I didn't imagine eyes staring at me and people whispering. Nothing to do about it. Hold my head high.

I stood alone, sipping on a glass of Beaujolais and waiting for Andy and Lance to come back from their reconnoiter of the hors d'oeuvres, when I noticed Peter Angelini heading in my direction. His black, curly hair was stylishly cut and lightly threaded with silver, and he sported a hand-tailored suit much like the ones I used to see in the expensive men's tailor shops in Chicago. His suit was from New York City or possibly Europe, and it appeared to be imported linen with a silk and cashmere tie matching the shirt. His shoes were Ferragamo Oxfords, going for fifteen hundred dollars. The only reason I knew this was because a wealthy friend of mine in Chicago used to buy all his shoes in Italy. I always teased him, saying he was a shoe snob. In Apple Grove, Angelini stuck out like a shiny Ferrari in a bed of used cars.

"Ah, the young painter." He took my hand and brushed the lightest kiss across the back. "I understand you are now the person in charge. Congratulations." His perfect smile lit up his face, and I wondered how many women were melted by those white, straight teeth set against his olive complexion. His voice had a trace of Italian in it. Was it manufactured? I'd met him a couple of times when he dealt with the judge. Angelini had sought out and bought paintings for Judge Spivey in the last ten or so years of his life.

"Mr. Angelini."

"Oh, call me Peter. We've met before and are both friends of Ron's. I've heard you are the executor of his will, a tough job even for an extremely capable woman."

If he thought flattery would get him somewhere, he was wrong. How old would he be? I guessed forty-something. Call me suspicious. I didn't say anything but waited for him to go in whatever direction he had obviously plotted.

"I hope our relationship will move forward as the judge's friends. From what I hear in the gossip around town, you will manage the judge's collection.

And, by the way, the judge's children are not at all happy. You might want to purchase a security system for your residence. But I am at your service if you should want to buy or sell. The judge always depended on me to negotiate his purchases."

I thought about his offer for a few seconds. Did the judge trust him? Obviously, Angelini wanted to continue the gravy train. I took a deep breath. "Peter, that's truly kind of you. I'm only beginning to catalog the collection. As executor of his will, I'll send all the artwork out for appraisal, to be sure all the paintings are genuine, and their provenances are accurate."

His face narrowed into a picture of concern and puzzlement. "Appraisal?"

"Yes. I've already contacted a forensic appraiser."

"But why?" he asked.

I could see it in his face—the concern deepening. "It's the law. Before I can ascertain the worth of his estate, I must have his artwork appraised. I've contacted a national group of appraisers. They'll check the provenance of each painting and sale and produce a figure of its worth. Must be done." I wondered what direction he'd go in next, and it wasn't but a few seconds before he had changed his plan.

"I'll be glad to take care of it for you. I have extensive connections in the art industry, particularly in New York City. My gallery is there. Pulling a few strings, I can even shorten the time for the appraisals."

I put on my best grateful face. "Thank you, Peter, but I've made the arrangements. You seem a bit worried. Is all fine in your world?"

Immediately he was all assurance. "Oh, absolutely. Here's a card for my business. If you have questions, please let me know. I encourage you to contact me if you need any help whatsoever. I'll be in touch. Ron always trusted me to find whatever he wanted to buy or to find buyers for his own collection."

"I'm curious," I said. "He asked me to find a forensic appraiser a few days before his death. Did he ask you about that?"

He blinked his eyes a bit too much. "No. Nothing."

Did I detect a wee hesitation there? I was sure he was lying. "Thanks. I appreciate your offer."

About that time, Lance and Andy returned with plates of maple caramelized figs topped with smoky bacon and carrot tarts with ricotta and almond filling. They watched as Angelini turned and walked toward the wine bar.

Andy held out his plate so I could see the food. "Angelini's face wore a scowl if I ever saw one. Did you rain on his parade, sis?"

I sighed. "The wolves are already at the door. He wanted to help me with the judge's paintings. Don't think he was happy when I turned him down. He knows more than he is about to reveal. I didn't mention I was picking up the shipping boxes from UPS later today, and the paintings will be on their way for appraisal on Monday morning. Shh. It's a secret."

"Mum's the word," said Lance. He held out his plate like Andy had done. "Great eats. We'll find a table if you want to go load up."

"Perfect."

They turned and walked over in the general direction of tables dressed in a sea of white linen tablecloths.

I was about to leave for the long banquet table filled with food when someone tapped me on the shoulder. It was Chad. He was dressed in dark trousers rather than his usual jeans, and instead of a Cardinals hat, he had a Vietnam hat. Probably to honor the judge's service. Next to him was a man I'd not seen before.

"Hi, boss," Chad said. "Figured you'd be here today."

I smiled, glancing at his companion. He was a big guy with a stomach like a huge pillow and a red T-shirt with an American flag on it above the words "Made in America." He sported a cap emblazoned with "Combat Infantryman Vietnam Veteran." Khaki shorts completed the ensemble with tennis shoes that should have been scrapped years ago. He had a white beard cut short and an equally white moustache. His glasses were tinted pink, and the eyes they covered studied me with interest, but the rest of his face was highlighted by a scowl. Chad must have known him from the service.

"This here's Reggie Patterson. He's a vet too, and we knew each other in Nam."

I held out my hand, and he shook it.

"Hello, ma'am. Happy to meet you."

"Hi, Mr. Patterson. Thanks for coming to remember the judge. I'm sure he'd be pleased some of his friends from the service are here to honor him."

He glanced at Chad with narrowed eyes. "Oh, well, I been here a week or two, just a visit. I mainly come today to make sure the man's actually dead. Didn't surprise me none someone offed him."

I didn't know what to say. Shock must have shown on my face because Chad turned and put a hand under his elbow, suggesting they leave, but Reggie wasn't ready.

"I'm sorry you feel that way," I said. "The judge has done a great deal of philanthropic good in this town. He'll be sorely missed."

"Not by me. Forgive me, miss. You had nothing to do with it. I done knew the man in another life. He ruined my life in the service. People like you who were never over there have no clue about the war. We grunts in Nam heard a lot, and secrets die with the dead, don't they? Unlike these other folks, I'm glad he's gone. I hope he roasts in hell."

"Wha—t?" I looked at Chad.

"Come on, Reggie. What say we go get food and find something to drink."

Reggie's face changed from narrowed eyes, an unsmiling mouth, and a stuck-out chin. As I watched him turn around and shuffle toward the banquet table with Chad, I wondered why he had come to the judge's funeral if he harbored such ill feelings toward him. Must be a story there somewhere. I'd have to ask Chad about it. It seemed strange to me no one else from the judge's Vietnam platoon had come to the funeral. I guess it was a long time ago. Past history.

After filling a plate with food, I wandered over to a table where Tom and Mary sat. Lance and Andy occupied a small table next to them, so I set my plate on their table and joined them. I glanced around. People immediately averted their eyes.

"I think you're a pariah," said Andy.

Lance reached out and patted my hand. "Don't let those idiots bother you."

"I haven't done anything wrong."

Andy glanced beyond my shoulder. "Let's hope we never have to find twelve of your peers in Apple Grove to decide your innocence. Might be a tough haul."

"I do seem to notice a lot of stares. And then there's Ivan Truelove, over in the far corner holding court. I think he's with Erika Prather."

"Who's the other guy with them?" asked Lance.

I glanced around, trying not to appear too obvious. "I think it's her husband, Owen."

"I thought they got divorced," Andy said, right on the tail end of swallowing an egg with pickled shallot and parsley.

"No, separated," said Lance. "Tom mentioned he showed up at the first whiff of future money."

"Conferring with Ivan cannot be good. It's like the conspiracy at Priscilla's Pub with Jezbhel Gushman." I took some sidelong glances. "And you ask why I feel paranoid." I popped a carrot tart in my mouth, determined to scan the crowd as if I had nothing to fear.

Chapter Thirteen

Wandering to work on Saturday morning, I spied three young girls on bicycles, possibly ages eight or so, at the stop sign on Mary Street. They chatted and laughed, one of them checking the chain on her bike. They could've been Angie, our friend Carolyn, and me twenty-two years ago on a Saturday morning with the freedom to do anything we wanted. When I was young, I didn't realize how special it was to grow up in a small town surrounded by corn and bean fields, loved by two parents, teased by two brothers, and able to ride anywhere on our bikes. Later, when I left for college and made friends with people from bigger cities, I realized I was the lucky one who'd played through my childhood in Apple Grove. My niece and nephew, Tom and Mary's kids, had a similar fortunate childhood. I loved to watch Emily's softball games and was looking forward to Jim's basketball games at the junior high. If for no other reason, I cherished being back here in my hometown to watch them grow. Working at an art center that continued my mother's legacy was a bonus.

Rounding the last corner before the square, I ticked off in my mind our agenda for the day. A class was going on upstairs. Donna Filbert, she with the corkscrew red curls all over her head, would be teaching a fused glass class on autumn leaves. Her class in August had students making flags for Labor Day in September, and it was so popular we added this new one today. Ivan had only texted me three times over the weekend with concerns about trash cans, roof tiles, and the national exhibit. I should text him back saying someone set a fire in the trash can in front of the building and burned part of the wood on the window behind it, roof tiles fell on the ground so fast we couldn't keep up, and the national exhibit had been canceled. Then I came to my senses, remembering those screwy messages might rocket him in person to the art center, a disaster to be avoided at all costs.

Walking through the front door, I smiled as I remembered we had a new alarm system purchased with a grant. Now that was excitement to be savored, especially because our old system was terrible and mid-twentieth century. Ivan couldn't complain when it didn't cost the art center a dime. Sometimes I won.

"Good morning, Jill," Louise Sandoval called as I walked back toward our offices.

"It is, Louise. How was your date last night?"

She walked over to where I stopped near a sculpture. "Dreadful. Early forties, not bad looking, but hardly said a word all night. I mentally went through my roster of possible topics, but nothing worked, not even sports or politics. It was a far cry from last weekend, when Mr. Possible talked all evening, never stopped, and always talked about himself. I swear if I hadn't been there, he would've chatted with the walls. I changed his name from Mr. Possible to Mr. Take-a-Breath."

"Why?"

"Why what?"

"Why do you continue to torture yourself like this?"

Her eyes stared over my shoulder toward the front of the gallery. "I ask myself that too, Jill. It takes me five minutes to figure out if it's a workable date. Don't know why I stick around after those first five minutes. Speaking of dates, how are things with the doctor?"

I smiled. "So far, so good, but mainly over the phone. Busy man. He plans to stop in today if he gets a few minutes off. His schedule's crazy. Between the hospital and the ER, he hardly has a small block of time to go anywhere. Oh, and thanks for sending him my way. Nice surprise."

"Speaking of surprises, I would've put money on the possibility the Spivey duo would have served you with a legal paper by now. The funeral was traditional and filled with closure, but I figured it meant the end of a truce. Wish we knew what they were planning."

As always, when totally focused on an idea, the index finger of my right hand tapped a staccato beat on my lips. "Angie called me last night to say she overheard them at Priscilla's. They've hired a lawyer—some important woman from Chicago—who plans to take me to court. Claims I had undue influence on the judge, as if anyone could make up his mind for him."

Louise laughed. "Where did they find the money to hire an expensive lawyer? From what I understand, they blow through money like a category-five hurricane. I could've saved them and told them to hire my ex-brother-in-law's uncle. He'd be cheap."

I put my hand lightly on her arm, moving us both back toward our offices beyond the gallery. "I might stand a chance then."

For the next two hours, Louise and I worked together on the national exhibit. It wouldn't be long before we'd celebrate artwork on the walls. The deadline to get pieces in was only six days away, and we were still waiting for five in transit. Louise shot out an email blast to the artists, warning them we needed all entries in by September 23. Part of the time we spent unpacking artwork and checking it for damage. Anthony, the juror, had chosen sixty pieces from an initial six hundred. We'd install the exhibit on the 26th and 27th using volunteers and board members. The hospitality committee was busy with decorations and food with a harvest theme. I was scheduled to meet with them one more time.

As we worked, we could hear voices from the classroom upstairs or occasionally the scrape of a chair moving. I was overjoyed with how well our classes were going. Growing up in Apple Grove, I hadn't had the kind of classes and support we were able to offer here. It excited me to see it come together. Since Louise and I had already done a first exhibit of regional artists, my stomach wasn't nearly as finicky as I worked on this one. It was much bigger, and pieces arrived from all over the country. *The country*, mind you, to tiny Apple Grove, Illinois. It would be our first juried exhibit, and I wanted it to go smoothly. Pulling several pieces out of the storage area, we considered how to arrange them. Composition, color, and medium filled our conversations. Soon the clock said three, and we'd been at this for hours. Amazing how quickly time flew when I loved my work.

The bell on the door chimed, and Sam ambled through the gallery. Such confidence. I almost expected one of those sparkly pings from the perfect, white-toothed smile on his face. He was casually dressed in a burgundy T-shirt and jeans.

"Afternoon, ladies. I think it's ice cream time. How's the big exhibit coming along?"

Placing a small, framed painting on a table, Louise winked at me and said, "Quite well. In fact, we've accomplished so much, I think it's time for Jill to take a break. You go ahead, Jill."

I set down a small sculpture. "Alright. But you're on a break as soon as I return."

Apple Grove had its own version of a multiple-flavor ice cream store called Angela's Ice Cream. It was a mom-and-pop operation owned for decades by the Trinh family. Cam and Minh, Vietnamese immigrants in the early seventies, came to this small town sponsored by a church group. They'd been American collaborators during the war and had to flee for their lives when Saigon fell. The town literally opened its arms, and the Trinhs began their own ice cream business a few years later. In the intervening years, it had become part of the fabric of the town. I introduced Sam to them, and we engaged in small talk before we ordered butter pecan and peach ice cream cones. We wandered out to an umbrella table on the sidewalk.

"They know everyone because they've been here for years. Their kids grew up here and left, so now they close twice a year to go see them in California."

He crunched on the pecans in his ice cream. "I'll bet you have plenty of stories like that about your neighbors. It seems to me fifteen thousand people is the perfect size for a town." He licked the side of his cone to keep it from melting all over his hand. "By the way, I like your yellow dress. It's a great color for you, Ms. Artist."

I crossed one leg and sat back. "Thank you. It's Cadmium yellow pale. Color's my bailiwick." I tried to keep the peach ice cream from dripping down the side of my own cone. Licking away at it, I paused, adding, "Had any emergencies this morning?"

He shook his head. "Quiet morning, actually. I have a break now, and then a few hours tonight in the ER. It's a pleasant change not to deal with gunshot wounds or stabbings. When I worked in Chicago, those were typical nights. I love to walk out on the roof at the hospital, stare at the sky, and see all the stars I never saw when I lived in the city. So amazing and peaceful."

After crunching on part of the cone, I wiped my mouth with a napkin. "Guess I take a few of those things for granted." I leaned toward him, gazing directly into those cerulean blue eyes. "How did you happen to come to Apple Grove?"

His eyes left mine as if he were thinking about what to tell me. "Several events came together. I grew up in a small town in Michigan. Figured if I worked in the big city, it would be adventurous. It certainly was, but as time went by, I guess the small-town vibe called to me, and night after night of adrenaline surges and dealing with the worst side of humanity pushed me in this direction." He used his napkin to wipe his mouth and fingers, pausing while I waited. "Oh, there's more to the story, but I've told you the general framework. Apple Grove is part of a network of small towns that hires doctors in exchange for loan forgiveness. I possess plenty of those to forgive, so it seemed like a good exchange. Of course, my schedule's crazy, which means I hardly have time to appreciate what's here. And, once again, I apologize for canceling Wednesday."

I leaned over the table and took a chance. "Perhaps I can help you with a fabulous tour of the joys of my town if we can manage to fit our busy schedules together."

To my surprise, his hand on the table moved over to mine and touched it. He said, "I'd love to make that happen."

Melting, melting, melting…

Chapter Fourteen

I smiled as I thought about Sam's words while I did paperwork before going home. We closed around five on Saturdays, but I found it easier to stick around and do grant research or details for the exhibit when I was by myself in the quiet. I had finished the last column of statistics when my mind wandered back to those blue eyes. Sam had a whole history I knew nothing about. I didn't think I was wrong in feeling he could've said a lot more about why he moved here. It was early days, I told myself.

The quiet was broken by the turn of a key in the lock of the alley door. Chad's voice filled the air, a greeting he always used when he figured I might be here because the lights were on in my office. He didn't want to scare me.

"Jill, it's me. Showing up for work, General."

I stood and left the office, meeting him on the edge of the gallery. My work was done, so a little conversation was welcome after all the mental gymnastics. "I hope you took advantage of the beautiful day while I was slaving away."

He hung his keys on his belt, walked over, and chuckled. "Grandkids. Took them fishin'. Didn't catch much, but I got to listen to all their worries about school being different this year." He shook his head. "They'll be fine after a few weeks. It's fear of the unknown."

"I understand. Kinda like my life."

"I imagine you're gittin' a bit of that too, what with the crazy Spiveys in town. Never know what's happening there."

"So true. I get hints they're considering a lawsuit."

Chad walked over to a closet and pulled out a bucket, mop, and dusting rags. Then he turned, uttering a noise like he was disgusted. "Yeah. Cleary, the EMT guy, heard them plotting about it at the bar the other night. They've got a big-city attorney gonna charge something about undue influence. I believe he heard your name mentioned."

I laughed. "Oh, yes. I'm in the thick of it. But saying and proving are two different things. At least the court system demands actual evidence. Thank goodness."

"I s'pose you'll still have to go through crap before they're done with their anger. People like that." His teeth clicked softly as he shook his head. "Actually, I saw the Prather woman in the Thai restaurant a couple of days before the judge was murdered."

"The restaurant here in town?"

"Yeah. She didn't appear happy, although can't say I've ever seen her smile."

I glanced out at the street when the streetlights blinked on. "Me either. You know, there's something I've been wondering about. How did you happen to know the judge? Were you in the same company or platoon in Vietnam?"

He took off his hat and scratched his head before putting it back on. "Now you've hit on an interesting story."

"I have time. Let's go back to the classroom."

After we were seated, Chad said, "I grew up here. My mom stayed home, and Dad did several jobs to pay the bills. Had two brothers, three sisters. One's dead now. The others left here quick as they could. But me, I wanted more. Grew up hungry."

I walked over to the small refrigerator, pulled out a bottle of water, and handed it to him.

"Thanks." He turned the top and took a long swallow. "Me, I was never much good with the book stuff, but I loved to watch people. Soon as I got through high school, I signed the papers and shipped out to Nam. Seemed like an adventure at the time. Never met the judge there, but I'd heard his name via the jungle telegraph, so I was surprised when he moved here to town. I thought it couldn't be the same guy, but darned if it wasn't. After a while, I decided I'd seen enough of the world. I come back here after my tour. Spent some time thinkin' about what I could do. People, I'd always watched people and thought about what made them tick. I got a job selling cars at Wendorff's. Done well and was able to help my parents. They're gone now, of course."

"I'm sorry."

He took another swallow of water. "It's the way it goes, you know. I'm sixty-six now and was near the end of the line of siblings, so it's no wonder."

"And you're married?"

"Oh, yeah. Me and Sandy been married thirty-nine years, two kids, four grandkids. Met her at the county fair when I was back from Nam. We rub along fine, but now I'm retired, she'd rather have me out of the house doing something rather than sitting around moping."

I laughed. "Sounds like things turned out quite well for you."

"I ain't complaining."

"I'm curious. How did you meet the judge if you didn't know him in Vietnam?"

Chad shifted his left leg over his right knee and stared at the table for a moment. Then he smiled as if remembering. "Sold him a car. Kinda funny. He came in looking for a car for his wife, and we struck up a conversation. I thought I'd heard his name before, but they'd just moved to town. Turned out he was a lawyer then, so I figured he might be a good person to know. It's never bad to have the phone number of a lawyer. After a while, we ran into each other occasionally around town and grew into a nice relationship. Oh, he always bought cars from me after the first one."

I smiled at him. "Sounds like the judge I knew. He was a friend of my parents when I was growing up. Then, of course, a friend of mine. I miss him terribly."

"I'm sorry. It's such a shame."

"We can't change the past." For a moment, neither of us spoke. I was about to push back my chair and go home for the night when another thought occurred to me. "The man you were with at the funeral, the one who had been in Vietnam, how did you know him? He seemed bitter."

"Oh, Patterson. Don't pay no attention to stuff he says. He's ain't someone to believe about anything."

I considered his words. "I've rarely met anyone who hated the judge. He must have quite a story behind his venom."

The janitor swallowed the last of the water. "He thinks he does. Back in the day, he was a medic with my company in Nam. I didn't like him much. He was always trying to figure out the angles. Get whatever for himself. Anyway, long story short, he got involved in the black market. Hush, hush stuff. Underground. He ain't smart, so he got caught. The guy who turned him in was rumored to be Ron Spivey, second lieutenant. At least it was what was goin' around. Patterson was drummed out. Dishonorable discharge. Never forgave the army, the judge, or the circumstances."

"Seems rather a big deal he came back here for the funeral then."

"He's been here a couple weeks. The judge was still around when he arrived. I figured his sudden appearance in town was taking his anger a bit far. He lives in Georgia now, so it was a trip. I've no idea why he came here, although he mentioned visiting a cousin. The judge's death was bad timing, I s'pose. Anyways, I steer clear of him whenever I see him."

"I can understand. He's a thoroughly unlikable character. You know, I've run into this Cleary with you several times. He seems like a likable guy. How did he end up here?"

"Good question. He's quiet. I get the feeling he's lived in a lot of places. Not sure where he grew up. His dad died a while back, and Cleary talks about being in the Middle East a lot."

"Oh. It might be that's why he's kind of a rolling stone. Sometimes it takes a while to settle in after you've been over there."

Chad nodded. "You're right. I had best get to work, and you need to go home and eat dinner. Put some meat on those bones of yours."

He meant well. "Yes, you're right. I was about to leave."

It was on my walk home when I thought back through our conversation. What Patterson's job was in the army—now, that was something to consider.

Chapter Fifteen

After parking my Austin Mini on the street in front of the judge's house, I pulled out my tote bag armed with legal pads and several pens. Marching up the walk, I noticed no newspapers on the porch, so they must've canceled his subscription after my phone call. The Sunday newspaper was usually big, and I would've noticed it if it had been anywhere near the porch swing. The air had the crisp feel of fall, and fluffy clouds filled the sky on a perfect autumn morning. But I had work to do. I couldn't dally around admiring the trees and sky.

Once in the house, I locked the door per Tom's instructions. Nothing was disturbed, and I found a note from Tilda in the kitchen saying she'd left a few brownies for me. Ground coffee was in the canister next to the coffeemaker. On the counter near the sink was a plate with three small brownies. Ahhhh, heaven. I'd work for a while first and then reward myself. Wish I knew what she put in those brownies.

Pulling my legal pad and pens out of my tote, I turned on the overhead light in the judge's office. I opened the curtains and watched as the sunlight brought out the mahogany tones of his huge desk. "Well," I said to no one, "time to get busy."

I'd check for the provenance papers on the paintings, the documents showing their history of ownership. Even though unscrupulous people could falsify records, those documents indicated how the artwork came to be in the judge's possession. They were invaluable when it came to the sale of artwork. Often a document was a signed statement by the artist or an expert, or it could be an original gallery sales receipt. Sometimes an artist would sign a receipt, and an art expert might later verify it. Knowing the judge's connections in the art world, I imagined he would've been cautious when it came to proving the worth of the paintings he owned. I expected to find documents confirmed by qualified experts who might even have significant background and history with the artists or their relatives.

I was not disappointed. Files filled the second drawer of the desk, and several held legal papers showing the provenance of his paintings. He had left a carefully written list of the works he owned, when he acquired them, a photograph, and how much he'd paid for them. Peter Angelini arranged many of the sales, especially the more recent ones. I worked slowly, making sure I matched documents with his collection list. It didn't surprise me he'd put together these papers in a clear, organized manner. His legal mind would've made sure all these files were in order. He'd accounted for every painting. If I'd added their worth in one lengthy list, their value would have staggered me. Millions. Goosebumps suddenly appeared on my arms as I considered all this wealth in one house.

I'd twisted a few arms to get help packing the artwork to ship to the appraiser in Chicago. I'd made the arrangements with UPS to collect them Monday morning. The value of the paintings meant they'd have their own truck and make a nonstop journey for the three hours to Chicago.

I found a box in the closet that would hold the provenance papers, which would accompany the paintings. I'd made copies to be safe. Experts in Chicago would check the papers verifying their authenticity. I set the box of papers on the desk. Time to get moving, have a brownie, and brew a cup of coffee.

As I rose, I glanced out the window and saw movement on the far side of the street. The judge's house was on a corner, and the cross street was Locust. A large black SUV with tinted windows and a second black SUV came to a halt just around the corner. Two people—a woman and a man—got out of each vehicle. I stared at the woman wearing skinny jeans, a blue T-shirt, and sporting red hair. Erika Spivey-Prather! The man could be Owen. They stood in the street talking. Erika gestured wildly and pointed at the house. His body language said he was trying to placate her.

She started toward me and the house, but he pulled her back by the arm. More talking. What would I do if they came here and pounded on the door? I could call Tom. Or I suppose I could call 9-1-1. I looked again.

A police car cruised slowly around the corner and parked behind the Prather cars. They both stared at it. I could see Jake Singleton calling the department on his car radio. Then he hung up and got out of the car. They were too far away from me, so I couldn't hear anything. Now a three-way conversation was going on. It was obvious Erika was arguing about her right to come to her father's house. Several times she pointed to the house. Singleton put one hand on his handcuffs and spoke into the radio on his shoulder. Then Erika's shoulders slumped and she turned to get back into her car, but not before a last remark to Jake. Probably a four-letter word. Prather also got into his car, and they both left. Crisis averted. I let out my breath. Guess I hadn't realized I'd been holding it. My shoulders felt stiff where my anxiety had held them, and I took several deep breaths.

Now I left for the kitchen and coffee. Ten minutes later, with my mind cleared, I stopped by the bookshelves, glancing at the photo of the judge's friends from his Vietnam days. How young they were! I wondered how many of them were still alive, or if they even knew about the judge's demise. None of them came forward or introduced themselves at the funeral. But life was like that—intense friendships sometimes weakened and disappeared. It was a lifetime ago. Setting the photo back, I stared out the window at the fluffy, white clouds resting together like cotton balls. How many times had he looked out these very windows when he took a break from his work?

I sat again and opened the middle drawer. The sticky note I'd found before was still lying in the drawer, stuck to paper clips. Ted Bender. No idea who he was. I grabbed the phone directory under the landline phone, paging through to the "B's." No Benders. Maybe he was one of the judge's clients. He could be someone from his days in New York City, or he could be a person from among art acquaintances. Boy, a great detective I was. No matter.

Pulling open the second drawer of vertical files, I brought out a file with "Owen Prather" on the tab. I opened it. The judge had hired an investigator to check on him. This was a file of information he'd found out about Owen Prather prior to and during his marriage to Erika. Work history, school records, personal details, family information…I glanced through it and understood why the judge was worried. Prather had skirmishes with the law in his late teen years. DUIs, shoplifting, an assault charge. Wow. He'd had a series of jobs that should've paid well, but the investigator said he had little in the bank. He was seriously hospitalized at age twenty- nine. He was diabetic and lapsed into a coma. Nothing after that. Maybe it was a hard lesson to take care of himself better. Then I came upon a shocking revelation from the investigator's notes—he had a cocaine habit. Better care—guess not.

I took another sip of coffee and checked out the windows again. Cars moved down the street slowly on a Sunday morning drive. Glancing at my watch, I figured it was the church crowd leaving services. Now I knew where the money went. Right up Owen Prather's nose.

What about Erika? Did she also have a coke habit? Did this come from the time they spent in New York City? The clubs they haunted? Could the judge have confronted her about it? If she decided to stay with Owen, was her decision the final blow that caused their rift? Who might know about it? John? But he'd side with his sister. Who might the judge have confided in? I searched through my brain archives. Abe. He might've talked to Abe Calipher. Was there such a thing as friend/coroner privileged information? I thought not. I'd have to find a way to mention this to Abe. Hmmm. Might bear thought.

It would help to send my brain in a different direction. I pulled open the top drawer containing the handgun. It was still there. But I noticed an envelope underneath it. Sliding it carefully out from under the gun, I opened it. A gun registration. I glanced through the details. The date was June 2, 2016. Three months ago. What happened back in June that would've made him buy a gun? I remembered an organizer resting on the far corner of the desk. Opening it, I examined May and June. Nothing. Ordinary scribbles about haircut appointments, people who'd come to see the judge, and notes to himself. Nothing made the hair on my neck stand on end. A dead end. I put the organizer back in its spot, returned the gun registration to its drawer, and closed the Prather file. I decided I should tell Tom about the gun.

I stuck the Prather file back into the desk drawer and noticed it had been pulling another one out from behind it. The tab said "threats." Taking out the papers, I noticed some of them were ancient, from the late nineties. But a more recent one held a name I knew—Reggie Patterson.

It was dated August twentieth of this year and written with a black pen in childish script. I glanced at the calendar on the desk. This was about three weeks before the judge was killed. Scanning it, I winced at the grammar and bad spelling.

> Dear Second Lewey Spivey,
>
> Don't know if you rememmber me, but my name is Reggie Patterson. We was in Vietnam together. I ain't forgotten you, and I am writing this letter to tell you that you done ruined my life. I didn't sell no guns to the VC. I didn't deserve no dishonorable discharge. You done that to me. You testified and made sure an innocent man's life was runed. I was set up.
>
> My hole life that discharge has followed me. I got no VA benefits when I was sick, and I've had to go from one lousy job to another. Why? Because of you and your lies.
>
> I will be seeing you soon. I know lots of ways to kill arrogant guys like you. You'd better wacch your back. I got nothin to lose.
>
> Signed, Reginald Patterson

Now, I felt the hair on my neck stand on end.

Chapter Sixteen

"Seriously? Do you mean this painting I'm holding here in my hands—right here—me, Andy Madison, is worth thousands and thousands of dollars?"

"Do not drop it. Do not take your gloves off or touch it," I said, admonishing my brother, the weakest link in this enterprise. It was Sunday night. I'd rounded up Andy, Lance, and Louise to help me pack the paintings at the judge's house to ship out tomorrow morning. "They're going to the IAAF in Chicago."

"The whatsit?" Andy replied.

"The International Art Appraisal Foundation. They're a reputable organization that appraises artwork. After they evaluate it, they'll get back to me in two or three weeks. But in the meantime, we must pack these babies carefully and ship them tomorrow morning. UPS has special packages to use for sending artwork, and I ordered enough to ship these."

Andy's partner, Lance, stared at the other paintings on the wall in the judge's secret hideaway. "Don't they have to be in a temperature-controlled conveyance? I mean, the judge's gallery is a certain temperature and humidity."

I nodded. "If I were sending them somewhere like California, they would. But we're about three hours from Chicago. I've arranged to have only these paintings in the UPS truck, so they'll be fine until they reach the foundation."

Louise chimed in. "Do you have any armed guards or the FBI following them?"

I laughed. "I think they'll be fine. We often packed and shipped valuable paintings when I worked in a gallery in Chicago. UPS has assured me of their confidentiality, and I'm not at all worried about the IAAF. They're highly reputable. Everything is invoiced. I'll have them not simply appraise these works, but also do forensic tests to make sure they're the genuine article."

"What? You think they might be fake?" Louise stared at the painting in front of her.

I realized it was a painting made by abstract expressionist Grace Hartigan.

"How would you ever figure it out?" Louise asked.

"I wouldn't, but these appraisers have a whole spectrum of forensic analysis technology at their fingertips. They'll decide which techniques to use. It's called a 'multi-analytical approach.' For example, they can use something called infrared reflectography to examine the paint layers, which often reveal underdrawings or changes in the layers."

Andy stared at the painting he was holding. "You mean kinda like a person getting an MRI?"

I nodded. "Yes. They also study the pigments so they know which ones were more commonly used in a certain time. For example, artists stopped using lead white pigment at the end of the nineteenth century because of its toxicity. If you were studying a twentieth-century painting like many of these, you wouldn't expect to find lead in the layers of white pigments. Forensic appraisers have studied past materials and artists' styles, so they know what they're looking for. Even the framing is important."

Louise examined a colorful abstract on the wall near the door we'd come in. "Now, this is obviously an abstract painting. Who's the artist?"

"It's a Kandinsky. Wassily Kandinsky. He was a Russian abstract painter influenced by Van Gogh and Picasso. He died in 1944, but not before some of his pieces were stolen from their owners by the Nazis. I remember reading a Kandinsky painting titled *Fugue* was auctioned by Sotheby's in 1990 and went for $20.9 million."

Louise gasped and took a few steps away from the painting. "Are—are all these paintings so valuable?"

"Mmm—some are worth more, some less. I have all the legal papers demonstrating provenance, and they'll go with them to Chicago."

Andy set the canvas he was holding against the wall. Then he stepped back beside Lance. "I can't believe you'd trust me to do this."

I smiled at him. "I can't believe I am either, but any port in a storm. We must pack these and get them ready to go. I know I can trust the three of you to help with this and not mention it to anyone." I gave Andy my best stern stare.

"Absolutely," Lance said. "Let's get started."

"I already went to UPS and ordered the shipping boxes in the correct sizes. Watch carefully. I'll demonstrate with this painting by Lee Krasner. We might be smart to work in pairs." Before I ordered the boxes, I measured each painting and added six inches around each side. UPS provided a double-wall corrugated box. I put blue painter's tape over the glass on top of the Krasner in a crisscrossed design. Then I laid a piece of glassine paper over the glass. To that, I added a piece of corrugated board on top of the frame. Then I put a sheet of bubble wrap on top. "Kind of like making a sandwich," I said.

"Finally, you wrap a bubble pack around this about six times to make a three-inch-thick protection. Tape the ends of the bubble wrap so it has three inches at either end. Slide it into the box and fill any space between the painting and box with bubble wrap. The idea is to minimize movement. Close the box, tape it securely, and put the label on it for the correct painting. I have all the packing materials measured and filled out. Should be easy-peasy."

Andy looked at me, his eyes glassed over. "Easy-peasy? You didn't tell me I'd be completing thirty steps of wrapping something worth millions of dollars. Lance won't let me pack a vase for shipping."

"I must admit it's true." Lance grabbed Andy's arm. "We'll work on them together. No problem. We got this, Jill."

"Good. Louise and I will work together. We'll have this done in no time at all."

It was almost ten o'clock when we finished all but the last painting, *Death in a Bygone Hue.* We'd lined the packing boxes in a row, leaning them against the wall in the first room. Glancing around at our packing crew, I could see we were all exhausted. We'd taken a couple of breaks for water and the bathroom, but mostly we'd stayed at it, wanting to get it finished.

Now we all stared at this last oil painting, its dark colors reflecting our exhaustion. *Death in a Bygone Hue.* I guess I'd never noticed it or studied it before. It was a night background, the stars twinkling in a cobalt violet sky. In the foreground was an army Howitzer crew, four men, firing into the night. They wore the army drab green with helmets of khaki and deep brown army boots. Sandbags were all around in rows on the ground. But the tone values made it all seem like a long-ago dream. What made it powerful were the sepia tones of the foreground. Lots of browns, tans, fallow, and taupe. The title was perfect—*Death in a Bygone Hue.* It was about the years that chip away at human memory, forgetting the thousands of lives lost on both sides of the conflict. A filmy curtain covers the entire scene, taking away our memories of the details and statistics. It was about the irony of what time does to sacrifice. A reminder our lives and deaths were such a small slice of the continuum of time.

Andy was the first to speak. "I remember Mom and Dad talking about this war as the first 'television war' because it was brought home to them every night on the news, as if they were there."

"We were all born long after the sixties," I said. "This was about Mom and Dad's generation."

"Do you think the judge bought it to remind himself of what they'd all been through?" Louise asked.

"That I don't know. He never talked to me about this painting. But I keep thinking there's something wrong about it. I'm not sure what. Call it an instinct, a visceral reaction. I've been working in the art business for ten years now. I can't put my finger on what it is, but I'll tell them to really examine this one closely."

Lance picked up the packaging and said, "Let's get this last one done. Morning's coming early, and we have to be at the gift shop."

Once we finished, I stood back, studying the lengthy line of boxes. I took a long, tired breath. "I'll be here at eight in the morning to open so they can load them in the truck. Thank you all for helping me." I gave each of them sweaty hugs.

Louise patted me on the back. "Great job. This place will seem awfully empty for a while."

I nodded. "But I'll be relieved when they're on their way because the Spiveys are in town. Better to have them off on their way to a safe location." I didn't mention I wondered if this painting was the one Peter Angelini was so anxious to have appraised himself. It was the last painting the judge had bought, and after its delivery, he'd asked me about a forensic appraiser. Could there be a connection?

Chapter Seventeen

After a night of poor sleep with paintings and UPS boxes floating through my dreams, I walked to the art center after meeting the UPS pickup. I treasured these walks alone so I could organize my thoughts for the day. A week from this Thursday, we'd install the juried exhibit. I had too many details to wind up before the installation happened. I glanced at my whiteboard and cursed at the way this murder investigation had taken me off course. Not today. Today, I'd focus, making sure nothing distracted me.

I'd just settled to work on the program for the exhibit when Louise appeared.

"Jill," she said as she rushed into my office. "Have you seen the newspaper this morning?"

"No. What is it?"

"That slimebucket Gushman is at it again with her stupid editorials. Here, I brought you a copy. I'll go unlock my office and unload because I don't want to be here when you read it." She dropped the newspaper on my desk and backed out of the room. I could tell she planned to stay out of my line of fire.

Once again, Gushman had an editorial with an inflammatory headline. "Undue Influence?"

We at the *Apple Grove Ledger* have watched with dismay at the cruel machinations of the legal system and the ineptitude of our local law enforcement. It has been nine days—nine long days—since one of our influential citizens was cut down in the midst of life with no police press conferences or information about the perpetrator of such a ghastly deed. "No comment" is all they could say. What are we to think? How safe are we in our own homes?

To add to this heinous crime, we have learned, through a court document filing, the large estate of Judge Ronald Spivey will be handed on a platter to someone with whom he shares no blood relationship while his two legitimate children are passed over. The Spivey children have undertaken every legal step to find out why this terrible injustice has occurred. But to no avail. However, we will not give up, and yours truly will do a deep dive into the lives of the players in this scheme.

The police are not talking, nor is their detective, Tom Madison, who is related to a legatee of the judge's immense estate. The citizens of this town deserve better! Why are they—and we of the Fourth Estate—kept in the dark? You ask about our dog in this fight? It's because we journalists are considered the Fourth Estate.

In medieval England, the concept of three estates included the clergy, nobility, and commoners, the Three Estates of the Realm. When Thomas Carlyle, Victorian writer, came along, he named the "4th Estate of the Realm," which meant the press, whose job it is to provide an unbiased dispersion of the news. We are also to hold officials accountable. The *Apple Grove Ledger*, proud member of the Fourth Estate, will do exactly that. We will not let the citizens of Apple Grove down.

We have become aware the Spivey family will pursue this matter by hiring an attorney and will strongly object to their father's will. They believe the current legatee has exerted undue influence on their father's mind or this whole nefarious web of deceit would never have occurred. Undue influence, readers, means the judge left a large portion of his estate to someone who had influence over his judgment. Undue influence also means this person estranged the judge from his family and defrauded them by her influence on the judge. It has become apparent to us the relationship between the judge and this legatee was "quite close." We'll leave our readers to decide what that means.

As we have previously stated, we have been drawn into the fray, hoping to pursue our quest for justice for this family. We intend to continue researching this whole situation and the principal people involved. We will dig to the bottom of this matter. Stay tuned for more developments. WE WILL NOT LET YOU DOWN.

Jezbhel Gushman, Executive Editor

I let out a scream. It was the least I could do under the circumstances. Then I took the page the editorial was on, shredding it into pieces. I despised the woman. Who did she think she was? A famous barrister who knew everything about the law? The fourth estate indeed!

A text pinged on my phone. Maybe it was Tom because I hadn't heard from him lately. I glanced down, unlocked the cell phone window, and checked. Argh! Ivan the Terrible. Could my day get any better?

Ms. Madison. Sorry the editor at the LOCAL RAG is railing against you. I understand the Spiveys being clangy, but this publicity for the PARTS CENTER is NOT good. Please tell me you have a LAWYER.

IVAN F. TRUELOVE III

Seriously, Ivan. Autocorrect turned my "ART" CENTER into a PARTS CENTER? Clangy instead of angry?

What? Had the earth shifted on its axis? Ivan the Bean Counter was on my side for once? Why? I stared at the shredded newsprint on the floor. Should I go home and come back again? Have a reboot?

Motives. I thought about motives. Ah, it was the judge's will. The art center was due to get millions of dollars. If the family proved undue influence and threw out the will, it ended the bonanza. Aha! That's why he was so conciliatory. On the other hand, I relaxed and smiled at this new development. It would only last five minutes before he texted me with his usual complaints, but, hey, five minutes is better than none at all.

"What's happened here?" My brother's voice came from somewhere behind me.

I turned around. He was staring at the shredded newspaper. "It's a critique of the latest Gushman editorial."

He laughed. "Don't let her upset you. It's all bluff and bluster. She's trying to sell more papers. They don't have a chance of proving undue influence."

"At my expense." I threw out my arms in an expression of disaster. "It's not that so much as what the town thinks about me. Once it's in print, they'll believe it's true."

Tom moved out of the doorway, into my office, and sat on the loveseat after moving my usual pile of stuff stacked on top of it. "I thought I'd stop in. We could put our heads together. I've found new information, and I thought you'd worked long enough in the judge's office to discover interesting tidbits."

"You first," I said, sitting back in my desk chair. "But you'd better close the door."

Tom reached over, pulled the door shut, and shifted his weight back to the loveseat. "After Tilda told me about the coffee cups and saucers at Ron's house, I checked it out. She was right. Someone sat in a chair in Ron's office, had coffee, and then killed him. He must've known whoever the killer was because why would they have coffee together? The autopsy showed the traces of coffee in his stomach and caffeine in his bloodstream. That means he did sit and have coffee with his murderer. The question is who? Whoever killed him washed the cups, wiped off any prints, and put them back in the cupboard, not quite in sync with the other dishes. Tilda was a perfectionist. Whoever this was had a conversation with Ron before he—or she—killed him."

"How cold-blooded. Do you think his kids could've done it? Either of them? I know they were desperate for money, but to murder your own father?"

Tom raised one eyebrow, pressing his lips together. "Their alibis are shaky.

John said he was at his office on a Saturday morning, but no one could verify it. The place was empty on a Saturday. He was supposedly catching up on insurance paperwork. He easily could've driven three hours and come here to kill Ron. He could've parked a block away or more, but no one we've canvassed saw his car."

"His motive would be the estate?"

"Yes. He was up to his neck in debt and had both alcohol and gambling problems. He'd already sold a house in New York to pay off debts to loan sharks."

I thought about it. "I found several letters in the judge's files from debt collectors."

"It's likely, but my guess is he also owed people who didn't send letters."

"You think he was desperate?"

"My contacts in New York City and Chicago mentioned the same pattern. A gambling addiction might mean he owed scary people. Where else could he get money quickly?"

I shook my head slowly. "Remember I told you he was shocked when I mentioned the probate period? Maybe that's why. He figured he'd liquidate the estate and come into a fortune. I imagine Erika felt the same way."

Tom nodded. "Erika lied to me. Royally. Said she hadn't seen her father in months, but she was seen here in town by any number of people a couple of days before his death. Both she and her husband have drug problems—cocaine. It's an awfully expensive habit."

"Does she have an alibi for that morning?"

"Depends on where she was, Chicago or Apple Grove. She swears she was only here for a day to ask Ron if he'd help her finance a divorce from Owen Prather. The timing of Ron's death wasn't helpful. She's still married to Prather, so anything she might get from a settlement would also go partly to him. If she were to kill her father for the money, it would've been better to wait until she was divorced. Erika isn't stupid. I'm not sure about her husband, Owen. Since he wasn't divorced yet, he might have thought he was still in line for handouts."

"On the other hand, if the judge said no, she might've thought part of her inheritance was better than none." My phone pinged, and I turned it over on my desk. "Where was she the day of the murder?"

"She works for a pharmaceutical company in the suburbs. I think she's a secretary or personal assistant. Says she was nursing a hangover in her apartment in Lake Forest."

"She works for a pharmaceutical corporation? Might her job give her connections to someone who could find her digitalis?"

"Possibly. I'd still like to know why Ron banished the two of them after Laura's funeral. It might be because of the money situation, but that had gone on for a while. It had to be more." Tom leaned forward on the loveseat. "So far, they've no alibis, strong motives, the opportunity, but the means is another thing. Whoever killed the judge was cautious and took care of details. Have you found anything unusual in Ron's files?"

I handed him the Patterson letter. "Only this. The grammar alone will make you cringe." After he read it, cringing indeed, I added, "So far, nothing appears peculiar with the artwork, but I shipped it out to the appraiser in Chicago early this morning. I'm a little suspicious about a particular painting Peter Angelini acquired for him. It's called *Death in a Bygone Hue*. An interpretation of the army in Vietnam. Angelini was not only nervous when I told him about the appraisal, but he was also anxious to do it himself. I nixed his suggestion, but you might check on him. I know the judge wanted something appraised, and he hadn't had the Vietnam painting long when he died. Do you think there could be a shaky story about how Angelini acquired it, or possibly its authenticity is questionable?"

"I'll check on his financials. You'd know more about art fraud. I'll deal with his money, and you let me know what the appraisal says."

"Perhaps he pulled a fast one on the judge who found out. Then Angelini killed him to salvage his reputation as an art dealer."

Tom nodded. "His reputation could be a powerful motive."

"By the way, I found a report the judge had done on Prather, and it mentioned his cocaine habit."

My phone indicated a call as it vibrated on the desk, but I let it go to voicemail. "Tom," I said quietly, "do you think I need to worry about this undue influence charge?"

"No. It's a tricky thing to prove, and they've no evidence. Put it out of your mind."

"All right."

"Let me know if you find anything else suspicious."

Despite my brother's soothing words, I couldn't put a possible lawsuit from the Spiveys out of my mind.

Tom had no sooner left my office than my phone vibrated again, jolting me out of my thoughts. It was Ken Winters.

"Hi, Ken. What can I do for you?"

"Hi. After reading Gushman's editorial today, I thought I should check on you. She's such a terrible journalist." He paused. "I keep thinking the Chamber of Commerce could exert a little pressure with the ownership to get rid of her."

"I'm fine. Tom was over and told me to ignore it. Gushman's a lot of hot air, but I worry about what people in town might think of me."

He paused. "People in town who know you or the Spiveys already know what to believe. It'll be fine. Besides, they haven't a leg to stand on with this undue influence claim."

"I'd like to believe that, but I understand they hired a Chicago lawyer. He or she might know a few tricks."

Ken laughed. "The law is the law. To prove undue influence, they'd have to show he wasn't in his right mind, or you alienated him from his children and spent too much time with him. They can't show either of those."

I blew a soft breath through my mouth. "Oh. I always feel so much more confident after I listen to you."

"That's why I'm calling. I received a call from their lawyer, Calista Mildeway-Whitlock. They want to meet in my office tomorrow at one thirty. If it's only the lawyer, it'll be easy, but I'll bet the Spiveys will be there too. Any lawyer worth his salt would rather not have clients there."

I pondered the possibility. "Do you want me there?"

"No. I can manage it. You keep doing what you're doing at the art center. Your work provides far more benefit to the town. Don't worry. No problem."

"Thanks, Ken." I punched the end button and sat back in my chair. It was so wonderful to be able to leave it all to him. I was kidding myself. The Spiveys were not going to stop coming after me over this will.

Chapter Eighteen

After I'd hung up with Ken, I thought about the threatening letter I'd found from Reggie Patterson in the judge's desk. Tom might want to see who this mysterious cousin in town could be, the one Chad said Patterson was visiting. I sent him a quick text.

I sat back in my chair and thought about my brother Tom. How did he do it? He grew up here like me, but he had to be aware his job took him into shadowy corners and dark secrets hidden by the very people he knew when he was young. Apple Grove didn't have high-end crime like multiple murders. The town had the usual robberies, car thefts, abuse, and domestic violence. Oh, underage drinking—Angie and I would've raised those statistics considerably in high school, but we didn't get caught. People he knew and investigated committed all those criminal acts. How could he do that?

How did he manage to keep all those dark secrets in his head without them breaking him? How did he deal with childhood acquaintances who disappointed him? People he had respected suddenly became people he only thought he knew. He was always so steady, maintained a wealth of advice for his children, never took his job home to them, always pushed on despite the darker aspects of his detective work. Unlike Tom, I never noticed splinters or nails as a kid. I was oblivious even now.

I had settled in to check the graphic artwork on my computer, double-checking the gallery catalog for the exhibit, when the art center phone rang. Maybe Ken forgot something. It was a number I didn't recognize.

"Adele Marsden Center for the Arts. How may I help you?"

There was a pause. Then, "Is this Jill Madison?"

"Yes."

"Jezbhel Gushman here."

My breath stopped, and I almost shivered. This would have been a fun opportunity to slam the phone down, but I didn't. "Yes, Ms. Gushman."

"I hope you caught my editorial this morning."

I was sure she paused to let her words sink in.

"Actually, I've far more important things to do this morning than read the drivel you put out as a newspaper." A quiet chuckle caught my ear.

"Puts you in a minority in this fine town. People are concerned with your actions and your silence. Thought I'd offer you an opportunity to give me a statement because the family of Judge Spivey plans to take you to court. Journalists need to print both sides of the story. Any reaction? Any comments on your part? I'm all ears."

What should I do? Or say? I considered Tom and what he'd tell me to do. "No comment, Ms. Gushman. I wouldn't lower myself." That was when I slammed down the receiver. I sat there shaking. She was no "journalist." I suddenly felt like the temperature in my office had become chilly with her slimy statements. She'd print whatever she wanted. Even if I did make a statement, she'd probably screw it all up or turn it around. It was a problem when her newspaper was the only news outlet in the area.

I sat back, tapping my lips with my finger. What to do? What to do? My question reminded me of the early days when I read *Winnie-the-Pooh* to my niece, Emily. What to do? I thought about Judge Spivey, what advice he would've given me. Didn't he have the right to distribute his estate the way he wanted? It was possible one of these Spiveys committed patricide. I smiled at the word. I hadn't entirely forgotten all my Latin from high school. It was time to be proactive, meet this problem where it lived.

I grabbed my cell and stabbed the button for Ken Winters. When he answered, I said, "Sign me up, Ken. I'll be there tomorrow, one thirty, to hear what this drug-addicted, divorcing, alcoholic, gambling, spendthrift family says. They make it obvious why the judge decided to skip over them in his will. It's about time I faced this head-on."

I hung up and thought about which direction to take next. Louise was out in the gallery near the front door rearranging items in the gift shop. I walked over to see the latest new items.

"Look at this jewelry Anna Snodgrass brought in," Louise said.

I leaned over the glass display case. "Wow!" She was arranging gorgeous glass pendants that hung from necklace chains. They were myriad colors, each with a darker surface color with small pieces of different colors of glass underneath the smooth glass surface. Some had floral designs also. They were examples of fused glass, and currently, we had such a class going on upstairs. I loved one of the pendants with azure pieces.

Wandering over to our front display window, I checked out the fall and winter scarves made by the weavers' group. I particularly liked a lightweight woven scarf in various colors of blue edged with white. Betsy Sanders made these Indigo-dyed, handwoven, rayon chenille scarves. I had several in shades of red or blue. I loved them.

"Look, Louise. This scarf is exactly the earth tones you love to wear—a color combination of cadmium orange mixed with permanent green light. It's a beautiful olive shade."

"I've had my eyes on that for a couple weeks now," she said. "Maybe it will be an early birthday present to myself."

"Or you could wear it on your next date."

"And that would be this coming weekend."

I held up the scarf. "Oh, the dating site strikes again?"

She came over, took the scarf, and examined the olive hue. "I think this might go perfectly with a blouse and jacket I have." Rolling it back up, Louise said, "Yes, Mr.-Flavor-of-the-Week is a fencing instructor from Edgington."

"A fencing instructor! Do you see lessons in your future?"

"Probably not. I'll stick with the mace in my purse. A sword might be a bit awkward to carry around."

I nodded. You never knew what Louise's weekend dates were like. There had been times when I thought she should ask for a refund from whatever dating site she used.

"I think I'll go up and check on Donna Filbert. Her fused glass class has just started."

Donna Filbert, a retired art teacher, taught several classes, including this one. I climbed the stairs and stopped outside her door, listening to her explanation to the all-adult class.

"Fused glass is the heat bonding of separate pieces of glass to make beautiful artwork. Here are examples of fused glass items done by students in some of my other classes."

I looked through the doorway as she held up a gorgeous mauve plate. About a third of it contained small pieces of fused glass in pinks, reds, white, and lilac. Next were coasters in yellow and orange hues, their smooth polished surfaces shining in the light from a window.

I smiled as I listened to her calm, expert voice. The class sat in rapt silence while she showed them pieces of artwork. Goosebumps. I had goosebumps on my arms. People creating art—I loved it!

Donna continued in her expert voice, "One class made Christmas ornaments. Aren't these wonderful?" She held up oblong ornaments with snowflakes and evergreens melted into them. A hum of excitement buzzed through the room.

We could do a class on that before Christmas. I logged that away in my brain.

The remaining projects she raised in the air were a couple of night lights for kids' bedrooms, a round wall clock with a red background and white hands, and three floral panels.

"All these pieces are made of fused glass," she repeated. "Folks, you too can be artists and create beautiful fused-glass pieces. Today is just the beginning."

I quietly moved into the room and sat in one of the chairs near the back so I could watch her demonstration. We'd installed a table in the front with excellent lighting and a mirror above it, slanted so the class could see the top of the table and her hands as she worked. After explaining safety rules, since we were cutting glass, she held up a box of Band-Aids.

"Hopefully, we won't need these if you're careful handling the glass pieces, focused, and armed with safety glasses. No exception on that last piece of equipment. Oh, and your phones should be put away and the sound off. Otherwise, a phone will go off, and someone will jump and end up with a cut finger."

Everyone chuckled nervously.

"Now," Donna continued, "we're starting easy today with a three-by-three-inch base. This class is an introduction. See these bins with different colored glass pieces?"

Everyone's eyes followed her to a bin on the side table marked "glass bases."

"You'll choose a color for your base. After that, the middle layer is how you create your design, which will be glued to the glass base. These bins have all different sizes and colors of glass to create your composition. You use these nippers or wheel cutters to cut the glass to your own liking." She held up both tools.

We watched as she used the nippers on some larger pieces of glass and then a wheel cutter on a smaller glass piece, firmly breaking the glass into pieces at the fissure line she'd cut. Gluing the small pieces onto the glass base, she created a design in different colors, shapes, and sizes.

"Now," she said, "you go to this other glass bin and pick out a clear piece of glass slightly larger than your design. You can trim it down just like you did earlier, so it's the right size. Then glue it onto the design you created, kind of like a sandwich."

I watched the class. They were focused intently on Donna.

A man near the front raised his hand, and Donna called on him. "So, I assume you fire these up in a kiln next. How do we remember which one is ours?"

"Good question." Donna smiled. "Over on this table to my right are small trays and masking tape. You'll write your name on a piece of tape and put it and your project on one of the small trays. Then I'll take all the trays home, fire the kiln to 1490 degrees, and fuse the pieces."

Another hand. "How long until we can come get them?"

"It'll take twenty-four hours for them to cool after the kiln fuses everything. I'll bring them back here"—she looked at her sports watch— "on Friday. You can stop in on Friday, be totally excited by your artistic endeavor, and glue a magnet to the back. That makes them ready for the refrigerator door. Any other questions?"

Everyone looked around.

"OK, let's start with the front row here."

After watching this class and listening to their excitement, I knew coming home from Chicago was all worthwhile. In my memory, I could hear my mom talking to me about why art was important in people's lives. In grade school, third or fourth grade, she'd said, "Jill, creating something that never existed before, except in your own mind, is an amazing feat. A wise author once said imagination is the beginning of creation. You imagine what you desire, you will what you imagine, and, at last, you create what you will." Years later, I read the same quotation in a play in one of my college classes. It was by the British playwright George Bernard Shaw. I've never forgotten my mother quoting his words that day or the intensity in her eyes when she examined a clay bowl I'd made in school and brought home to her for Mother's Day. I was so proud, and she looked at me with such love.

Deep inside, I was sure she somehow knew what we were doing here in a place with her name on the door, and she was smiling.

Chapter Nineteen

I didn't sleep well thinking about facing the Spiveys or their lawyer. Ken said it would all be fine, they didn't have a case, but I wasn't so sure. I glanced up from the judge's desk and stared at the calendar. September 20. Tuesday. It didn't seem possible he'd been gone ten days. Time was playing out like a spool of thread rolling away from me.

Get a grip on yourself, Jill. I stared down at the folders in the drawer I was cleaning. One of them had handwritten notes about his art collection. The actual documents proving provenance I'd sent off with the paintings after scanning copies. I opened the folder with his notes, wondering what I'd find.

Seeing his familiar writing on the top piece of paper, I closed the folder and stared out one of the office windows. Now, I found myself in a place like Tom, combing through the details of someone else's life. A person I thought I knew, but now I was no longer a teenager whose concerns stopped in a small circle around my feet. I believed I better understood the complexity of people's lives. What else would I find in the judge's life? Hidden secrets? Notations here and there on receipts detailing his attitude about his family and artwork? Thoughts about his wife or kids? I hadn't found a journal or diary. I didn't expect him to have information I'd need to go through about his legal cases. But I still felt like an interloper who would comb through his personal papers, explore the hidden edges and creases of their surfaces, discovering things I might not want to know about this mentor who had been my friend and counselor. The judge must've thought I could discover his failings but still believe in his goodness.

"Jill?"

I jumped and blinked at Tilda standing in the doorway.

"Oh, sorry. I was deep in thought. What's up?"

"Didn't mean to surprise you." She walked into the office a few feet, a worried expression on her face. "I've discovered something's missing."

"Missing?"

"Yes. An ornamental dagger the judge bought on a trip to Japan. It was in his bedroom, hanging on the east wall. It's small, but part of a collection. Only this one is missing."

"Oh. Has it been gone long, or could he have sold it or sent it somewhere before he died?"

Tilda sat next to the desk. She swept a hand over her hair, smoothing it back from her face. "That's the problem. I can't remember. I hadn't noticed, but I was dusting his bedroom, looked up, and realized it was gone."

I pulled open a desk drawer. "Let me check." The judge had a partial inventory of things in the house. It should make my work a bit easier. I found the right file, lifted it from the drawer, and spread it out on the desk. Using my finger to follow down the spreadsheet, I found a notation for a group of four daggers, the smallest called a kaiken. They were weapons used by Samurai for close self-defense. "He lists four here."

She shook her head. "Now there are only three."

"Hmm. Usually, the judge made a notation if he sold something or sent it out to a museum. This has no notation. I'll have to think about it. Thanks, Tilda."

"Could be those Spiveys are involved with this missing knife." Her face had a skeptical expression. "Since the smallest is missing, they could've slipped it into a pocket."

"As far as I know, they haven't been around lately, oh, except for Erika. Hmm. Let me know if you find anything else that seems irregular or is missing."

"Will do." She stood and was about to leave, but she turned around instead. "Don't trust those Spiveys." Then, she was out the door.

Strange. Judge Spivey was incredibly careful with his artwork and purchases, this inventory proving the truth of that fact. I put the inventory folder back in the drawer and opened the information about his art collection. Here, there were handwritten notes about all kinds of artwork. His handwriting resembled scribbles he'd written as he was thinking about pieces he owned or sales he was considering.

He had stipulated in his will at least five of his paintings must rotate on a six-month public display each year. We'd talked about this at a few of our lunches. Artwork is meant to be viewed—a precept we both agreed upon. He'd received five paintings back two months ago that he'd lent to a museum in San Francisco, fortunate timing as all the works were back at his death. I'd called two other museums that were expecting artwork and explained, apologetically, the artwork was part of a will in probate. I'd heard all the artwork had arrived safely, without incident, from the appraiser in Chicago. They'd get back to me with their findings in a couple of weeks.

When appraisers evaluated pieces of art, they investigated recent prices paid for comparable items in the world. These prices included the fair market value, the insurance value, and the market value for liquidation. I was sure the last one was the option of interest to the Spivey sibs. The appraisers would also put the paintings through forensic tests, studying the provenance of each. It meant they'd check out the chain of ownership. Were they sold at auction? Acquired in what year? Documents? Since they were aware of the paintings of artists and kept extensive libraries of research, they'd be able to use their information to check the documents alleging the paintings were legitimate. If artists were known to use certain techniques, materials, or brushstrokes, they would have to research sources about each artist. It would also help with forensic testing like ultraviolet analysis, x-ray fluorescent analysis, and microscopic examination.

While I wasn't an expert on finding forgeries, I'd actually taken part in a microscopic examination of paintings one summer in an internship I'd done. It involved putting a tiny paint chip to the test to see if pigments in a painting were true. We'd shine a laser over the paint chip, and it would tell us about the binder. Acrylic, for example, was a binder. Knowing when acrylics were first used, and what colors were available, could help us figure out if a forger had done the work.

Certain variants of colors came into play. Research on color variants and their date of use helped decide if a painting was a forgery. I remembered reading about a forgery where the artist had used a yellow pigment called Hansa yellow in a 1938 painting he forged in the 1970s. Unfortunately, Hansa Yellow was not used in 1938. We checked for inconsistencies. Knowing those kinds of facts helped detect forgeries. I knew our appraiser had a vast research database, so they could check the judge's paintings carefully.

The question in my own mind concerned his last buy, *Death in a Bygone Hue*. Something about it seemed off. I wished I could put my finger on it. I began leafing through the pages of the judge's notes. Certain papers had dates when he'd written the notes, others didn't. He'd jotted phrases and descriptions, sometimes with question marks. I think he was checking the provenance documents. I turned several pages and still saw nothing about the Vietnam painting.

Then I hit pay dirt. I found a one-page description of the artist the judge must've researched. Calvin Dexter Saphstone [1948-1975]. He was born April 18, 1948, and grew up in Milford, Massachusetts, an only child. I scanned the information, focusing on what seemed significant. He went to public schools. Upon his graduation, he was invited to enroll in the Rhode Island School of Design in Providence. Spent a semester abroad in Italy while at the RISD. His work earned high praise, and the school exhibited it on campus his senior year. In 1969, the US government drafted him and sent him to Vietnam.

I sighed and looked up for a few minutes. For someone so sensitive and deep into art, I couldn't imagine what a horrifying experience Vietnam must've been. I read on.

His Vietnam experience had a considerable influence on his thinking and his art. He created a series of paintings reflecting his time in-country. *Sunrise Over Pleiku, Death Stalks the Market Place, Death in a Bygone Hue,* and *Fires in the Central Highland* were paintings that won honors and were valued at thousands of dollars. By 1974, his work became more erratic. Alcohol and drugs contributed to his suicide on February 4, 1975. Following his death, his works rose in value. Some sold at auction recently for $1 million each.

I flipped through more pages, a few of them legible, some not. Finally, after squinting at the judge's squiggly handwriting, I came upon a page with the painting's title. He'd written several phrases about provenance documents. He must've been checking to see if they were legitimate.

"Gallery sticker attached Aberstrom Gallery of Art 612.555.4976," he'd written. He'd scribbled dates where he'd tried to reach the gallery. Several question marks followed. A gallery sticker is one form of authentication, but if it can't be checked, it's worthless. In another place on the page, he'd written "previous owner" and Barnstable Art Center and Museum. Another phone number followed: 508.555.2913. Again, several dates and a question mark. He must've tried to call this art center listed as a previous owner. Under "previous owner" was a second name and number: "Fenton Ivy 319.555.4701." Several scribbled dates. No other notes.

Right behind this page was a gallery catalog for the Museum of Fine Arts, Minneapolis. He had folded it back to reveal a description of *Death in a Bygone Hue*. But there was little information beyond these small tidbits. The museum's phone number was jotted down in the judge's handwriting. But again, he scribbled dates next to it with no other information. Three question marks.

At the bottom of the page, he'd scribbled, "Check with Angelini." The date was in late August before his death. As someone who was well-educated in checking on the provenance of paintings, my first reaction was to suspect the judge was having no luck checking on whether the documents with this painting were authentic. He was obviously suspicious. Had he been careless? Had he paid big money for a fake painting? Had he confronted Angelini before his sudden death?

Most buyers who work through a dealer like Angelini were cautious about checking on the provenance of anything they purchased. He'd collaborated with Peter for quite a few years since he'd moved to Apple Grove. I would think the judge trusted him. Had Angelini made a mistake? Why was Spivey suspicious about this particular oil painting? I felt the same way, but it was a gut feeling, an intuitive spasm. Perhaps the appraiser in Chicago would have answers.

I decided to make a folder of things I didn't understand. Perhaps Ken Winters could help me. Placing the scribbly paper in it, I opened the center desk drawer and found the sticky note with "Ted Bender." I slid it into the folder.

Trying to step into someone else's life and figure out what was happening could be impossible at times.

Glancing up at the clock, I realized I'd better appear at the art center before lunch. Louise was being terribly patient with me. She'd covered on several occasions when I'd had to check on the judge's estate. I added hours at night to make sure I didn't short the art center on my weekly hours. But now, as I waited for the appraisal, I didn't have much to do except be patient.

I reached down to put the folder back in the drawer, but something grazed the top of my hand. Momentarily surprised, I pulled my hand out quickly. What was it?

Rolling my chair back, I leaned over. An envelope was partly hanging from the bottom of the drawer above the one where I'd replaced the folder. What the heck? I pulled on the piece of envelope hanging down. It came out in one piece. The tape had attached it to the bottom of the drawer, obviously hidden. Yellowed and old, the tape had little reason to stick to anything. There was nothing on the envelope, no address, no name.

I sat up and pulled out the flap. A piece of folded paper fell out. I opened it, laying it on the desk. A familiar scent enveloped me. Adrenaline rushed through my body. I gasped. My mother's handwriting stared me in the face. My hand flew to my chest because I couldn't breathe. Why would the judge have a letter in my mother's handwriting? Why would he hide it? Sitting back in the chair, I took several deep breaths, my arms filled with goosebumps. Spreading it out, I began to read.

Chapter Twenty

Ken Winters had asked me to be at his office around one o'clock. The meeting was at one thirty, but he wanted to talk with me first. It was hard to even think about seeing the Spiveys after what I'd read in my mother's letter. My stomach was roiling, and I hadn't eaten lunch, which didn't help. My hands shook a little because I was anxious about dealing with this Chicago lawyer. Before starting up the stairs to Ken's office, I took a deep breath. I'd have to concentrate and put that letter into a separate compartment in my brain. Wasn't easy, but I'd have to try. I was already thinking about calling Angie after all this. She'd know what to do. We'd figure it out. How many times had we solved problems like that over the years?

Entering Winters' door, I spoke to his secretary, Doris, and sat in a chair near the door. She made a call, and in a few minutes, the door to his office opened, and he walked toward me and stopped. There was a concerned expression on his face.

"Are you all right, Jill?"

I stood. Pulling myself together, I said, "Sure. I'm ready for this. Just a little shaky."

He smiled. "Nothing to worry about. Come on into my office."

I followed him and sat in the same chair in front of his desk, the chair where I'd heard the news about becoming the judge's executor. What had the judge gotten me into? I stared across the desk and felt comforted by his confident face. He took several papers out of a folder.

"You don't need to be concerned about this meeting. Ron made sure his will was in perfect legal shape. His signature was witnessed by Tilda Swanson and Abe Calipher. If worse came to worst, they'll be excellent witnesses, but I don't anticipate it will come to that."

I swallowed. "Why?"

"Everything has been done correctly to set up probate, the will was witnessed legally, and there is no way they can prove undue influence. They'd have to show Ron Spivey was not able to withstand your pressure to leave his estate to you and the art center. They have no proof."

"Good. However, no one was at those lunches we had for several months. Only the judge and me."

"And did you unduly pressure him to put you in his will?"

"No."

"Did you know the contents of his will before I disclosed them to you in my office?"

"No."

Ken sat back in his chair, putting his hands behind his neck. "You have nothing to worry about."

If he only knew what I'd just read in my mother's letter. Sweat broke out on my forehead thinking about it.

"The paintings are all off to the appraiser, I hear. Excellent. When do you expect to receive word about their value?"

"I believe they said two to three weeks, but I think that estimate is a bit premature."

The phone on his desk buzzed, and Ken picked up the receiver and listened. "I'll be right out." He looked at me and said, "Follow me. You don't have to say a word. I'll take care of this discussion. Let's go to the conference room, where we'll have a table with plenty of room to spread out. We can face the enemy across a table."

As I followed him out of the office, my stomach dropped. The Spiveys were here. They were with a tall, slender woman who wore a black suit, a mauve silk blouse, and black spike heels. She was all business as she gave Ken a stilted smile and shook his hand. Erika's eyes were gleaming at me, as if she were headed into a battle, and her lawyer was wearing armor as she got ready to charge. John followed behind her, a guarded expression on his face.

Once we settled in the conference room, Ken introduced me to the Spivey lawyer, Calista Mildeway-Whitlock. And yes, she was from the Chicago firm of Sampson, Lockhart, Praxis, and Whitlock. I had to admit she seemed a little scary. I hoped Ken was ready.

"What can we do for you, Ms. Mildeway-Whitlock?" Ken began.

The lawyer set several folders down on the table, opened one, and began. Erika and John were seated on either side of her. "My clients believe your client, Ms. Madison, exerted undue influence on Judge Spivey, their father, to change his will and unfairly exclude them from their inheritance. You would, of course, agree they have standing with the court?"

Ken nodded. "They are mentioned at the beginning of the will, and, as his children, have standing with the court. But there is no evidence whatsoever Ms. Madison was a part of putting that will together."

"And yet, here we are. We were hoping to discuss this sensibly rather than moving to a court case immediately."

Erika Spivey stared at me, pointed her finger, and said, "She's the one. Our father loved us, left us his estate, and then she made him cut us out." The last few words were said with venom.

Mildeway-Whitlock turned to her and said, "I'll take care of this, Erika." Then she turned to us again and said, "How do you explain the fact that Erika and John both have copies of a previous will where their father's estate was left, in its entirety, to them? Ms. Madison or the art center were never mentioned."

"Have you asked your clients that question?" Ken said.

I glanced at Erika, who was smirking, and John, who moved uncomfortably in his chair. Erika blasted out again, "You should be ashamed, taking advantage of our father at his age! You're nothing but a—" This time, her lawyer glared at her and put her hand around Erika's arm. Tightly.

I could feel my face turning bright red at her implication, but Ken's hand touched my arm as if to say, "I'll handle this."

"Ms. Mildeway-Whitlock. We both resent your client's implication. Judge

Spivey was a mentor to Ms. Madison, and he was the treasurer of her art center board. They had a business relationship. Furthermore, he and his wife knew Ms. Madison's parents for years prior to his death. You have no evidentiary basis for any of these outrageous claims. The judge was not dependent, isolated, or vulnerable."

Ken's words sounded very legal-ly to me. Score one for my great lawyer. John, who had been quiet since we started this discussion, leaned toward me, and said, "Then why did he change his will?"

Before I could say a word, Ken addressed the other lawyer. "The original will was drawn prior to his wife Laura's death. What is the date of his current will?"

She checked her papers. "July 25, 2005."

Ken sat back in his chair and crossed his arms. He stared specifically at Erika, his face serious and his eyes narrowing. "And what happened two weeks before the date of that will in 2005, Erika?"

Her face showed she recognized his point. Narrowing her own eyes, she said in a low but scathing voice, "Our mother died."

I understood her pain and almost felt sad for her. Then I remembered she had threatened me.

Ken resumed. "Now, I can see why you thought Jill had undue influence because she has had meetings with Ron to discuss art center business, but this decision to make her executor of his will was eleven years ago, when Jill was nineteen and in college. After college, she resided in Chicago. She didn't even speak with the judge until recently, when she returned home to run the art center. It would be tough to prove undue influence. Then a few months ago, he made the change that included the art center. He was, after all, in his right mind. I would swear to that, as would his doctor."

"Then she tricked him, defrauded him—" Erika spurted.

"Ms. Madison-Whitlock. As Ron's lawyer, I'm quite aware his relationship with his children was strained and has been after the death of his wife. While she was alive, Erika and John received substantial financial benefits from their parents. But something must have happened after their mother's death. Maybe they can explain that to you." He looked at Erika, then back at her

128

lawyer. "I'd suggest you explain to your client those kinds of statements about Ms. Madison will land her in court with a charge of slander. And if she knows what's good for her, she'll stop giving our local newspaper editor slanderous words as well." He turned his head to the lawyer. "Now, is there anything else you feel is germane?"

She glanced at the two Spivey adults. "We'll discuss your points, Mr. Winters, and I'll get back to you."

Now, I stared at Erika and said, "Oh, and Tilda Swanson says a ceremonial Japanese knife has been missing from your father's bedroom since you came back to see him a couple of days before his death. Would you know anything about that?"

Her face immediately took on a guilty expression before she straightened herself out and snarled at me, "No. But you've been in the house a lot from what I hear."

Ken studied the lawyer, whose face remained impassive. Then he said, "Easy, Erika. The investigation into your father's death is still going on, and both you and John have millions of reasons adding up to motive."

Erika stood, stared at me, and said, "I know a thing or two about the law too, Mr. High-and-Mighty Lawyer. The slayer statute says she dies, we win everything. So, watch your back, Jill Madison."

"Erika, shut up," said her lawyer. "I apologize for my client's difficulty in controlling her behavior, Mr. Winters and Ms. Madison."

"You'd better watch your back," Erika repeated. She stood, stomped her foot, and opened the door, slamming it behind her.

Everyone around the table breathed a sigh except me. She was right about watching my back.

John Bradford stood. "I apologize for my sister. She is a difficult woman with a temper she tries hard to control. I've never been able to get her to understand compromise. On the other hand, we both have reasons to be angry about this. Not being allowed in our own father's house is suspicious. Could be there's another will there, but we'll never be allowed to see it. It'll be destroyed."

"What did happen after your mother's death, John?" Ken asked, deflecting the direction of the conversation.

"Nothing," John practically shouted.

"I think we're done here," their lawyer said. She stood and shepherded John out of the room, closing the door behind them.

"You were magnificent, Ken."

"I hope we've heard the last of the Spiveys, but I never discount what greed does to people. Ms. Mildeway-Whitlock took on their case for some reason. I wonder if she owed one of them. But it's obvious even she realizes they don't have a leg to stand on."

"Did you mean that about slander?"

"I think Erika believes it, so you'll get a rest from her nastiness. Editor Gushman knows just how far to go with her intimations. She's a wordsmith. She'll phrase things so we can't sue her for libel. You may have to put up with that."

"And the slayer thing?"

"It's Erika trying to make you worry. I wouldn't."

I thought about his words but remembered Erika Spivey's face as she spat out that sentence.

My mind was going in another direction, prompted by Ken Winters' words about being in college studying art when the judge made his latest will. Maybe he justified his executor choice in his own mind by my actions once I'd returned to run the art center. But on a deeper level, I thought there might be another reason, and only my best friend could talk me through that tangled web from the past.

Chapter Twenty-One

"That settles it," Angie said that evening at Priscilla's.

We were sitting in a booth at the back of the bar, surrounded by nothing but empty tables. It was early, so this was the perfect space to talk about shocking disasters.

"You're not going home alone tonight. If Erika Spivey can be so direct about murdering you, we'd better make sure you have some company."

I waved her off. "I'll be fine. Her mouthy threats are nothing. But I know she stole the dagger. I wonder what else she managed to take that we haven't found yet."

"A dagger? She even has a weapon. It's funny she's overt in her threats, and her brother is quiet, from what you say."

I nodded, then took another sip of my beer. "But, as my dad always said, it's the quiet ones you have to watch out for."

"Oh, great." She glanced over at the bar to make sure she wasn't needed. "Now that the overture part of your day is done, what's the first act? You said you found something troubling. I'm waiting."

I opened my tote bag and, with trembling hands, took out the letter I'd found taped to the judge's drawer. "I'll read it to you. I'd never have found it except the tape was so old the letter came loose at one end. Here goes." I opened the one page delicately, smoothing it out on the table as my mother's perfume hit me once again. Goosebumps down my arms. "The date is August 2, 2005."

"2005? That was shortly after Ms. Spivey died."

"Correct," I said and grimaced, "and the date may be crucial to this story."

Angie tilted her head, raised an eyebrow, and said, "Carry on."

"August 2, 2005. My dear Ron, I'm writing this note to once again tell you how sad I am about Laura's passing. If I was a help with your need to vent your sorrow the other night, I'm glad. That's what friends are for." I studied Angie's face, then started a new paragraph. "It's hard to believe it's been twenty years since we met at the Tansler Art Gallery exhibit. My sculpture, 'Two Hearts,' will always have a special place in my own heart and memory. So many years have passed since those days when I was struggling with my marriage and the two boys. You were there for me at a time when I needed someone to lean on. I remember you talking then about second chances. So lucky. I'll never forget the lost weekend or the afternoon we spent at Navy Pier. Long, long ago. Thank you for being there for me. I'll never forget. Love always, Adele."

Angie was silent. So was I, waiting for the true import to strike home.

"They were friends long before you guys moved here, and he helped her with her marriage. So what?"

"No, don't you see, Angie?"

"What? What don't I see?" She leaned closer, setting her empty beer bottle on the table.

"I did a little research this afternoon. The exhibit she's talking about was at the Tansler Art Gallery, an independent contemporary art museum in the West Loop. It was an up-and-coming place in the art world, and my mom's career was gaining steam then."

Angie thought a moment. "They met once before the Spiveys moved here. In fact, ten years or so before they moved here."

"Yes. I'll bet her death brought up my mother's memory of their meeting. I researched it. The Tansler Art Gallery had an opening for my mom's exhibit the night of August 6, 1985."

"OK. I don't understand why this is such a big deal."

I stared down at the letter in her handwriting. It almost made me cry. I was seeing a side of my mom's life I didn't know anything about. It brought back the heart-breaking fact that she had been gone six years. I took a deep breath. "I figure my parents had been married about ten years then. Tom was seven, and Andy, five. My mom was balancing a career teaching, two kids, exhibits, my dad, and the house. I imagine it's why she was going through a rough time and needed someone to lean on. Might be she and Dad were in a tough period of their marriage. It happens, you know."

"But what is this 'second chances' stuff? She said something about him mentioning second chances."

"What if it means she gave him a second chance at love?" I watched Angie's stunned expression, which seemed a lot like I'd felt when I first read this letter.

"Oh, that's crazy, Jill. No way. You think she and the judge did the dirty deed when they were both married to other people? No way. She'd never have done that to Howard."

"Exactly what I thought when I first read the letter. Then I reread her references to a 'lost weekend,' and 'never forgetting.' What else could it mean?"

Angie shook her head. "No, it's impossible. Not your mom."

I took a long swallow of my beer, setting down the bottle and feeling a wetness on my cheeks. "Why impossible? It sounds like their marriage was in trouble. She gave him a 'second chance,' for love? How do we ever know what our parents' personal lives were like?"

"No, no, no, no, no. I knew your mom and dad, almost as well as you. I spent weeks at your house growing up. Remember? This could never have happened. Give me one good reason I should believe this."

"I can give you several million reasons."

She paused. "You think it's why he left you so much money? Because you're his kid?"

"Why else? If he didn't plan to leave it to his own kids, he could've given it to charities or his old college or some art gallery in New York City. Why give it to me? What made me so special—unless I was actually his kid. In fact, Ken Winters told me the judge thought of me as a 'surrogate daughter.'"

She still shook her head. "No way."

"I counted, Angie. If they had a—a lost weekend around August 2, 1985, you count nine months, and what do you hit? April 17, 1986. Guess whose birthday that is?"

Now I had her attention.

Angie let out a long breath. "If that's true it would make you a half-sister to your brothers and even the Spiveys? Yuk on the Spivey connection. There must be a way to divorce them."

"Exactly. I'm mortified. I wasn't ever meant to see this letter. The judge didn't know he was going to die. There's no one to ask, no one who can verify what I'm thinking."

"How about your brothers? Do they know about this?"

"Are you crazy? I could never tell Tom or Andy. It would break their hearts. It's doing a number on mine as it is. The judge, my could-be father."

She reached over, putting her hand on mine. "Look, you don't know for sure. You should burn the letter and forget it."

"But what if I am the judge's kid? It would explain why he'd been so kind to me, why he helped save my job a few months ago, or why he's always fought with Ivan the Terrible to back my position at the art center. No one would know, well, except the judge and my mom, and they're no longer with us."

"That settles it. Each person who counts in this story is gone. Just forget it. Don't worry about it. No one will ever know."

I took a deep breath. I glanced down and said quietly, "I will."

We were both silent, as if sharing a moment of silence when someone died. In my case, it wasn't a death but a change in how I understood the people I loved.

"All right. How do we get confirmation? Who would know?"

I thought about it. Did I really want to know? Part of me believed I'd be better leaving everything like it was and destroying this letter. Angie was right. But then there was a niggling, tiny voice saying it would be better to know the truth. There was a way. "I think we can find out."

"How?"

"I read online about tests that can tell you if you're a full sibling or a half-sibling based on your DNA."

Angie's eyes were curious. "How do they work?"

"I would apply online for a test, swab my mouth and my brother's mouth, and send it in. They can tell if we have the same parents."

"Gosh, it sounds easy. Tell Tom, the law-and-order man, you need to swab his mouth. Or better, tell Captain Looney Tunes you need to swab his mouth to see if someone dropped him from a tree or left him on your doorstep. How would you ever find a way to check without telling them?"

"I'm working on that. Possibly Lance."

"Lance? He's not even related to you."

"No, I mean I'll talk to Lance, let him know my suspicions, and figure out a way to get Andy's DNA. There's no way to get Tom's."

Angie's head shook. "I can't imagine any explanation that would work there."

"Hmm." I touched my lips pensively with my index finger. "If there's a way, I can figure it out."

"What will you do if you get it back and it says you're only a half-sib?"

"I'll be devastated, Angie." Then I grimaced. "It will break my heart."

Chapter Twenty-Two

By Thursday evening, I was exhausted by all these loose threads and problems. The Spiveys, the judge's will, my suspicions about the artwork I'd sent to Chicago, the missing dagger, whether I was only a half-Madison, and internal squabbling among the weaver's group at the art center. Then there was the art exhibit coming up at a rapid rate. Too many things weighed me down, but in the back of my mind, the judge's killer and the DNA situation were first and foremost. I was still no closer to finding out who killed Judge Spivey, but Tom might have made progress. My brain was working on how to get Andy to give me a DNA swab so I could find out if we were siblings or only half-siblings.

For the past day, I'd experienced the same sadness grief imposed after my parents' deaths. Up and down like a rollercoaster. My motivation was flagging, I'd briefly cry at ridiculous points in the day, and I felt a huge betrayal on my mother's part. Had my father known? Then, I'd talk to myself and reason that I wasn't sure what had happened back then. Could this be my imagination working overtime?

Tom planned to stop in on his way home from work because he had news to talk about. I did too. I'd had a preliminary call from the appraiser in Chicago, and he confirmed my suspicions about the Vietnam painting. Not exactly confirmed. But of all the works I'd sent, the one I questioned was the one he'd zeroed in on. He'd get back to me in a few days about the findings. They had more tests to conduct.

I'd just opened a bottle of Savvy B when Tom knocked on the back door. I grabbed two wine glasses from the cupboard.

Unlike my quiet sadness, he was all bonhomie.

"Great news, Jill. I know you've been concerned about Ron's death. We've found two phone calls to follow up on that went to Ron's phone number."

"Phone calls?" I handed him a glass of wine, and he followed me out to the deck off the kitchen. When we were both seated in deck chairs, and I'd adjusted the umbrella on the table to keep the late afternoon sun out of our eyes, he pulled a paper out of his shirt pocket and unfolded it.

"The night before Ron died, he received a phone call from an unknown number. Likely a burner phone."

"A burner phone?"

"Yes. It's a phone you can buy cheap anywhere. It's only meant for temporary use, and then you throw it away. No contract, but you buy it with prepaid minutes."

"Can't you trace it?"

"Not back to its primary number with a listed owner. But we could tell this one bounced off a local cell tower, so whoever used it wasn't too far away." He took another sip of his wine.

"What you're saying is someone called the judge and didn't want to be traced?"

"Exactly. They talked for six minutes. Not long, but I figure long enough to make an appointment the next morning."

I gasped. "His killer?"

Tom nodded. "That's my theory. Of course, the question is who. Somehow it doesn't seem like something Erika or John would do. But possibly Erika's husband. I could be wrong."

I walked back into the house and grabbed the wine bottle, carrying it out to the deck. Refilling Tom's glass, I paused. "You said *two* calls were interesting?" I set the bottle on the table and sat again.

"The other call was from Peter Angelini."

"The judge's art dealer?"

"Yes. It showed up two days before the murder. It was much longer, about twenty minutes. What do you know about him?"

I hesitated. "He spoke with me at the funeral. All obsequious mannerisms as if he wanted to help me with the judge's artwork. I don't think I'm wrong when I say he was nervous the minute I mentioned the paintings had to be appraised. He offered to help, but I politely turned him down. Something about his manner put me off. But why would he use his own phone and then a burner phone?"

Tom took a deep breath and gazed out to the west where the sun was slowly dissolving into the landscape. "Could be the longer call was one he was returning and didn't have a clue about what the judge wanted to talk about. The burner phone might have set up the meeting, and he wouldn't want that traced. You think he might have sold the judge a fraudulent painting? And is there reason to be worried? Has the appraiser gotten back to you?"

I nodded. "Today. In fact, this morning. He called with a preliminary question. The last painting the judge bought through Peter Angelini, *Death in a Bygone Hue*, was an oil painting by an American who'd been in the Vietnam conflict. Calvin Dexter Saphstone. I have no idea how the judge felt about his wartime experiences, but he'd bought this painting, and something about it bothered me. Call it intuition. The artist had died, making his work more valuable. When I examined the notes the judge had made about the painting, it appeared he'd had trouble tracing the provenance of the work."

Tom set his glass down and turned to me. "They had trouble identifying whether this was the real thing?"

"Yes. I'm waiting to hear more. The appraiser said they'd do a more thorough dive into the background of the work. His question to me was if I knew anything about this particular painting. I only knew he bought it through Angelini. I'm not doing anything until I hear back from him."

"And then?"

I hesitated. "I've little experience with forgeries, but if they determine this painting is indeed a forgery, I contact the US Attorney for the Northern District of Illinois, and he'll contact the FBI after seeing the information from the appraisal."

"The FBI investigates art forgeries?"

"Fraud," I said. "They've had an FBI Art Crime Team since 2004. The last figure I read—if I'm remembering correctly—was $800 million dollars they'd recovered. I believe they deal more with theft than fraud, but in this case, it's the closest agency I can contact that would deal with the legal aspects."

"Is it easy to forge a painting?"

"The internet has made it easier than ever to make forged artwork and provenance documents."

Tom chuckled. "You know a lot about where our jobs intersect."

I smiled like a Cheshire cat. "I read about it."

A silence fell on our conversation, and both of us, after a long day, were willing to sit peacefully and watch the sun go down. After a while, Tom said, "You're being careful about Erika Prather threatening you, right?"

"Yes. I'm locking the doors and watching over my shoulder."

"Good. Erika lied to me about not seeing her father recently, and she needs money. You have her money, she believes. I'm having a police car come by a little more often, especially at night."

"Yes, brother dear. I'm being cautious. Thank you."

He rose slowly and picked up his glass and the wine bottle. "I'd better get home to my dear wife."

I followed him into the kitchen, closed and locked the sliding doors, and put a dowel rod in the track so no one could open them. "See, being careful."

"Good. Let me know what you hear."

"Thanks, Tom."

And with that, he was gone. As I waved from the front porch, I remembered I hadn't checked my mailbox. I grabbed the mail, heading back into the living room. Shuffling through the bills and junk mail, I set it down on the kitchen table, arranging the junk in a pile to throw into recycling. At the bottom of the pile was a hand-addressed envelope. I picked it up and opened it. No return address. Inside was a single piece of paper with silly letters cut out from magazines. So dramatic. As I read them, however, I sobered. The letters spelled out a horrifying message.

"You stole from me, now I steal from you. Your life should even things out."

Chapter Twenty-Three

I dropped the threatening letter at Tom's office on my way to work Friday morning. I'd been careful not to touch it any more than when I opened it, and I sealed it in a plastic bag. He was off somewhere doing his detective bit, and I left him a note with it.

At the art center, things were in full swing. Only two more days before we started installing the national exhibit. So exciting! Despite my enthusiasm, I'd spent the night thinking not about the exhibit, but instead about how to get Lance to collaborate with me on a DNA test for Andy.

Finally, I dialed his cell phone.

"Good morning, Jill."

What a pleasant voice he had. It sounded calm and reasonable. It must be true opposites attract. "Hi, Lance. How're things going?"

"Great so far. Just got in a new shipment of gift items I ordered in Chicago. In fact, I found a silver tray that would be perfect for your living room. Want to stop by?"

I paused. "Actually, I was thinking it would be nice if you'd stop by the art center because I have something I need to talk with you about." I paused. "Is Andy around?"

"He's in the backroom opening boxes. Do you want me to get him?"

"No. Absolutely not. In fact, do not tell him I called."

"Hmmm. Is Angie with you? Are you two plotting a nefarious deed?"

"No. Why would you think that? Totally innocent—Angie and me. I need to ask you a favor, and I don't want Andy to know about it. Is there any way you can get out of the store this morning on a pretense but stop by here instead?"

"Sure."

"Perfect. See you soon." I tapped off and sat back in my chair. I had devised a plan around three in the morning when I was tossing about in my bed. And I'd already overnighted my mouth swab to the company. It just needed Andy's for comparison.

Louise knocked on my office door.

I turned. "Yes, I'm ready." We spent the next hour examining the artwork for the exhibit. Making sure wires were in place and repairing anything damaged in transit, we studied each piece and discussed how we'd group them. We had today and tomorrow to do any last-minute fixes and get the gallery ready. Chad was a great help when it came to cleaning each night, but for this, we needed to go over every inch of the gallery and make sure it was sparkling. Just before we'd finished the sorting and mending, a boy from the printing company on the square came in with four huge stacks of gallery catalogs for the exhibit.

I opened the brown paper wrapping on one stack and pulled out the first catalog. Louise and I oohed and aahed at how wonderful it looked. We'd both given the catalog a proofread because two sets of eyes were better than one. *Harvest Time.* What a lovely theme. Leaves in the fall, fields ripe for harvest, and any number of imaginative ideas dealing with an aspect of that phrase. I was drawn to a watercolor painting of an older couple sitting on a bench staring out over a wheat field ready for harvest. Of course, I thought about my parents and how they'd been robbed of this moment. Before the thought made me angry, I stopped myself and glanced around the gallery.

The hospitality committee had done a smash-up job of planning decorations. There'd be cornstalks out in front of the main doorway, silk autumn leaves scattered in various places, pumpkins here and there, and sixty entries in the exhibit. The opening would be September 30, and we'd have apple cider, various cheeses, candy corn, pumpkin cookies, apple slices, pumpkin pie slivers, and white and red wines. We'd reuse the red-and-white-checkered tablecloths from our first exhibit at various stations. I couldn't wait to see how it all looked when it came together. Louise had lined up the volunteers, so we were ready to go.

"Perfect," said Louise. "I'll bet we'll have even more people at this exhibit than the first one."

"You've done a great job on promotion."

I studied the empty walls and thought about how they'd be full of paintings and photographs in a few days. Then the bell on the alley door jangled, interrupting my thoughts. It was Lance.

He glanced at all the piles of artwork in various groups around the gallery. "You two making plans for the upcoming exhibit?"

"Last-minute patching and taping. Come on back to my office."

Louise went ahead of me, saying she was taking the mail over to the post office. It was only a block away. Once she left, Lance and I settled into my office.

"What's the deep, dark secret this time?" he asked.

"What makes you think Angie and I've been up to anything?"

"I know that tone of voice on the phone."

I acted indignant. Then I told him I wanted to have him talk Andy into doing a mouth swab for a DNA test because I wanted to send it to one of those genealogy sites.

At first, he said nothing. Then his eyes narrowed. "What are you getting me into this time?"

I put on my best innocent face. "Nothing. Scout's honor."

He studied my face. "This isn't really a Christmas present, is it?"

I paused. "Well…not exactly."

Nothing. He thought about it. Then, he rubbed his hands together and said, "OK. But I don't want to know what you're planning." He paused. "It isn't illegal, is it?"

"Why would you ask?"

"Oh, please. If this were Andy asking, I'd know enough to say 'no.' You and Angie are just slightly under his name on my list when it comes to 'iffy' projects I should steer clear of."

"Then you'll do it?"

He sighed. "I suppose. What do I have to do?"

I handed him the remaining DNA testing kit from the package and a set of directions. "Bring the results to me. You won't regret this."

"What should I tell him about why?"

"Uh, let me think. First, let him know I gave this to you because I'm terribly busy with the upcoming art exhibit, and I happened to run into you. Tell him I'm going to send his DNA in to check our family ancestry and give the information to Tom as a Christmas present."

"And I won't regret this? The last time you asked me to pick you and Angie up on a dark country road after you evaded a police raid on a party, you were just under the legal age, and I was aiding and abetting."

I gave him a warm hug. "And I'll love you forever for your rescue. Tom still doesn't know."

"And why do you want this?"

"You need to trust me."

He gave me a quizzical look and a long sigh.

The rest of the day was an endless whirl of last-minute details to nail down before the installation of *Harvest Time*. But now Louise had left, the day was starting to get dark, and Chad was whistling as he worked upstairs. Time I should go home and fix something for dinner.

I glanced at the *Apple Grove Ledger* in the stack of mail on my loveseat. I could take a few minutes to look through it. As always, the police blotter was the best part.

10 a.m. The police department received a call from a resident of Gooseberry Lane who said someone had broken into the henhouse on his property and let all the hens out. They shouldn't be hard to track because of a trail of fluffy feathers.

11:44 a.m. A resident called saying their neighbor's dog, who was in heat, was chased by their dog, who broke through a glass sliding door to go after the female dog of his dreams. Broken glass was everywhere. They needed a police report to file an insurance claim. They also wanted the police to fill out some form saying they weren't responsible for any progeny that resulted from that chase.

Gee, what an exciting town I live in.

I glanced through the want ads and sports pages. The editorial page was once again filled with nasty innuendo by Jezbhel Gushman, Executive Editor. And her lies all pointed to me. Screaming one loud, angry reaction, I threw the paper on the floor in disgust. I was so angry I grabbed my phone and called Angie. She was the one who helped me at times like this. Was I being unreasonable? I thought not.

"That does it!" I said to her. I was sure my blood pressure was going up, up, up, and I could feel my heart pounding. "I'm going over to her office and tell her off. How can she continue to print these lies about my nonexistent part in the judge's death?"

"It sells papers," Angie said.

She was being too reasonable.

"Are you determined to go yell at her?"

"Yes," I said.

"Great! I'll meet you there. You'll need a witness in case she sues you."

"Keep me from slugging her, OK? I don't need an assault charge. She doesn't need more material."

"Gotcha. No assault."

I grabbed my car keys and purse and tromped out the back door and down the deck stairs. By the time I reached Gushman's office, I was a little calmer, but not much. Angie was already waiting in the parking lot.

"Who does she think she is?" I shouted. "I'll tell her a thing or two. Then, I'll talk to Ken Winters about libel."

"Right behind you," said Angie. "Carry on. No assault. Well, no physical assault."

We marched through the front door of the *Apple Grove Ledger*. Straight ahead of me, a counter contained a stack of newspapers. No one was sitting at the desk behind the counter. In fact, I glanced around the small newsroom, and while the computer screens were still on, no one was sitting at their desks. They must be out on errands, stories, or at dinner. I had no idea what hours newspaper people kept, but this was the dinner hour in Apple Grove.

Angie broke the silence. "We have met the enemy, and she is missing."

"Somebody has to be here. Let's find her office." Walking around the counter, I found a hallway with office doors. Two doors down, the window said, "Jezbhel Gushman, Executive Editor" in gold letters.

"This is it," said Angie. "What's the plan?"

"A straight-ahead attack." I paused, thinking. "Maybe we should knock on the door."

Angie nodded. "Sounds like the civil thing to do."

Pounding on the door, I noticed lights on through the frosted glass. Feeling my adrenaline pumping, I shouted, "I know you're in there, Gushman, you crummy excuse for a journalist!" The door was open a fraction of an inch, and I pushed my way in, Angie following behind me.

Shock was my first reaction. Papers all over the floor, books fallen off the desk, a lamp turned over and the bulb broken, two chairs on their sides, and general chaos.

"What the heck?"

"Terrible housekeeping," remarked Angie.

We gingerly walked around the papers and books and pulled up short at the side of the desk. Jezbhel Gushman was lying on her side on the floor, an ornamental dagger in her back and blood everywhere. So much blood. I felt light-headed. She wasn't dead, but her eyes were starting to get glassy.

I knelt beside her. "Hang on, Jezbhel. I'm dialing nine-one-one. Stay with me." I punched in the numbers on my phone and put my hand on her shoulder.

Angie whispered as she knelt beside me. "I never realized how good you were at finding bodies. Is she going to be alright?"

"She's still alive. Stay with me, Jezbhel," I repeated as I heard the dispatcher come on the line.

In my shock, the first thing I thought of was Ivan the Terrible, counting all the dead bodies I'd found in the last few months. I could see his text in my head:

AGAIN? ANOTHER BODY? How do you do this? You need to hire yourself out like one of those dogs who sniff out slugs, only you find bodies. God in heaven, what is going on in your life?
IVAN TRUELOVE III, CPA

I rolled my eyes at "slugs." Autocorrect strikes again.

Chapter Twenty-Four

Because of my endless evening, I was exhausted the next morning. Sitting in my office, I glanced at the calendar. Saturday. Only two more days until we started installing the *Harvest Time* exhibit. Maybe we shouldn't have exhibits anymore. Each time I scheduled an exhibit, someone was murdered. Or I was kidnapped. Or both. Why couldn't I have, say, an ordinary few days leading up to an exhibit? Was it too much to ask? My phone pinged with a text. Of course. Add Ivan to the list.

Ms. Madison. Do you have nothing better to do than find murder victims? CAN I MENTION ART EXUBERANCE COMING UP? If you'd stay at your job these things wouldn't happen. At least no more BAD PUBLICITY in the local rug.
IVAN F. TRUELOVE III CPA

This time I texted back. **She is in hospital. Not dead. Will survive. Could you say, "saved her life?"**

The man had not an ounce of human kindness. I didn't like Jezbhel Gushman either, but at least a quiet mention of her injuries might have been more appropriate. Another text popped up immediately. Oh, dear God. Save me from this idiot. He totally ignored what I'd texted.

Also, do not go down to the basement UNDER ANY CIRCUM-STANCES. I will be over early to inspect the gallery for the *Harvest Time* exhibit. Stay FOCUSED.

IVAN F. TRUELOVE III CPA

That's it. I turned off the sound on my phone and flipped it over, face down, on my desk. Andy always told me if you were good at something, people expected you to do it all your days. This might be one unusual time he was right, but I hadn't expected to be good at finding corpses. At least I didn't see dead people like that famous movie that scared me silly a few years back. Perhaps Jezbhel Gushman would survive to continue masquerading as a journalist. Might it be too much to think she would be a teeny, tiny bit grateful and stop printing such horrible things about me? Well, time to work. So done with you, Ivan.

I glanced at the photo of my parents. A lovely picture, and one I could use to erase the ugliness of what I had seen at the newspaper office yesterday. The only thing good I could say was red was a color that worked well with Jezbhel Gushman's pale face. Oh, I can't believe I just thought that. I needed to get a grip. Too much blood, and it was such a shock because my adrenaline had been pumping, rehearsing what I'd yell at her. I practiced the words all the way to the newspaper office. She was a slimy, stupid, illiterate hack of a journalist, and if I dug back far enough, I was sure I could find lawsuits pressed by victims of her total lack of ethics. I knew I'd cleverly created several great lines after that, but right now they'd flown out of my memory. Toad? I think the word toad was in one of them. But, alas, I lost the opportunity, and despite her idiotic editorials, I felt awful for her.

What a horrible memory it was. Last night, I tossed all night trying to find sleep, but the scene in carmine red kept coming back into my restless brain. And the dagger matched the three others at the judge's house, only it was the one that had been missing for a while. The small one. I was sure Erika had stolen it. But why would she have tried to kill the newspaper editor? She was on her side. The golden goose. It made no sense. I had work to do at the judge's this afternoon. That should keep my mind busy.

The phone vibrated. If it were Ivan on the other end, I would smash it. But it wasn't. My brother's beaming face shone on the glass, and the theme from "Law and Order" sounded its strident notes. "Hi, Tom."

"How are you doing this morning after your terrible experience yesterday?" His voice was conciliatory. He was worried about me. Mary brought me a loaf of banana-nut bread yesterday evening. Food was love and healing.

"I've had better days. I can't get that horrifying picture out of my mind. I know the dagger was the one Erika stole from the judge's house. She never admitted it, but her smirk said it all."

"I took it over to Tilda, and she identified it. Erika tried to blame it on you. She stole it, thinking she could sell it in Chicago. But she says you stole it from her hotel room. Of course, that didn't happen. Her fingerprints were not on it nor at the crime scene."

"What?"

"Yeah. She figures if you're in prison, you won't be able to spend any of her money. But she didn't push her case very hard."

"Now, is she in jail, where *she* should be?" I sat up a little straighter, pressing my case.

"No. I imagine she's on her way to Chicago to go back to work on Monday."

"What? How could you let her go? She threatened me and stabbed Gushman." My lips were pouty.

Tom paused, and I imagined he was thinking about how he'd phrase his next words. "She didn't do it, Jill."

"Which? The threatening letter or the murder?"

"Neither. We found other fingerprints on the letter, but they weren't a match in any of four databases. Erika's were not on the letter or the envelope. And, when Gushman was killed, she was over at Priscilla's with lots of witnesses. As was John. Besides, Gushman was their mouthpiece. Why would they kill her? I didn't have evidence to hold either of them. They both have alibis."

I pressed my lips together. Then, "I was thinking that, actually—about not having a reason to kill Gushman. Did Gushman see who tried to kill her?"

"No. She had her back to the door, pulling a book from the shelf behind her desk, and suddenly someone attacked her from behind. But she does remember a dark figure with a ski mask over his face. She thinks a guy, about six feet tall."

"Think of all the enemies she must have. She's written so many terrible opinions masquerading as facts. She's ruined lives...or livelihoods, for that matter. You would have a long line of people who might want to do her in. Now what? Make a long list?"

Tom's voice was silent.

"Tom?"

"Yes. Sorry. I was lost in thought. There's an item missing here. I can't quite find it in my brain, but I know I heard something over the last few days that sparked my thinking about both crimes. They're related, but maybe not in the way we're thinking."

"Makes perfect sense, kind of like pond scum. Lots of ugly details with both deaths but no clear picture. Disguising the judge's murder as a heart attack, missing objects, possible art fraud, children who are greedy, angry death threats, a gun in the judge's desk, pristine cups and saucers, and goodness, what else? I think I'm glad I don't have your job, Tom. How do you put all these pieces together?"

"Methodically. But I'm missing something. I can feel it. I've been going down a blind alley, and I need to change directions. Think I know just the person to help me sort it out."

"Oh, me? I'd be glad to help you."

He chuckled over the phone line. "Wish it were you, but no."

By the time I left the art center, it was dark and raining. I'd had details to put together in our financial accounts and lost track of time. Besides, this wasn't a nine-to-five job. The work had to be done, often by deadlines. I'd driven to work this morning because I needed to go out to Handleman's Grocery to pick up a few things. Handleman's was on the edge of town near the highway.

I was thinking about Jezbhel Gushman when I noticed a car coming behind me quickly. He was riding my trunk, a maneuver I hated. I decided to turn a corner and let him go on, but he followed me around the corner. What's with this driver?

Speeding up, I turned again to get back on the route to Handleman's. I pulled out onto the highway, and suddenly the driver switched to his bright lights, temporarily blinding me in my rearview mirror. I hit my brakes, skidded on the wet pavement, and went careening onto the shoulder and down into a ditch, coming to an abrupt stop. Before I got my wits about me, my airbag deployed, and I felt like I'd been socked in the face by a sumo wrestler. Fortunately, my car called 9-1-1. Gotta love twenty-first-century technology.

Sitting in the green-and-white ambulance, I held an icepack to my left cheek while the blond female EMT checked my vital signs. Her shirt said "Alissa" on it.

"Blood pressure's up. Not a surprise. But otherwise, your heart is pumping with a strong rhythm. Anything else hurt besides the bruises on your face and arm? Do your ribs hurt when you breathe?"

"No," I muttered, looking at the inside of my left arm. "What is this?" I asked, noting what looked like a rug burn.

A deep, male voice replied, "It's a surface abrasion from the airbag."

I glanced up and saw Sam, his eyes worried, his face reflecting his concern. My body relaxed, a feeling of warmth flooding through me. The EMT moved back, making room for Dr. Finch. He looked delectable, but then I was probably in shock. They spoke some medical jargon, she showed him a paper on her chart, and then she handed him a small flashlight.

"I'm checking your eyes," he said, touching my shoulder. The brightness of the light made me want to close them. "No, keep your eyes open." He skillfully moved the light and had my eyes follow it. "Good. No evidence of concussion. Does it hurt to breathe?"

"No," I said, feeling breathless for another reason.

He touched a spot on my face. "That's a bruise from the airbag. The ice pack will help."

"Seriously? I survive a crash, and my airbag tries to kill me?"

He chuckled. Then he turned both my arms over. "That will heal. But just to be sure, I'll follow the ambulance to the ER. The police will deal with your car. I believe you're going to live with very little damage."

By the time the police arrived at the ER, the nurses and ER doctor had already rechecked every moving and non-moving part of me. Officer Aubrey stopped in at the ER to question me about the accident. No, I hadn't seen the driver. No, I didn't know the make or model of the car. The headlights seemed high in my rearview mirror. Might have been an SUV or a truck.

Then Tom showed up, hugged me, and made worrying noises over me. He conferred with Sam. He was all business, asking me more questions and talking to Aubrey. Coming back to my bed, he said, "And you have no doubt this was deliberate, especially since the other car didn't stick around?"

By now I was exhausted, my eyes hurt, my arm and face hurt, and my brain was saying, *Sleep, please*. "No, Tom. No doubt this was on purpose." I told the story yet again.

Another familiar voice could be heard beyond the privacy curtain. "Which one is she in?" Angie. She came around the curtain, looked at the bruise on my face and my tired eyes, and said, "Oh, Jill." A huge hug followed. I was sure a hug magnet.

Over her shoulder, I saw Tom in a huddle with Sam, the EMT, and Officer Aubrey. Then he came over.

"They're going to send you home for now. I'll have Aubrey keep an eye on the house tonight, but I imagine the fireworks are over."

Angie and Sam glanced at each other. I speculated that they were in a silent tug-of-war about who would take me home. Then Angie said, "I'll take her home, Tom, and I can stay overnight. We'll open a bottle of bubbly and tell ghost stories just like the old days."

Sam smiled. "Uh, no alcohol. Wouldn't be a good idea right now."

I also smiled weakly. "Ah, you take all the fun out of attempted assault."

Maybe Sam wasn't in the mood to be silly. His eyes were serious when he said, "I'll check on you in the morning. For now, sleep would be helpful."

I considered how nice it might be to have my own doctor on call.

The last thing I remembered saying to Angie when I was snug in my bed at home was "Maybe we should take this threat a little more seriously. Someone doesn't want me to spend the judge's money at the art center." I felt like I was dozing off, but I remembered my buddy's last words as she pulled the bed sheet up closer around my shoulders.

"They've no idea who they're dealing with, Jill. We take down killers before they've proofread their death threats."

Chapter Twenty-Five

I was still thinking of Tom's comment about going down a blind alley when I climbed the steps to the Spivey house. I didn't see Tilda's car. I planned to tackle the closet behind the desk for a change of pace. It was jammed full of odds and ends, and a lot of what was in it could probably be thrown in the trash. Always organized, I had a box of trash bags in my bottomless tote. Angie said she'd stop by and help me, so it wouldn't take so long. I bet she was planning to girl-talk about my date with Sam tonight.

I stopped a moment, studying the bruise on my cheek reflected in the glass outer door. I was fine, my little car was in the car hospital, and Tom was threatening to have me followed by Officer Ned Fisher for the rest of our lives—depending on which of us succumbed first.

I walked in and locked the door behind me, as was my habit. It was quiet, with the drapes closed and the judge's rooms simply waiting. I didn't bother opening the drapes but walked back to the office after grabbing a bottle of water from the refrigerator. This would take an hour or two at the most with Angie helping, and I'd still have lots of time to shower and get ready for my date with Sam. I repeated that out loud. *My date with Sam.*

The office was just as I'd left it, and I turned on the lights and moved over to the desk, taking my phone and the trash bags out of my tote. Then I opened the drapes and let in the September light. The days were getting shorter, and the sunshine was at a premium. Soon we'd be counting the brief sunny hours of winter. I wasn't excited about Midwest winters, but now that I had Sam in my life, it seemed like I could deal with anything.

I considered last night. I didn't see the car's make or model or the color.

It was raining too hard. Who could have done this? Tom said it might have been road rage, but I didn't do anything to cause the accident, not even a teeny, tiny obscene gesture. Angie would have stopped the car, flown out, and given him a piece of her mind. Or maybe it wasn't a "he." This was a weekend. Perhaps Erika was back for a surprise visit. She drove a dark SUV, as did her husband, Owen. I recalled Tom's warning that if I died, the Spiveys got the jackpot. This seemed less like a death threat and more like a warning. I glanced around the study.

I'd just set my water on the office desk when the doorbell rang. Angie. Turning, I walked back to the living room. Angie was in the window of the door making silly faces. I unlocked the door. "Enter," I said, bowing in a mock salute. "Thanks, pal, for coming."

She threw her arms out. "At your service." She looked over my shoulder at all the paintings in the living room. "Wow. This is amazing. I've never been in the judge's house before. Oh, my."

I followed her glance to an abstract painting hanging behind the sofa. It had bold splotches of various red hues. She seemed frozen.

"Angie?"

She stared at the painting. Then she whispered, "Carmingle?"

"What?"

"Isn't that the red paint you always talk about?"

"Oh, carmine."

"Whatever. I had this horrible nightmare last night. I was at the newspaper office, but I was alone. Walking down this never-ending corridor, I saw door after door with carmingle handprints on the inside of the glass door windows."

"Oh, gee. That sounds awful."

She gave me a skeptical look. "It gets worse. You came down the hallway driving your Austin Mini, and I tried to warn you, but you waved and smiled and honked your horn. Practically ran me down. After I squeezed up against the wall, you drove by, and I heard a screeching crash. But you were gone. Disappeared. I couldn't stop you."

"I'm fine. Just a little bruise."

Angie grimaced. "You remember those old jack-in-the-box toys?"

"Sure, where you cranked the handle on the metal box, and then a clown popped out?"

"Yes. I turned around from watching the taillights of your car, and a huge box was sitting there playing 'Pop Goes the Weasel.'"

"Let me guess. Weasel. Jezbhel Gushman?"

"How did you guess? She popped out of the box with red yarn hair, a big red bulb for a nose, and carmingle splashed all over her."

I laughed. "I'd love to have seen that."

"Even though she looked like Gushman, I knew she wasn't."

"Why?"

"She had a dictionary in one hand and a thesaurus in the other."

I stared at Angie, and we both laughed. "Seriously."

"Seriously. I kept repeating this dream in my head today so I wouldn't forget to tell you."

"I guess that discovery of the editor's body shocked you more than I realized. I'm sorry."

Angie shook her head slowly. "I don't know how you do that—find bodies. Don't you have nightmares?"

"Sometimes. But mine are more satisfying. It's usually Ivan Truelove the Third who's been murdered. Then I wake up, he texts, and I realize it was only a dream."

Angie set her keys and billfold on the coffee table. "Time to get to work. No murder victims today."

We walked back to the office. Standing on a stepstool, I started at the top of the closet behind the judge's desk and worked my way down, handing stuff to Angie. Boxes of Christmas decorations were near the top, and I could tell they hadn't been used for a while. Probably older objects Laura had decorated with prior to her death. "Here, pitch these," I said to Angie, handing her the decorations.

On the middle shelves were scrapbooks, and I pulled a pile of four out, handing them to her so she could set them on the desk. There weren't a lot of things to save that would interest the family, but I thought if the scrapbooks had pictures the Spiveys might want, I'd save them. They hadn't been decent to me, but this was their past, and I could value that even if they didn't.

"OK, got them," Angie said as she lined them up on the desk. "Think they're family photos?"

"We can look at them later and see. For now, let's take a break."

We headed for the kitchen. Possibly Tilda had left something yummy in the refrigerator we could snack on. But no. Dashed hopes. I opened a cupboard and glanced at the cups and saucers. A few were missing. Figuring those were the ones Tom had taken to check on, I grabbed two cups and saucers and set them on the counter.

"Slim pickin's in the refrigerator. How about coffee?"

"Sure," said Angie.

We sat at the kitchen table drinking coffee and talking about the car accident. I didn't know any more now than I had last night.

"So, where are you going tonight with dreamy Dr. Sam?" asked Angie.

"Some new place in town he's come up with."

"Andy and Lance's band is playing at the bar tonight. You could stop by for a nightcap."

"I'm not sure if he's up to meeting Andy yet. Sam is so normal."

"Has to happen sometime," said Angie, stirring her coffee. "At least it would be in a public place."

"When has that ever stopped Andy from being bonkers?" I drained the last of my coffee. "Well, I'll think about it. Come on, let's get back to work on the closet. We're almost done."

An hour later, we'd cleaned out most of the items in the judge's closet and had eight trash bags to put out in the back.

Angie eyed the scrapbooks on the desk. "Let's look at those and see what his wife saved."

"Sure. Maybe take them out to the living room."

The first one was of the Spivey children when they were young. It was fascinating to see their lives through photos from long ago. Several colors were faded, but each child was still recognizable. The second scrapbook was the same.

By the time we'd checked out the third and fourth, I realized they were all past photos of the family as the children grew and the judge and Laura aged. She was such a beautiful woman.

"I think I should give these to the Spivey brood. No reason for me to keep them, and they might want them since they're family history."

"After the way they've talked about their father, I can see Erika and John burning them," Angie said.

I scratched my head. "You may be right. I guess I can't be responsible for what they do with them after I turn them over." We were on the last two pages of the fourth scrapbook when an object fell out the bottom of the album and landed on the floor. I bent over and picked it up. It was an envelope addressed to the judge and postmarked March 2, 2016. He'd obviously opened it with a letter opener. "Should we or shouldn't we read it?" I asked.

Angie hesitated. Then she said, "He's gone now. Who would know?"

I pulled out the letter and opened it. A white stationery card, ordinary card stock, stared me in the face, but what was in it was strange. A dried, black flower petal. The message in black ink was brief.

"November 17. A hard date to forget. If you have, you'll remember it soon."

"That's weird," said Angie. "No signature, no return address, nothing."

I put the card and petal back in the envelope and set it on the coffee table. Then I turned the last two pages of the scrapbook to the end. Sure enough. Someone had stuffed three more envelopes into the scrapbook between the last page and the back cover.

Angie watched me as I pulled them out and put them in order by postmarks: May 2, 2016, June 2, 2016, and August 2, 2016. "That wasn't long ago. The judge must have hidden them here. Each postmark was from a zip code in New York," I said, turning them over in my hand.

"Could they connect to John? He'd lived in New York City for quite a while, as had Erika. Did they have something to do with these? And why a black petal? Why would he have stuck those cards in an old scrapbook?

158

Funny they weren't in his desk. Had he wanted to hide them?" Angie turned each of them over, looking at the address.

"But these postmarks are recent. They live in Chicago now. Who do we know who lives in New York?"

"Angelini maybe?"

I took a deep breath and opened the one postmarked May 2. As I pulled out the card, another black petal fell out. This one said, in the same handwriting with black ink, "Revenge is an act of passion. Crimes are avenged. 11.17." Again, no signature.

"This is even weirder," I said. "Revenge?"

The other two cards had similar black lines of writing and a black flower petal. Each had something to do with revenge, and each had the date 11.17.

"What year?" I said out loud.

Angie stacked them into a pile, and I knew I must give them to Tom. Maybe he could figure out something about the handwriting or about fingerprints.

They were puzzles. Who sent them? Was it a person he'd sentenced? Were they out for revenge? Could it be a family member? Angelini? It didn't seem like an item the Spivey adult children would have sent.

Now Angie stirred. "Could it have been the Patterson guy whose life he said the judge had ruined? He was in town before the judge's death if Chad was right. Did the threats have anything to do with the judge's murder? And why black flower petals?"

"I'm beginning to think whoever killed him sent these and is mentally unstable. He—or she—tortured the judge with these weird threats before coming after him. This is scary."

I looked at the pile on the desk. "One thing's for sure: he'd stuck these cards away where no one could find them. Someone was methodically threatening him, and the postmarks were prior to this death."

"That's creepy," said Angie. "You'd think the judge would have been more guarded about letting someone into his house after he received these, especially someone he didn't know."

"Unless it was someone he did know."

Chapter Twenty-Six

Sam picked me up for a lovely dinner at The Getaway, the newest, trendy restaurant on the western edge of Apple Grove. The bruise from the car crash was green these days.

We'd dined on salmon and followed it with after-dinner drinks. He was so handsome in an open-necked shirt and dark jeans. Presentable. That's what Angie had said to me last week. It was important to find a guy you liked but who was also presentable. And he was highly presentable.

"You're not on call tonight at the hospital?"

"No. Jennifer Holmes is, and unless there's a five-alarm fire with casualties or a thirty-car pileup out on the highway, I'm all yours." He smiled, inched his fingers over the table, and laid them on my hand. They felt soft and warm.

The waitress came back. "Dessert? We have a fantastic tiramisu layer cake. Any takers?"

I smiled at Sam skeptically, and he caught my thoughts on my dessert-free zone.

"No," he said. "I think just the check. And thanks. The meal was amazing."

"I'll be sure to tell the chef and be right back."

"So. Did you mean it when you said you'd like to hear Andy and Lance's band?"

He laughed. "Absolutely. I'm all in. Is it time to meet the crazy brother and Lance?"

"He promised he'd be on his best behavior, but that's like asking the tide not to rise."

"Think I'll chance it."

"Let's go."

He paid the check, grabbed a couple of mints, and we headed out the door. We popped the mints in our mouths and drove through Apple Grove. Not much traffic. Streetlights were shining their pale beams in little islands on Main Street as we cruised through the quiet town. Two police cars were nestled next to each other on a quadrant of the square, the officers talking, and an occasional person passed down the sidewalk under the streetlights. So different from my years in Chicago, where life went on nonstop, and sirens were a constant. The stores on Main Street had their security lights on around the windows or doors. I could almost imagine a century ago when a policeman or patrol officer walked the sidewalks and checked to make sure the doors were locked. They'd have passed under streetlamps that might have been gas or electric, depending on how soon the town had managed to switch from one to the other. It was a comfortable feeling moving quietly through the night with Sam. Almost magical.

"A penny for your thoughts," Sam said.

I turned to him and said, "Go left at the next corner."

"That's what you were thinking?"

I chuckled. "I was imagining Apple Grove a century ago, and I bet it was just as quiet downtown at night back then too."

"I imagine so. I've been to Priscilla's Pub before." He paused. "Think I can find it. Yes, this is a far cry from Chicago or Minneapolis. I like this small town. Apart from the occasional accident, the cases we get at the ER aren't violent episodes. We do get a few domestic situations. But nothing like my last place. I think the pace here is about right."

"I'd agree."

He took my hand from my lap and put it up to his lips with a lightly brushed kiss. It felt perfect, and my fingers tingled as I closed my eyes for a few seconds. When I opened them, I said, "Oh, wait. Stop."

He hit the brakes, and I lurched forward. "What's wrong?"

"No, it's all right. We just went by the corner where we needed to turn. I was...distracted."

He laughed as we sat there in the middle of the street. Then he turned and kissed me lightly on the lips. Perfect. "You're right. I was distracted too. I'll turn around."

Priscilla's was rocking. Wiley saw us come through the door and motioned us to the bar.

"Hi, Wiley," I said.

"Hi, Sam, Jill. Come to see the boys?"

"Of course."

"They took a break, but lots of dancing's going on. They're in the zone tonight."

We ordered drinks and found a table near the bandstand area. Lance saw us sit down and came over to the table.

"Sit," I said to him. "Lance, this is Sam Finch. Lance Hughes." They shook hands.

"I think Jill's mentioned your name once or twice."

Sam smiled. "Only once or twice?"

"Ha, ha," I murmured.

"Where's Andy?" I asked.

Lance glanced toward the back door. "He went outside to get a breath of fresh air after the last set. He'll be in soon. We've had a few interesting characters in the bar tonight. The Spiveys were here, but now only John is left, sitting over there with Cleary, the EMT, and Chad."

I followed where he was nodding. "Ah, I see. I thought the Spiveys were out of town by now."

"John's been drinking steadily all evening."

Andy came in the back door about that time, and his face lit up when he saw us. "Jill, you finally brought the doc to see us. Fantastic." He stuck out his hand, and Sam shook it.

"Nice to meet the renowned brother."

Andy puffed out his chest and smirked at me. "See. He knows who has standing in this family. Good to meet you too, Dr. Finch."

"Oh, just Sam."

"All right, Just Sam."

162

CHAPTER TWENTY-SIX

"What are you playing next? We'll stick around for a set," I said.

Lance glanced at Andy. "I think it's time for country. A little Keith Urban, a bit of Jason Aldean, and a few songs of Faith Hill?"

Andy checked his watch. "That about sums it up. You two need to get out on the dance floor. We'll be watching. Remember, Jill, I have a microphone."

"Do not do anything to embarrass me," I said, staring at him.

"Me? Nah. Best behavior. Come on, Lance, let's go."

"He seems pretty normal to me," Sam said as we watched them fiddle with the microphones and check their instruments.

"We'll see how long it lasts."

Ten minutes later, Sam left to take a phone call, so I took the chance to go over and talk with John Spivey. Cleary and Chad had both left, and Spivey was sitting at a table by himself, nursing a beer.

"May I sit?" I asked.

Spivey pulled out a chair. "Your brother plays a mean guitar."

I nodded. "I think so. He actually plays several musical instruments and likes to remind me I only took piano lessons for a few weeks." I glanced over at Andy and Lance, who were now playing a slow number. "Have Erika and her husband gone back to Chicago?"

He set his glass down, swallowing his beer. "Yeah. They needed to get back to their jobs."

"And you're still speaking to me?"

He smiled. "Of course. Not sure Erika feels the same. I love my sister, but she's had to take several anger management classes. She's likely to show up again."

I relaxed a bit, hoping it was true. "I'm curious."

"About what?"

"About what caused such a terrible estrangement between you, Erika, and your father." I hoped the beers had loosened his tongue. Several empty bottles sat on the table.

"Oh. I s'pose it doesn't matter now. In my case, I made a few bad investments, you might say."

"Investments?"

"Well, gambling. Never could stay away from a deck of cards or a horse to bet on. Started in college. Fast company. The old man couldn't abide my 'bad habits,' as he put it. He and Mom bailed me out, but I guess the last time was one too many." He shook his head. "I'm sure your art center is a much better investment than my sorry life."

I didn't say anything. What could I say?

"Something about my dad near the end. I've thought about it a lot. I don't know. The last few times I talked with him on the phone, he seemed a bit sad. I don't know why. Whether he was lonely without anyone here, or if he thought a lot about our mom. I don't know. There was a kind of melancholy about him. Could be he was thinking about the past."

"I'm sorry, John." I paused. "But I want you to know I never put any pressure on your father to leave me anything. I was as surprised as you. Actually, shocked."

"The old man always did like surprises. Me, not so much, and Erika not at all."

I glanced over toward the door to see if Sam had come back in yet, but he hadn't. I should take a chance and ask about Erika. "And your sister. Did she have a gambling problem too?"

He laughed. "No. Not Erika. She has a man problem. Right now, she'd like to divest herself of Owen, and he can be a mean, uncooperative son of a gun. But that will take some cash for lawyers. And her other problem goes right up her nose."

"Cocaine?"

"Yeah. She and Owen both. Drug use was what finally cut the string between her and the judge. He found several lines of coke in her bedroom when she was back for Mom's funeral. Terrible argument. Screaming at him. It drove her crazy he could be so calm when she was so hysterical, but, after all, he was a judge. All those years growing up, and I'm not sure I ever saw him lose his temper. That was the end of their relationship. I know she tried to heal it a few days before his death, but it wasn't going to happen."

"And she came back why?"

He pushed the beer bottles into a neat line and took a sip from the one he was drinking. "I think she wanted him to help her pay for a lawyer to divorce Owen. He's been a millstone around her neck. But the old man said no. The last time I talked with her, she was desperate. A killer? I'm not sure. If her back was against the wall, maybe. Her life has been a mess lately, and she needs money. Both of us are a couple of losers. Too bad." He paused. "Too bad. The last time she saw Jezbhel Gushman, they had a terrible argument. Erika thought she should put more pressure on the investigation of our father's death. Oh, I don't know."

I almost felt sorry for him. But then I remembered. "Then who sent me a threatening note? I was sure it was Erika."

"A note? Perhaps. She could do that. I wouldn't put it past her."

About that time, Sam came in the front door. I had to ask one last question. "What will you do?"

"Oh, go back to Chicago. Stick with my job. Try to stay sober. One foot in front of the other."

"Good luck, John. I hope things go better for you."

He nodded. "Thanks." Then he seemed to have a sober moment. "You don't know how Erika responds to desperation. Her loser husband has an expensive habit too, and his anger is coiled tightly until it explodes. Better be careful."

Chapter Twenty-Seven

I arrived at the art center on Monday morning to a bustle of activity. We would begin installing the national exhibit, and several of the weavers were coming in after lunch to put in an extra weaving session. It would be quite a busy day.

I'd stopped by the bank, so Louise had opened, and three of our volunteers were out in the gallery arranging sculptures, paintings, and mixed-media artwork. There would be more help later. We set the pieces against the walls. That way, we could get a better idea of their placement. Louise was directing traffic, and two of the volunteers were moving ladders into the gallery from the storeroom. For the next two hours, I was installing artwork, fielding phone calls, and bustling back to the gallery from my office. By late morning, we were ahead of schedule, thanks to our helpers.

"Jill," Louise called from the office hallway. "Phone for you. It's Tom."

I gave one last direction to the volunteers, and then I left for my office. I'd given Tom the "black petal cards" yesterday morning. Could be this call was about those, or perhaps he had new information about the Spiveys.

"Hi, Tom."

I heard a pause, then, "Good morning. Hope I'm not taking you away from anything important."

"Oh, no. Just an exhibit installation. And it is important. We're ahead, so I have a minute. What's up?"

"The cards you gave me. The ones with black flower petals...."

"Weird, huh? Did they tell you anything?"

"Hang on a minute."

I could hear his muffled voice as he put his hand over the phone receiver and said something to another person.

"Sorry. Jake was just leaving, and I had to mention a couple of things to him. Anyway, yes. It's obvious he was being threatened for several months prior to his murder. No fingerprints or other clues as to who wrote them. When did you say he bought the gun you found in his drawer?"

"Oh. I hadn't thought about that. If I remember correctly, the paperwork on the gun was June 2, this year."

"The paperwork would be after he'd had two of those threatening letters, and they were dated the second of each month. I don't like coincidences, so I believe those notes led to the gun purchase. He was frightened and bought the gun for protection."

"Then why didn't he use it?"

"Lots of possibilities. Could he have been taken by surprise? Could be he knew the person he was talking to and didn't see them as a threat. We're getting closer. Whoever called him from the burner phone was the same perp who sent the notes. I'm sure. But why black rose petals in each one?"

I sat back in my office chair. "Something about those black rose petals seems familiar to me, but I can't think why. It'll come to me eventually. What about the date? November 17. Does the date have any special significance in the judge's life?"

"Not that I know, but it's obviously connected to the idea of revenge. I'll check with the courthouse and see if I can find out whether the judge handed down a significant sentence on that date. It might give me an idea of whether it's an angry former criminal he sentenced."

"Then I'll talk with the Vietnam vet you met at the funeral. He's still in town, and I think I know where to find him. That's one direction to take, and the other will be to check the judge's cases. I must admit I'm at a loss for the moment. But I still have grunt work to do to chase down possibilities."

"I'm so busy right now no one could catch me in one place for more than a few seconds."

"Oh, one other thing."

"What?" I asked.

"Erika and her husband were seen here this weekend. They were together and drove down from Chicago in his car. I checked his SUV at the hotel parking lot. It has a scrape across the front paint below the grill."

I held my breath. "Does it have paint from my car on it?"

"No. He says he scraped it on a fence railing in a Chicago parking lot and hasn't had time to fix it yet."

"Alibis for Saturday night?"

"Of course, they were together."

I thought for a moment. "Was the scrape in the right place to have hit my Austin Mini?"

"I'd say so. But I don't have enough evidence to get a search warrant and haul it in to do a paint check. They have alibis, whether they're true or not."

Later that afternoon, I walked down the stairs from the classroom just as Tom came in the door with a woman I'd never seen before. Looking very official, she was wearing a navy suit with a bulge near her underarm indicating a gun. At least, that was my first thought. Her hair was short, dark brown, and nicely styled. The pleasant smile on her face made me think she was making her best effort. She wasn't from Apple Grove. She had a big-city look I recognized from my years in Chicago.

"Jill Madison," said my brother. "This is Special Agent Frieda Powers of the FBI."

She extended her hand, and I shook it. "Good afternoon, Ms. Powers. I take it you've heard from the appraisal company in Chicago."

"Yes."

"Come on into my office."

Once there, I indicated the loveseat and an extra chair near the desk.

"Special Agent Powers is here because the IAAF called her after talking with you and finishing their appraisal of Judge Spivey's collection. Your gut instinct was correct about the Saphstone painting being a forgery."

"Yes," Powers said. "Two of the pigments used in the painting were not typical of the work of Calvin Dexter Saphstone. The signature on the painting was also suspect. We've been investigating Peter Angelini for some time, suspecting his business was used as a front to launder money."

"Wow," Tom said. "Artwork and money laundering?"

She turned to my brother. "Oh, yes. Art fraud and theft is the third highest-grossing criminal trade in the world over the last forty years. That's why the FBI began their special art crime team, and we have agents in New York City. We executed a search warrant two days ago at Angelini's gallery there. It will result in a criminal case. We'll see shortly what it turned up."

"I didn't realize it was such a big deal," Tom said. "Art is my sister's area."

At that, I piped up. "Art crimes are a six-billion-dollar industry worldwide."

"She's right," said the agent. "It's a precarious industry to buy into because it's highly unregulated in online marketplaces. Lack of transparency or regulations on art transactions make it a target-rich environment for thieves and forgers."

"You're saying someone forged this painting?" Tom said.

"Yes. And who knows how many others? Angelini had ties to a crime family to whom he owed money. They were taking it out in money laundering through his lucrative business."

I could see the confusion on Tom's face, and, for once, I was the expert. "Oh, it isn't a crime to copy a work of art or an artist's style or even their signature. But if you do that and say it's the genuine article, then it's a crime. Angelini sold this to the judge, and I could tell there were also problems with tracing the ownership, or provenance. That, too, made me suspicious."

"You were so right to be suspicious," she said.

Tom turned to Special Agent Powers. "Judge Spivey's death might be related to Angelini, and I'll need to know if he has an alibi for the morning of September 10. Angelini called him prior to the tenth, and if the judge suspected his crime—and we know he was suspicious about its provenance—Angelini would be a prime suspect. Can you check on that for me?"

"I sure will." The agent exchanged business cards with Tom. Then she turned to me with a business card. "We're pleased you recommended the IAAF call us. Thanks, Ms. Madison. We'll follow through and let your brother know what we find out. He can relay it to you. In relation to the Angelini case, if we need a deposition from you about the sale of the Saphstone painting, we'll get back to you. Otherwise, you have my card. Feel free to call if you have questions, or I can help you with further information." She rose, indicating the interview was over.

After Tom and the agent left, I sat there in a daze. Art forgery. My first and only personal involvement with a fake painting. Oh, I knew galleries often had forgeries, but they usually quietly disposed of them once they were revealed as fakes. No gallery or auction house wanted to admit they'd housed or sold a forgery. I couldn't wait to hear what Tom found out from them about Peter Angelini's alibi. I thought he was a sleazy character. Maybe, years ago, when the judge first met him, he was honest and not involved in forgeries. More recently, even the judge wasn't fooled by his acquisition of *Death in a Bygone Hue*. But the question was, could the judge's suspicions have gotten him murdered by the art dealer? I wish I knew the contents of the phone call between them prior to the judge's death. Once the murder occurred, Peter Angelini must have thought he was home free. That would be more than enough reward to allow Angelini to go on with his illegal activities. Did he kill the judge, did he hire someone to do it, or did a person totally unconnected to Angelini do it? I thought my brain would explode. So many unanswered questions.

Chapter Twenty-Eight

Tuesday was an uneventful day except for getting my Austin Mini back sans dents. We'd finished installing the exhibit, and I'd called Anthony Arteaga in Philadelphia and arranged to pick him up at the airport in Peoria on Thursday morning. The opening was Friday night, so I had time to make sure the gallery was perfect. Now that we'd installed the artwork, I could relax a little. The hospitality committee was handling the refreshments, and I had the catalogs ready to go. We'd do quite a bit more publicity now that the opening was in sight.

Angie called, and we arranged to go to lunch today. I was waiting for her to show up at the Casa Mia Mexican Restaurant. I glanced at my watch, and it was exactly eleven thirty. There she was, coming through the door.

"Hi, Jill. I have soooo looked forward to lunch today. Tuesday couldn't come soon enough. Wiley's been in a poopy mood all morning. Good to get away. How's the exhibit going?" Angie was always perfectly put together. Jeans, hooded sweatshirt in a gorgeous mint green, and dangling earrings hanging down among her blond hair. She sat across from me at a small table I'd picked because we could see out a window. The trees were beginning to turn colors, and the soft maples and oak leaves were lovely.

"All is done."

"Wow. There's a switch from the exhibit in the summer where everything that could go wrong did, including your kidnapping."

"Uh, yeah. Somehow, I figured this would be easier."

"And how's the doctor with the gorgeous smile?"

"Sam? He's still gorgeous. We don't get to see each other much because his hours at the hospital are crazy."

"I can tell from the smile on your face. You are so into him, girl."

We gave the waitress our orders and sat back once she left.

I took a sip of my water. "I never could keep a poker face. Oh, well. How are things going at the bar, other than the black cloud over Wiley?"

"Slowed down, believe me, after the Spiveys left town." She stirred her iced tea. "I imagine they'll be back. Hope springs eternal that they will inherit their father's fortune. Man, they were drinkers."

"And a few other things too. Say, have you seen that Vietnam vet, Patterson, lately?"

"Oh, him. Sure, he's in most nights early, around five thirty or six. Why?"

I considered how much to tell Angie, but we rarely kept secrets from each other. "I believe Tom is thinking about the judge's past and whether it might have something to do with his murder. This Patterson had a grudge against the judge. He got Patterson kicked out of the army, not that he didn't deserve it. And now he shows up here a few weeks before the judge's murder. I think I'll mosey into the bar later, when he'll be there, and see if I can pry information out of him. Tom's checking cases the judge decided in his last years on the bench. Something to do with November seventeenth."

"I still can't figure it out. Why would someone send him black rose petals?" Angie asked. "That seems morbid."

"Tom and I both think it had to do with who killed him. Revenge. Then there's the fake painting Angelini sold him. It was about Vietnam, at least that was the subject. A guy shows up in town who was a Vietnam vet and hated the judge. Doesn't this indicate a pattern?"

"Someone who was in Vietnam hated him and came back to kill him? But why wait till now? That was years and years ago."

The waitress came with our food, and we dug in with gusto. No more talk for a few minutes while we devoured our salads.

I wiped my mouth with my napkin. "Have you thought any more about November 17? Does that date seem significant for any reason?"

"No, not to me. You?"

I shook my head. "It's significant to the writer of the black petal notes. No year. Not sure why. But it must have something to do with the judge and an event happening on that date. The person wants revenge."

"Clear as mud."

I set my fork down, looking thoughtfully at Angie. "If I'm remembering correctly, someone told me Jezbhel Gushman was planning to research the judge's past. I wonder if her decision had anything to do with the attempted murder. If a person told me that, it could be all around town. But there's something else, something I'm not remembering."

"First sign of dementia. You can count on me to take care of you."

"Seems ominous. You, my caretaker."

"We'd have cocktails every day precisely at four."

I chuckled. "It's a date. Meanwhile, I think I'll stop over and see this Patterson character later after work. He must be a creature of habit, so I should be able to find him there."

"Each day. Five or five-thirty."

"It's a date."

"And the thing you were stewing about?"

"Which thing?"

She whispered. "You know, the 'Is-he-my-father?' thing."

"Nothing yet."

"Patience is not your virtue."

I sighed. "So true. And I haven't figured out what to do with the results once they come."

"What to do with them?"

"Yeah. Whether to open the test results or leave them forever forgotten."

"Call me. I'll open it."

"All right. That's a date too. What would I do without you, my friend?"

"You would be dead because I was the one who tracked your phone last summer when you disappeared."

"True. Like I said, what would I do without you?"

That afternoon, it suddenly hit me. The thing I couldn't remember buzzing around my head with no success. The black rose petals. By three o'clock, I couldn't stand it anymore. I stuck my head in the door of Louise's office.

"Louise, I'm going to run over to the judge's house to check on something. I'll be back right away."

Deep in a gift shop inventory, she turned around and said, "No problem."

I drove over, figuring it would save time. I made sure I locked the front door as Tom had instructed, even though the Spiveys were gone for now. I walked quickly back to the office and turned on the overhead light. Staring at the bookshelves, my eyes landed on the sepia picture of the judge's Vietnam buddies. But that was all. I was sure I'd seen a silk flower, a black rose lying next to it. But there was nothing. Was I crazy?

Walking out to the kitchen, I whipped my phone out of my pocket and tapped in Tilda's phone number. It rang three times. "Be there, Tilda," I whispered.

"Hello, Jill."

"Hi, Tilda. Are you busy? Can you talk?"

"Sure. What do you need?"

"I think I'm going crazy. I was sure there was a black silk rose on the bookshelf at the judge's house the day I found him in his study. It was lying next to his photo from Vietnam. But it isn't there now. Did you see that too, or am I remembering things wrong?"

There was a pause. "Oh, yes."

"Yes? I'm imagining things?"

"No, you're not. I threw it away."

"Oh."

"You have to understand, I've cleaned the judge's office for years. I don't know why he'd put a cheap, artificial flower there, so I threw it out. It didn't fit the other lovely objects he'd collected."

My breath caught. "Tilda. This is important. When did you see it there and throw it out? I don't know how long it had been there."

"Not long. Let me think. It wasn't there the last time I cleaned before his death, but it was there after he died, and the police had come and gone. I threw it out. Was it important?"

"I'm not sure. But thanks. Thanks for telling me I'm not seeing things."

"No problem."

After I tapped off, I sat in the desk chair. A photo from Vietnam, a black silk rose, black rose petals in threatening notes, a painting called *Death in a Bygone Hue*. Were these clues pointing to something from the judge's past? Was that Patterson, the Vietnam vet, the killer? He was the only one I knew in town who had anything to do with the judge's past in Vietnam. My first impression of him was that he wasn't too smart, but I could be wrong. Could he have been stalking the judge, shown up in town a few weeks before his death, and killed him at an opportune time? He was a medic. He'd know about giving injections. There was the attempt on Jezbhel Gushman's life. The editor might have heard a connection between the two men at the bar and mentioned she planned to research the judge's past. Could Patterson have heard Gushman's plan? Later this evening would tell the tale. I should tell Tom, but this might be another amazing opportunity to show him how good I was at being a junior detective.

Chapter Twenty-Nine

Sam had to work late. I drove over to Priscilla's by myself, hoping to find Reggie Patterson. My phone played the theme from *Law and Order*. Tom. I had a hands-free system for my phone, so I answered his call while I was driving.

"Yes, Tom."

"Hi. Are you driving?"

"Yes. I'm going over to Priscilla's to see Angie." It was a small, white lie. Sometimes I had to protect myself from overprotection.

"I heard from Special Agent Powers. Angelini doesn't have an alibi for the day the judge died. He had flown to Chicago a few days ahead of that, so it's possible he drove down to Apple Grove. They checked rental cars, and he rented one. He returned it with enough mileage to indicate he could have been down here. But no one remembers seeing him. Apple Grove isn't terribly big. We now know he had a reason to go after the judge, but I don't see any connection between Angelini and Jezbhel Gushman."

"I'm not sure that makes sense. Did Angelini know how to use a syringe to kill the judge? It might be something you'd want to think about. So many murders, so little time."

"For sure. And this murder and attempted murder are in a tangled web of people and facts that don't fit together yet in my mind."

"I figure the paintings will come back from Chicago any day now. With my luck, they'll send them the day of the opening for my *Harvest Time* exhibit. Life is all about timing, isn't it?"

"Yes. The older you get, the more you notice that. Have a good time. Bye."

I heard his call disconnect. Could Peter Angelini have killed the judge? He sure had a motive. If the judge discovered the Vietnam painting was a fraud, it would affect Angelini's reputation, and in the art world, reputation was everything. I could see him writing me a threatening note. If he was here when the judge was murdered, it wouldn't be hard for him to set an appointment with the judge and slip in and out quickly. He'd been here often and knew about the judge's house and his tendency to leave doors unlocked. They'd had a conversation prior to the judge's death, and the phone log indicated that call. Angelini is someone the judge might have sat and had coffee with that morning. Could the judge have confronted him about the authenticity of the painting?

I felt like I was going in multiple directions with so many possible suspects who had motives. Pulling into the parking lot at Priscilla's, I parked my car near the side. An ancient Buick with lots of old stickers on it about Vietnam and POWs sat in front of the building. A piece of wire was holding the muffler up, and rust decorated the wheel wells or held them together. It could be Patterson's car. He sure had a thing for the Vietnam War. Did that mean his discharge preyed on his mind? I parked and walked into the bar. Angie was working, but the place wasn't packed like on the weekends. She walked over to a booth with me, and we sat.

"Ready to interrogate the suspect?" she asked.

"Where is he?"

"In a back booth over there." She nodded her head toward the area where the stage was. "He's on his first beer. I'm hoping it will loosen his tongue."

"What does he drink?"

Angie walked over to the refrigerator and pulled out a bottle. She came back, set it on the bar, and said, "PBR. I'll get your fav on tap too."

"All right. Wish me luck."

"He's a sleazy guy. I'll keep my eye on you."

"Thanks, partner."

After Angie had drawn me a beer, I crossed the vacant floor and moved over to a series of booths usually full on the nights Andy and Lance played. It was a Wednesday night and early. I checked my phone. Five thirty. Then he looked up, saw my pair of beers, and smiled. He appeared as disheveled as he had when I met him at the funeral. Old jeans that needed a good washing or ten, a T-shirt with a logo on it, and his hat indicating a Vietnam vet. I moved slowly, placed the beer on the table, and said, "Hi, Mr. Patterson. I thought I recognized you from the funeral."

He gestured to me to take a seat. "Uh, yeah. You're the woman the judge left his bucks to. Can't remember your name."

"Jill. Jill Madison. And yes, the judge did leave my art center a bunch of money. Quite unexpected."

He laughed, but with a kind of nasty scowl on his face. "I s'pose the judge could leave his dough wherever he wanted, but I'm surprised he cut off his kids. Don't seem quite fair."

I decided to take the open-and-honest approach. "To be honest, Mr. Patterson, I had no idea he was planning to do that. I'm as shocked as anyone else."

He snorted and shook his head. "Don't seem right to cut off kin. But that was the kinda scumbucket he was. Don't surprise me."

I swallowed a good-sized mouthful of beer and considered his thoughts. Then I gave him my most earnest facial expression. "You seem to have a terrible opinion of the judge. Care to share details? You came quite a way to visit. Was it a cousin you were visiting?" I watched as he glanced over my shoulder, seeming to consider.

"Yeah, yeah. Got me a cousin over in the town east of here—Edgeburg. Hadn't seen him in years. Thought I'd visit."

"You mean in Edgington?"

"Yup. I don't always remember names or places well. That PSTD stuff." He looked around at anyone but me. "Saw the judge too. Happened onto him at the grocery store. He didn't remember me. I was only a grunt, not worth his exalted time. He ain't no different now than he was back then."

"Why did you hate him? What did he do that made you so angry?"

"Do? He ruined my life. You got any idea what a dishonorable discharge does to you once you're back home?"

I shook my head.

"I'll tell ya. It's followed me around forever. It's like a felony. I don't got no rights to VA benefits, so when I fell a few years ago and broke my hip, I didn't get no healthcare rights like I should of. Thank you, Judge Ron Spivey." He glanced up at the ceiling and made an obscene gesture. Then he stared back at me. "And I couldn't get a federal job with benefits. They checked my military record. Ended up in prison for months and months stateside. It's been hell getting work 'cause anybody who might hire me can check my record. That don't make jobs easy to get."

I nodded in an empathetic way, thinking about the state of his car in the parking lot. "What did you do to cause your discharge?" I couldn't add "dishonorable" because it might set him off.

He took a long pull on his beer and glanced all around the bar as if he expected someone to be listening. It could be he was thinking about the story he'd tell me.

"Nothin'. It was a setup. Hadn't been over in-country for very long. Been out on recon missions in the boonies where we'd cleared out quite a few VC hiding places."

"VC?"

"Victor Charlie. Viet Cong. The enemy." He took a swig of his beer. "Didn't take no brains to see this was a losing situation. Firefights, DH5s...uh, them was Claymore mines. Never knew what you might step on or get into. After a while, I'd clean my M-16 and consider what I might be able to do to make boo-koo bucks. I didn't sign up to go to that purgatory. The army sent me a 'Greetings from Uncle Sam' notice. So, being me, I studied the situation and thought about how I might get out of it alive with a bit on the side."

I noted his weasely eyes and red-veined nose. What a piece of work. "How did you meet Judge Spivey?"

"He weren't no judge in Nam. But he'd gone to OCS—Officer Candidate School—was a second lewey, and thought he was so smart. Second lieutenants. They was a dime a dozen and had a target on their backs in Nam. But somehow, he had'da charmed life. He swore I'd sold carbines to the VC. Now why would I do that? Them're the ones shooting at me! Someone was selling them guns, but it wasn't me. We found plenty of them in dead VC hands. But, no. He was a high-and-mighty officer. No one was gonna believe me."

He paused a moment, examined his now-empty beer bottle, and set it back down on the table. "Had me court-martialed, thrown in the clink, and out of the army. His say-so. Ruined my life forever. I figured he'd never make it out alive from that jungle hell, but I read a story in the paper in Georgia saying he got a kinda award, and I figgered it was him. How many Ron Spiveys could there be? I come here to see if it was the same second lewey I remembered, and sure enough. While I spent my life trying to keep food in my stomach and a roof over my head, he's living the grand style. Figgers." His eyes narrowed. "What about Gushman, the newspaper woman? Is she gonna be all right?"

I wondered why he was curious about Gushman. Guilt? Wondering if he'd been seen as the almost-killer. "I believe so."

"That's another one people don't much like."

"And you? Did you like her?"

His eyes shifted again. "She wasn't nothing to me."

I could imagine a conversation between him and Judge Spivey. That would have been something to behold. He hated him enough. Could he have called him the night before our lunch, gone over ahead of me, and shot the judge full of digitalis? Where would he have gotten it? Brought it with him? He obviously knew how to give shots because he'd been a medic. Why would the judge let Patterson come to see him? His conscience? By Patterson's own admission, he hadn't known the judge was alive until recently. That might explain the decades-old lapse.

He was lying to me. The shifty movement of his eyes, the occasional tongue licking his lips as he paused and considered what to say—and I doubted Judge Spivey would have turned him in if he didn't have evidence on him. Patterson had a temper but was trying to control it as he talked to me about his war crimes. He'd chosen his words with care, and I didn't believe him for a minute. He might not be so smart, but he had a crafty look to his eyes. Why come all the way from Georgia to Illinois to see someone he'd known long in the past? He seemed to have unfinished business. Maybe now he'd finished it.

"Since you've been here a while, I'd assume you're going back to Georgia?"

He tilted his head slightly as if he were thinking. "Prob'ly. I kinda like this town. Apple Grove. But I got a job to git back to, such as it is, so I'm starting to think about going home. We'll see."

I rose, thinking I'd better let Tom know Patterson was considering leaving town. "Nice talking to you, Mr. Patterson. Perhaps you'll come visit again." I left and walked back across the dance floor, moving toward the bar. Angie was leaning against the cash register behind the bar.

"Leaving so soon?" she said.

"Need to go home and get sleep. Tomorrow's a big day. I'll be picking up the curator for our exhibit, fixing last-minute details, and praying a lot."

She leaned close and whispered, "How was Patterson? Scary?"

I thought for a moment. "I'd say he has a pretty bad temper, a motive to kill the judge, and an expertise with medical things. He's a possibility."

"Hmm. Yeah, that is a problem. You know, because Gushman could never keep her mouth shut, it's quite possible a suspect like Patterson tried to kill her when she said something she shouldn't have said. I've seen them drinking together. I wouldn't rule him out."

"So many crimes, so little time. The editor said she was going to research the judge's past—that might include when he crossed paths with Patterson. Paranoid Patterson, Smarmy Angelini, Avaricious Erika, and Too Quiet John. Alibis and motives are all over the place. I think I should just quit."

Chapter Thirty

"Oh, I love your gallery," Anthony Arteaga said as I led him into the Adele Marsden Center for the Arts.

I had picked him up at the Peoria airport on a flight from Philadelphia this morning. He looked as crisp as autumn felt when I spotted him in a polo shirt with a logo from the Philadelphia Museum of Art and crisply creased khaki slacks. Not overly tall, he was Hispanic with a short dark beard, dark downward-pointing moustache, and a receding hairline. He was, maybe, in his mid-thirties, and when he smiled, his face lit up. Dark, penetrating eyes met mine, and he was easy to talk to during the hour's drive to Apple Grove. A light-hearted manner about him put me at ease.

Now, in the art center, I wanted to impress him with what we could do in a small town in the heartland. I watched as his eyes glanced throughout the exhibit, moving from the left side of the gallery to the right. He was speechless.

"Amazing!" He set a shoulder bag on the floor and walked slowly around the gallery as if he were memorizing each of the exhibit entries.

I watched him silently while he stopped before some of the pieces, taking them in as if inhaling them. Then he'd move on and walk past others, pausing only briefly. Unmoving, I waited until he'd made a circuit of the entire gallery. It was then he turned to me.

"It's been a while since I saw these online, but, as always, they are astonishing in real life. The internet never does them justice. This is so impressive. How many people live in Apple Grove?"

"About fifteen thousand, give or take a few. It's a small town, and I grew up here."

"This is breathtaking for such a rural town in the middle of Illinois. Do these fifteen thousand people realize what a gem this is, this art center named for your talented, artistic mother?"

I smiled. "I hope so. Our whole region supports the art center. We live on grants, as you'd guess, but also on memberships and connections with corporate sponsors in the area. Fortunately, we have a liberal arts college that collaborates with us. Our endowment is healthy."

"And this is thanks to a foundation set up by your family, right?"

"Yes. My late parents set aside money for this venture."

He glanced around the room again and whistled gently. "Amazing."

"Thank you. So, I thought you might want to do some judging this morning for an hour or so, then take a break, and we'll drop off your overnight bag at the hotel and go out for lunch. Does that sound like a plan to suit you?"

"Absolutely. I'd love to walk around and do some judging because I've been sitting on a plane all morning, and you know how comfortable flying these days is."

"So true. What might you need? A clipboard? Paper? Pen? iPad?"

He walked back to his messenger bag and pulled out several items. "I have all I need. Just turn me loose."

I handed him a list of artwork and left him to it. The artwork had tags next to each with the title and medium but no names of artists. "I'll be back here in my office if you need me. And thanks so much for agreeing to come help us."

"My pleasure, for sure," he said, looking around at the walls again.

Forty-five minutes went by, and I could see him out in the gallery taking notes, turning his head this way and that, backing away and moving toward different pieces. Sometimes he walked right up close as if examining specific details or brush marks. I decided to go out and ask him to tell me his thoughts about a few of the entries. It always intrigued me to hear how jurors understood and judged artwork. Each one I'd ever listened to came from their own background, sensibilities, and interests. There was no objective about it. Anthony had a background in rural life and agriculture, and I'd chosen him for exactly that reason. Anything he told me would be private and confidential.

He was standing in front of a painting called *Bringing in the Harvest*.

"Mind if I tag along and listen to you talk about what you're seeing?"

"Not at all," he said. "I noticed this oil painting immediately when we came in. These are my thoughts. It's a rustic pastoral of workers in the field, equipment from the early 1900s, and a harvest of golden wheat. While there are many workers, the one in the middle foreground is the focal point. His face is concentrating so hard, but there's also joy there. The red bandana brings to life his work clothes and his pride in what he's doing.

"The horse-drawn combine with two huge draft horses is the predecessor of steam-powered tractors, but they're not yet here in the breadbasket of the country. This is hard manual labor. Notice the other workers and their slumped shoulders. Despite the discrimination of the railroad rates and the tariffs that tear away his farm profits, he comes alive as he works his land. I'd estimate about forty percent of Americans were living on farms in the time depicted in this painting. Now the percentage is two. I love the artist's use of color, especially the way the light plays on his face and on the grain. His brushstrokes are strong and confident. He feels what he is painting. There is such humanity here."

"Amazing. You are the perfect juror for this exhibit!"

He smiled. "I grew up on a small farm in the Southwest. Such a struggle. My professional interests and certainly the topic of many of my lectures is rural America and the plight of small communities in a time when urbanization, corporations, and large-scale farm interests are squeezing out the small, family-owned farms." He laughed. "Sounds like the thesis for a dissertation, doesn't it?"

I nodded, then turned slightly. "What do you think of this sculpture? Since my mom was a sculptor, I'm always drawn toward three-dimensional artwork." I was pointing at a bronze cast sculpture called *Day is Almost Done*.

We walked over toward the stand holding the piece.

"This is intriguing to me. It's an elderly Black man, bending over tall grass with a scythe. Every part of his body shows his weariness. He's probably been at this all day, and his shoulders are slumped, his knees are about to give out, and his hands hold the scythe as if they hurt. Maybe blisters? Look at his face up close. So many wrinkles, almost like a road map. What must he have been like as a young boy? His carpenter's jeans hold a handkerchief in one pocket, and the pocket on the other side is partially torn. I can feel every ache in his body. The details are simply so real.

"I like the title too, because the day is almost done for this way of life and also for this elderly man. You can see a few small tufts of hair over his ears, and if this were a painting, they'd be white. This creative artist really knows his or her medium. I can almost feel his presence as he added these details to make this old man come alive for us."

"Yes. What technique, experience, and knowledge this artist has." I took a deep breath. "Are you ready to take a break yet?"

"Hmm." He scanned the wall. "Let me check out this fused glass piece, and then I'll be ready."

"*Leaf-Peeping Season*. Ah, this abstract panel's backstory could be set in New England."

"Yes. I've done some leaf-peeping there myself in the autumn. This concept is totally different from the other two I talked about. It's an abstract, so the colors and design simply suggest the gorgeous hues of fall. The composition is what captures my eyes. Notice the dark red over in the lower right corner? Both the shape and size draw your eye because they contrast completely with every other color in the work. You have browns, yellows, and oranges, and a small tint of green, but the red draws your focus. It's slightly off balance. The focus is diagonal, and your eyes sweep from the lower right diagonally across to the upper left. Perfectly composed. The artist has used such an exuberance of color, emphasizing how our world goes from brown and green into all these glorious shades. It's the last spectacular exhibit of nature's color before we sink into darkness and short hours of daylight. Leaf-peeping indeed! And the technique is perfect. Whoever did this fused glass panel knew what they were doing when it came to composition, color, and technique. Wow."

"Thanks, Anthony. I enjoy hearing your take on these entries. Your enthusiasm warms me, and I have no idea how you're going to make choices for awards."

"Don't you worry, Jill. I can do that, even though it's like apples and oranges."

"Come on. I'm going to take you to lunch."

I checked the clock. Nine p.m. After cleaning my office so it would appear halfway organized when I brought Anthony Arteaga here, I now noticed how quickly it filled with piles of work once again. Louise, I, and several members of the board had taken Anthony out for dinner at the Tuscany Bistro, named by owners who had immigrated from that region. We had a lovely dinner, excellent wine, scintillating conversation, and lots of laughter. After dropping Anthony at his hotel, I'd come back over to the art center to make sure all was well and clear up a few details.

I peeked out my window into the gallery. Louise and I would put the tags next to the artwork tomorrow. Since the judging was over, these tags would identify the artist and give the title. The list of winners was sitting on my desk, and Anthony would announce them tomorrow night. Volunteers would be in and out all day tomorrow, setting up stations for food and wine and making sure all was ready to go. After yawning, I let out a huge breath. So far, so good.

I heard Chad's radio playing country tunes on the second floor, and then the music was accompanied by footsteps on the stairs. Soon, his head popped around the corner.

"Ain't you gonna go home at some point? Big day tomorrow." He set down a bucket of mop water and wiped his forehead. "All's well upstairs, but that's not the most important part, is it? I'll start here in a few minutes. I'm gonna take a break and eat a sandwich."

"Sounds good. I'll bring my coffee and come join you. Is that all right?"

He smiled. "Absolutely. It's kind of quiet and lonely here at night."

I followed him down the hallway and into the room where the weaving group had placed their looms, all covered now with colorful pieces of material. Turning on the lights as we went, I set my coffee on the table and waited as Chad pulled his dinner out of the refrigerator.

"I'm glad you're here, Chad. I've spent a lot of nights here in my office alone, and at times it's a little spooky. Old buildings. Lots of creaks and groans. Now that we have the new security system in, I feel much safer, but I still hear the creaks and groans."

He unwrapped his sandwich, opened a bottle of water, and pulled a couple of pills out of his pocket. Seeing my face, he said, "Blood pressure pills. Take two each night."

"Ah."

Setting the sandwich on the cellophane, he nodded. "You have a good security system. I s'pose it was a grant too?"

"Yes. After a burglary earlier in the year, it seemed like a security system should be a grant I'd get on top of right away." I watched as he took a bite of his sandwich. Then he pulled out a small knife from his pocket and cut up an apple. "I had a talk with Reggie Patterson the other night."

He glanced at me quickly, a worried look on his face. "Really. That must have been an experience. Where'd ya see him?"

I quickly explained about our conversation at Priscilla's. "You knew him before he came to town. Do you think he's capable of murdering a person?"

Chad thought about it for a moment. Then he raised his eyebrows as if he were considering conflicting opinions. "I seen him kill people in Nam, but they were VC. It was a war. He didn't have a problem with it. But if you mean the judge, I don't know. Seems a bit coincidental he shows up here slightly before the judge's death."

"But Jezbhel Gushman? Patterson didn't even know her."

He stopped, a slice of apple midair. "That there's another story. He does spend time at Priscilla's Pub, and Gushman's there a lot. I've seen 'em at a table together on many occasions, and those were only the nights I happened to stop in. Gushman was a big blowhard. Didn't have a filter. She might have said anything. Whether she said something that set Reggie off, I don't know." He took a long swallow from his water bottle. "She might'a found a lot of info on the judge's war record. It ain't hard for a newspaper writer ta do that with the laws about freedom of information. Gushman spouted about facts and research too."

"But I thought you said he—the judge—was right about turning Patterson in."

He nodded and swallowed a bite of the sandwich. "Oh, he was right for sure. Patterson had gotten into black-market stuff involving guns. None of the guys in the squad was happy about that. He deserved what he got. Who'd wanna be next to a guy in a battle when the guy had sold guns to the people who were shooting at you? He's lucky friendly fire didn't kill him."

"Friendly fire?"

"It's the term used when you're killed by your own side."

Now I was shocked. "Your own side?"

"Yeah. It wasn't unusual. You've never been in a war. Things git chaotic and mixed up. People end up in a spot where they shouldn't be. Artillery rounds go in the wrong direction. Stuff like that happened all the time." He paused. "And sometimes, I'd guess, it happened when one guy hated another one for whatever reason."

"Well—well, that's just murder."

Now he stopped chewing and swallowed. "I hate to tell ya, but in war, murder and the job you're hired to do are the same."

I paused, thinking about his words. Taking a sip of my coffee, I set it down. "Chad, did you ever hear any Vietnam rumors about black roses or black rose petals?"

He rubbed his chin and thought about it. "Back of my brain there might be something. Gosh, that was so long ago. I was over there in sixty-eight and sixty-nine. Something."

He stared over my shoulder, and a change came over his face as he remembered.

"I heard about a bunch of guys in a kinda crazy unit. Called themselves the rose tattoo group. I don't know about black roses. Seems kinda weird. Never seen a black rose. It was a rumor, that was all. They was big drinkers and weedies." He thought about it more. Then he shook his head. I noticed he hadn't looked me in the eyes as he told this story. Avoiding my gaze still, he added, "Course a lotta guys were drinkers and smoked weed. I can't remember much more. You know, it's been decades ago. I think there was a death or deaths involved. Can't remember any more than that. Sorry."

"That's OK."

"I suppose you're a little anxious about tomorrow. The opening?"

"Oh, I'd put my anxiety level about as high as One World Trade Center in New York."

He took a deep breath. "It's gonna be fine. You've thought of everything."

I laughed. "You have no idea what my road record is with openings!"

Chapter Thirty-One

"This is Anthony Arteaga, our juror for *Harvest Time*," I said for the umpteenth time, this time to a board member. Our opening was in full swing after the first hour, and people were drinking wine, milling around conversing, and checking out the artwork. I scanned the gallery and smiled at the decorations put together by the hospitality committee. Cornstalks out on either side of the front door, silk leaves on the tables of hors d'oeuvres, apple cider, and wines, and pumpkins everywhere.

I saw Louise at the other side of the room, mingling with the crowd also. The board members were all here, as was most of my family. At least I didn't have to look at the face of the local newspaper editor tonight, although I saw one of the stringers she'd hired. Anthony was deep in conversation with one of the art professors from the college, so I walked over to Sam, who was talking with Andy and Lance.

"I like the painting over there that looks like someone took a toilet plunger and made lots of concentric circles in different fall colors," Andy said. "I could do that."

Sam laughed because he knew I was right behind Andy.

"Nice review," I said. "It's a specific technique in oils, and it doesn't involve toilet plungers."

"Oh, hi, Jill," Andy said, his expression a bit sheepish.

Sam came over to my side and grabbed my hand. "Nice crowd you have. I'd guess a hundred and fifty people, at least at the moment, and more coming through the door."

"Great exhibit," Lance said. "All the fall colors and designs are amazing.

So many landscapes, which I, personally, like."

Tom and Mary were coming in the door. I waved at them and turned to my circle of friends. "It's time to do my thing. Introduce Anthony and get on with the awards."

Sam squeezed my hand gently and let go. "By now, some of them should have a glass or two of wine, so maybe they won't take defeat too dearly."

I laughed. "If they do, we have a doctor in the crowd. Gotta go."

I walked over to the far side of the gallery and grabbed a microphone.

"If I could have your attention, please." I waited for the crowd to get quiet, and when most of them were, I started my remarks.

"I'm enormously proud of this first national exhibit. I know my mother, Adele Marsden, would be so excited to gaze down on us and know art is alive and well in Apple Grove. Just think, folks, artwork from all over the United States is here in our gallery tonight, and our juror is from a distinguished museum in Philadelphia. Many of the artists are new to the exhibition world, so they'll have great networking possibilities and additions to their resumes after tonight. I would like to thank Louise Sandoval, our manager"—I pointed her out—"and all the board members who are volunteers. Please raise your hand if you're a board member."

I scanned the crowd and saw board members with their hands up as people clapped. Even Ivan was smiling.

"I'd like to thank our corporate sponsors too, and you'll find their names in your gallery catalog. We also have many volunteers who installed this exhibit and put together the decorations, wine, and food for your pleasure as you peruse the artwork. If you're a volunteer, please raise your hand."

I waited for the sounds to die out. "And now I would like to introduce our juror for the exhibit, Anthony Arteaga, and ask him to say a few words." I handed him the microphone.

"I'd like to express my gratitude to Jill Madison, her staff, and the board for my warm welcome and the opportunity to be a juror for *Harvest Time*. I understand this is your first national exhibit. As I told Ms. Madison, I am so impressed with your work. This beautiful art center is a jewel I hadn't expected in the middle of farm country. The amazing artwork mounted on these walls and sitting on pedestals represents the creative power and individual responses to the phrase 'harvest time.' I hope you'll immerse yourselves in these images as deeply as I did. They'll change your own perspectives on that theme."

And now it was his turn to speak and announce the winners.

"As I judged these works, I considered many facets of creativity. I thought about the craft and skill of the artists—their technical virtuosity. I studied their composition, color, design elements, and material choices. How did they thoughtfully place details? What was their artistic process? Finally, I was interested in how lovingly they chose to display their final work—their matting, framing, and mounting. With my background and interests, I was deeply drawn to these rural displays of the harvest. So now, let me announce the awards."

I followed him around the gallery, handing him ribbons and symbols to place next to the winners. He spoke briefly about each winning selection and a bit longer about the overall exhibition winners in each category. Then it was time for the prize-winning entry.

"And the Best of Show award, with a monetary prize of two thousand dollars, goes to Max Abernathy for his rustic oil painting, *Bringing in the Harvest*," announced Anthony Arteaga.

The audience applauded, and Max, who lived in a rural town on the west side of Iowa and had made the trip for the evening, walked forward and accepted the prize from Anthony. I felt tears roll down my cheeks. It was a thrilling and dramatic ending to the announcement of prizes. People surrounded Max and other winners, congratulating them.

My chest swelled with pride as I did a pirouette in one spot and checked out all the ribbons and prize announcements hanging next to artwork. It had been a grand occasion, and everything had worked like clockwork. Once people began talking again, I left Anthony, who was deep in conversation with the mayor.

"You're a star. Louise is too, and the two of you have brought this off," Sam said.

My cheeks were blushing. "I'm so excited. I wasn't here for the opening of the first exhibit we did. Now I've been able to see the end of all our work. Tomorrow, I'll feel a huge weight off my shoulders." Sam looked so amazing in a dark suit and open-collared blue shirt. Handsome. Then his beeper went off. I groaned.

"Oh, no," he said, consternation on his face.

"Use my office phone to call, or you can step into my office with your cell."

After he left, more people gathered around me.

They were congratulating me, telling me how wonderful the exhibit was, and shaking my hands or hugging me. We'd gone through bottles and bottles of wine, both red and white, and the partygoers were in great spirits by now, the apex of the evening. Louise would take Anthony back to the hotel and would drive him to the airport early tomorrow morning. I glanced toward my office door. Sam was coming back into the gallery.

"Rats," he said, as we were in hearing range. "I have to go in. Traffic accident on the edge of town and multiple injuries. I'm sorry."

"I understand. It's your job, and you must go save people. It's more crucial than curating artwork."

"Don't sell yourself short. Artwork saves humanity."

And that's why I found myself falling for him as he hugged me, kissed my forehead, and headed for the door. He actually thought my work was important. He could be a keeper.

An hour and a half later, most of the crowd had left, and a few of the board members remained, picking up discarded napkins and paper that had found its way to the floor and putting paper plates and napkins in the wastebaskets.

"Hey, everybody. Let's worry about cleaning this tomorrow. Tonight was about celebration. We'll deal with the chaos tomorrow afternoon. Thank you all for your hard work and for coming to see this opening to the end. This was such an exciting night. Let's not ruin our fun by having to clean the gallery. See you tomorrow afternoon." Quite a few volunteers nodded their heads, waved, and headed out the door. I suddenly realized I was exhausted. The night had been a huge high, and now I was coming down.

Chad walked over to me. "I'll check the upstairs rooms and the bathrooms to make sure everyone's out. "Cleary here will help me, won't you, Chance?"

"Absolutely. Come on." They both headed upstairs, and I checked the front door, locking it, and went back to my office. I sat for a moment at my desk in the solitary stillness. I wish Judge Spivey had been here tonight to see how his encouragement had made this all happen. I remembered our first exhibit. I'd shown up here the next day as the volunteers were cleaning, and he laughed and gave me anything I wanted for the art center. His eyes had twinkled, and he said I'd kept things "lively." That was the beginning of our adult friendship and the plan to have lunch together a couple times a month. We'd talk about the art center and about art itself. Why, oh why, did he have to die? A tear or two leaked out of my eyes. He would have loved this reception. After things were sorted out with the probate, we could put together a memorial prize in his name. It would keep him close to this art center he'd loved.

I heard footsteps coming down the stairs. Chad and Chance leaned around my office door, and Chance said, "No one here but us mice."

"Great! Thanks for your help."

"You about ready to go? We'll see you out to your car," Chance said.

"Yes." I stood and grabbed my light jacket and purse.

"Say," said Chad, "I have a thought about the art center."

"Oh? What's that?"

"You know I took a fused glass class with Donna Filbert."

I put my arm through my coat sleeve. "Yes. It was crowded. Donna thought an adult class during the week might work, and she sure was right."

Chad smiled. "We students in the class got to talking while we was working, so to speak, and we thought it would be a great idea to have a senior group at the art center."

"A senior group?"

"Yeah. You know, Apple Grove has a lot of older residents, and a group dedicated only to them would bring more people into the center. Some would even volunteer to help with things. But if we formed a group and they met once a month, we could have programs to talk about art things."

"Hmm. That's a great idea, Chad."

194

CHAPTER THIRTY-ONE

"It is?" His face lit up.

"Absolutely. I'm always looking for new programs and ways to get more people in the area to learn about art. This would be a perfect opportunity."

"Great! I had an idea." He glanced at Cleary, who smiled. "Let's plan a meeting. We could come up with a name for the group and think about meetings and programs."

"I'll get your proposal going," I said. I buttoned my jacket, locked my office, and we all set off for the alley door. They walked to my car with me, and once I was in and started the engine, they turned to walk back through the alley. I heard Chad say, "Whad'da you know. I thought of a good idea."

I smiled.

Chapter Thirty-Two

What was it about Judge Spivey's past, his death, and the attempted murder of Jezbhel Gushman? Somehow there must be a connection. But what? I should research Gushman. I pondered these questions as I sat behind the judge's desk on Sunday afternoon. We'd cleaned the art center yesterday, and I still felt the thrill of our first national exhibit. We would have a place on the map of the art world if these national exhibits continued, and they would. Who would have thought we could take a nineteenth-century building, make it safe, and have national art exhibits and bursting-at-the-seams classes in a small town like Apple Grove? I felt the excitement all over again. I thought about my parents, especially my sculptor mom. They would have loved this.

Now it was time to get back to my duties as an executor. Since the art exhibit opening was over, I'd need to get on top of this job. Also, I'd had a call from Tom. Because Angelini was under arrest, Tom planned to fly to New York City to interrogate him about the judge's murder and possibly Gushman's attack, although the latter was a long shot.

I was moving a couple of folders to a file cabinet when my cell phone began playing "Welcome to the Jungle." Andy. I punched the accept button. "Hi, bro."

"Just checking to see if it's a new day, a new week, and a relief now that the opening is over."

Interesting. Usually, he didn't show much curiosity. "Sure. All is well, and it's quiet at the art center. No classes starting for two weeks, and the opening of the exhibit over. Whew."

"I read the other night on the internet that genealogy is a huge passion these days, with millions being spent to find ancestors. Any progress on finding ours?"

Oh, I felt my heart drop. I'd forgotten I'd used it as a pretext to find out about my parents. I'd have to send my DNA in to one of those online businesses soon, so it would be back before Christmas. Then I could present it to Tom, and Andy would be none the wiser.

"Jill?"

"Oh, yes. Haven't heard anything yet. Boy, Tom will be excited. This is the best Christmas present ever. Thanks for helping me with it."

"I don't know why you couldn't have simply sent your own DNA. Why mine?"

Think fast. "Uh, it's for Tom, and because both of you are males, I thought it would make more sense." That was a whopper. I hoped he wouldn't consider the stupidity of my comment.

"Oh. Hmm. I heard Gushman got out of the hospital. S'pose she'll stick around and continue at the newspaper after that?"

"For our sakes, I hope not."

"You must admit her form of journalism is entertaining. Gotta go." And he ended the call.

I set my phone down and stared at the financial records on the desk, numbers I'd been pouring over for the past three hours. As Tom had instructed, I'd checked for any irregularities, but I hadn't seen any. Reviewing the huge figure he'd paid for *Death in a Bygone Hue*, I wondered what would happen now that Peter Angelini was under arrest and the painting had been determined to be a fraud. Would he have to return the money he'd stolen from the judge?

I'd had an initial report from the appraisers in Chicago, and the numbers constituting the total value of the paintings had blown my mind. It wasn't simply six figures, but more like eleven. I'd had to take multiple deep breaths. Unbelievable. The art center would have an endowment for life, and I'd have a wonderful nest egg. It didn't seem real. Nothing did until the six-month probate period finally ended.

For the tenth time, I wondered what I'd done to deserve this. The DNA information wasn't back yet. Why was it taking so long? Argh. I wasn't patient. That's another thing the judge used to say to me. The universe of art was a place where you had to be patient. The value of paintings and sculptures fluctuated over time. Periods came and went, and what remained was classic.

I rubbed my eyes, being careful not to screw up my contact lenses. Sitting back in the chair, I glanced around the office. It was beginning to feel like home. Light shining through the prisms of the Tiffany lamp reminded me color was nothing more than light being absorbed or not by the geometric panes of glass. Beautiful, warm. I glanced at all the legal books lined up on the shelves to my left. Wondering how often the judge had referred to them, I noticed they were well-worn. I glanced down at the shelf of photos of the judge's family. It must have made him sad to consider the lives and decisions of his two children. No families were perfect, but what disappointment he must have felt. He never let me know he had this sadness in his life.

It reminded me of what the judge had said about second chances. At lunch one day, we were talking about a story he'd told from his days in law school about a classmate who had almost been expelled. But he was given a last-minute reprieve. He went on to have a distinguished career and issued many stunning judgments that became legal precedents in jurisprudence. My mentor had finished his story by saying, "People's characters don't change much. But over time, they may evolve, grow, and realize more about the nature of humans. If you give a person a second chance, you might be surprised. Of course, sometimes you're disappointed, but I've seen lots of second chances from my days on the bench that ended up in lives well-lived. I prefer to live on hope."

It was only one of the pronouncements he'd made when we had lunch and discussed the world. I missed that. A lot. What a rotten thing someone didn't let the clock run out naturally on his life.

I stood and walked along the shelves filled with his mementos, picking up the photo of him and Laura. I envied their marriage. Despite the disappointment in their children, they sure lived the "in sickness and in health" part of those vows. Of course, the jury was still out on his relationship with my mother. I hoped the Spivey parents were together now. I'd like to think of them playing celestial bridge with my mom and dad.

Moving on to the sepia photo from Vietnam, I picked it up, staring at the faces. There was the judge at the top of the photo with three other soldiers. Of course, I didn't recognize anyone but the judge. They were so young. They stared at the camera, and I could see the dirt on their uniforms, the helmet straps hanging beside their cheeks, and the rifles on the ground next to them. Who had taken this photo? I wondered who the other three were, and why none of them had come to the judge's funeral.

At a chance thought, I turned the photo over, pushed the little pieces of metal holding the photo in the frame, and pulled the stand away from the glass. I took the picture over to the desk and sat, laying it under the light from the Tiffany lamp. Then I turned it over.

The judge—or someone—had written names behind the placement of each soldier in the photo. I read the names: Sid Graham, Liam Axel, Ted Bender. "Ted Bender." Where had I heard his name before? I scanned the office, my brain trying to pinpoint the memory. Then I opened a desk drawer, and there was the folder with the yellow sticky note saying, "Ted Bender." Why had the judge written that? Was he planning to call his old friend? Did he have a question for him? Was he planning to meet him somewhere? Had something occurred, causing him to think about his past in Vietnam?

I didn't remember ever hearing the names of the other two. Of course, the judge never talked about his experiences in Vietnam. Someone had placed a black silk rose next to this photo. Was it the judge? Was it the person who killed him? Chad had said he'd heard of a group of soldiers who'd drunk a lot and smoked weed. And...a death. They'd had something to do with black roses. I'd been fooled by people in the past. Was it possible Chad knew those guys in Vietnam? He seemed a bit evasive, not like his usual self, when he talked about this group of guys over there who were hell-raisers. I glanced at the photo again. But it couldn't be the judge. He was the farthest person I knew from someone who'd smoke weed or drink too much. I'd always seen him have a glass of wine, sometimes two, but that was it. I giggled. "Sober as a judge."

I clicked on the judge's computer screen, typing "black roses" into the search engine like I had before. Same answer. Their symbolism was myriad, but particularly death, despair, hatred, and tragedy. I considered the last symbolic meaning…revenge. A chill passed through me.

Sitting back, I thought about the notes I'd given to Tom with black rose petals in them. Was one of these soldiers angry with the judge? Did one of them send the notes? Why would they wait for decades to exact revenge? I found this confusing. It made no sense.

Staring at the screen, I considered where I could get help to sort this out. Who might know what this was all about? Then I remembered someone, someone who might have the answers. I picked up my phone and punched in the numbers.

Chapter Thirty-Three

onday was uneventful at work because the exhibit was up, the opening over. I'd managed to put out an email Saturday morning to all the members of the art center and tell them we'd have a meeting on October 5, Wednesday, at 10 a.m., of senior citizens who were interested in forming a new group at the center. By the end of the day, I'd had twenty RSVPs. The IAAF was planning to ship the paintings back to me on Wednesday. All was falling into place. I hoped by the end of today, I'd have answers to my questions about the photo in Judge Spivey's office. I planned to present the information to Tom, once he returned, as an accomplishment. The late afternoon meeting was on my mind all day as I worked.

Paige Lemon, the elementary school art teacher, stopped by. She was in her mid-thirties, enthusiastic about her classes, and always dressed in vibrant colors. A few weeks ago, she'd taught a watercolor class. That was the class in which the O'Connell twins painted the elevator. Today she had on a white top with splotches of mauve (translate white, phthalo red rose, and cobalt violet) with an asymmetrical hemline. This was over yellow ochre shorts and sandals with glittery straps. After some chitchat, we dug into the real reason for her visit.

"I've been doing some thinking," she said, "about some watercolor classes for the seniors who live at the nursing home. I know some of them are capable of painting, and it might be great for their mental acuity. Do you think the BCA might be willing to sponsor that, even if it weren't on site?"

"What time frame did you have in mind?"

"Well, not right this minute. I was thinking maybe spring break next year. I'd be off work, and we'd have plenty of time to talk it over with the director at Innovative Retirement Care. I'd be glad to go do some preliminary steps, like checking to see how many residents might be able to join the group. What do you think?"

I admired Paige's enthusiasm. She'd done marvelous work with our classes, and this would be an opportunity to branch out into the community and provide art services. "I think check with the director, come up with some figures and information, and if it looks good, I'll take it to the board and see what they say."

"Oh great," she said, clapping her hands. "I've had that on my mind for some time, and I think it would be a great opportunity."

As she left my office, I considered her plan. This was what I loved about my job at the art center. It gave me lots of opportunities to collaborate with community movers. Often, like Paige, they came to me with ideas. Occasionally, the board would turn them down because of resources or money, but usually, they were excited also.

After lunch, the art center was quiet. Louise had an appointment and left for the afternoon, and I finished some bookkeeping. A lot of loose ends weren't becoming any less loose. I still hadn't heard anything about the DNA sample. Jezbhel Gushman was recuperating at home, but word was she still planned to continue at the helm of the *Apple Grove Ledger*. Drats! No one was any closer to naming her assailant. Tom had left a message that they hadn't had any luck so far finding the vehicle that ran me off the road. Along the same line, Angie had called and mentioned that Owen Prather had a dark SUV and was still in town. Too many events with no resolution.

I was hoping to have some resolution later today about the Vietnam connection.

By 3:55 p.m., I was standing on the front porch of an old friend. I rang the bell of a comfortable ranch-style house about eight blocks from my place. I could hear his voice call, "Coming!"

Abe Calipher answered the door, welcoming me in, his face glancing at me with curiosity. He'd been surprised when I'd called and told him I had an important matter to talk about with him. He ushered me in, and I followed him to the kitchen, where he had the coffee heating and a plate of cookies on the table.

"What a pleasant surprise this is," he said. "I know you can't be asking me about art because it's not exactly my area of expertise, so it must be something else." As I sat, he turned, grabbed the coffeepot, and poured coffee into each of our cups. Once he sat, I could feel an air of anticipation.

How to start. "Abe, I know you were a close friend of the judge."

"Sure was. I'm still feeling the roller coaster ride of grief. Is Tom any closer to finding out who killed him?"

"Not sure." I poured a little creamer and a teaspoon of sugar in my cup and stirred it. "I think he's following new leads. Since the Spiveys left town, he's been going in multiple directions, as have I."

"You?"

"Sure, the judge was my friend. I remember him telling me one time he'd known a lot of talented people in the art world, but persistence and self-discipline made them rise above their competition. He tried to convince me to keep trying last summer when most events kept going wrong in my life, and I couldn't paint. I miss him and his advice. When it comes to his death, I'm trying to be persistent and keep my investigation on the down-low. Mostly I research, stay under Tom's radar, and think about connections. But yes, I do miss him terribly."

He nodded. "Me, too. We've been great friends in the years after our spouses died. His death's left a huge void in my life." He took a swallow of coffee and waited for me to continue.

"Did you ever meet Peter Angelini?"

"Once, quite a few years ago. Why?"

"He's been arrested by the FBI in New York on forgery and money-laundering charges."

Abe's face wore a shocked expression.

"Yeah," I punctuated the news.

Abe shook his head. "Then Ron was right. He thought Angelini might be selling him forgeries, or at least one he mentioned."

"Yes. He was right."

He picked up a cookie and examined it briefly. "You know, Angelini called Ron, oh, a few days before Ron's death. The judge told him he planned to hire a forensic appraiser to examine the painting about Vietnam and see if it was authentic. Angelini was angry at his accusations, but Ron told me he thought it was all bluster. Something was off about that painting. Does Tom think Angelini might have murdered Ron? He sure had a motive if the judge was planning to turn him in." He took a bite of his cookie. I popped mine in my mouth.

"I'm sure it's one line of inquiry. Millions were on the line, and Angelini's reputation. It's all moot now. He's in custody in New York. Tom's out there talking with him. I suppose it's possible Angelini knows a lot about this money laundering. I wouldn't put it past him to hold out for immunity or a witness protection gig."

"I'll be. I never liked that Angelini, and I only met him once. There was something about him, too smooth and charming."

I set down my empty cup, and Abe gestured as if to ask if I wanted more. "No, thanks. I've had enough coffee. I wanted to ask you about something else. When I was cleaning out a closet in the judge's office, I found several threatening notes. They were sent about a month apart and a few months before his death, and each one had a black rose petal. Mean anything to you?"

He was silent. Then, without looking up, he said, "They might."

I waited for him to ask a question, and when he didn't, I prodded him a bit. "Abe, what aren't you telling me? The judge is dead now. There isn't anything such as coroner/client privilege, right? Or a HIPAA law that says you can't talk?" I chuckled, but he wasn't laughing.

After several seconds, he said, "I do have a memory, but it was a long time ago and told in confidence. Don't know if he'd want you to know about the past. You had a close relationship, the two of you, and I'd hate to have you think badly of him." He studied me squarely, and I could see the indecision on his face.

I laid the spoon on the saucer with my coffee cup and took a deep breath. "Look, Abe, whoever murdered the judge had something to do with his past. More specifically, an incident from the Vietnam War, which he never talked about with me. I found a photo on his bookshelf of him and three buddies, and someone laid a black silk rose next to it near the time of his death. It seemed like quite a coincidence when I found these threatening notes with black rose petals. Not sure I believe in coincidences." I stopped talking, letting the facts lay before him, hoping he'd talk.

He pushed back his chair, stood up, and walked to a cupboard. Pulling out a bottle, he grabbed two glasses, returned, and poured a finger of deep amber liquid into each glass. "A talk like this calls for bourbon. Good bourbon." Then he picked up his glass, as did I, and we clinked them together.

I waited until he took a deep swallow, hoping it would give him courage. Then I joined him. It was expensive bourbon, smooth going down.

"It's a story. I don't think Ron would have wanted me to tell you about this, but if it will help find his killer, well, all right. But it goes no farther than you and maybe Tom."

"OK. I promise."

"The judge was not always the man you know, a distinguished member of the bar, and presiding, as a judge, over trials where he had to make difficult decisions. He was, once upon a time, a reckless teenager like all of us. In college, he joined ROTC and was later sent to Vietnam." He paused. "Something that happened there disturbed him and followed him the rest of his life. I knew he had a melancholy about him, a face he didn't show to other people. Finally, one night, after a couple drinks, he told me about it.

"When he first went to Vietnam, he was idealistic and on a mission. He hadn't been in- country long when he investigated the Patterson guy and turned him in for black-market gun sales."

I nodded. This sounded like the judge I knew.

"As time went by, though, what he saw in Vietnam disturbed him, as it did so many other young American kids who'd never seen death up close, nor had they caused it. He met three guys who were from small towns in America and equally as naïve and appalled by the horror of that war. As the months dragged on, the four of them formed a group that raised a lot of hell. Drinking, smoking weed, being generally irresponsible. It was the way they coped with being on a battlefield, thousands of miles from home, in mud, with leeches, monsoon rains, and death all around them, much of it very violent."

"Seriously? I can't imagine. Not the judge."

"You can't imagine Vietnam either. Three of them got black rose tattoos when the fourth died— to remember him. When Ron died, I know his tat was still on his right shoulder. I didn't do the autopsy, but he'd showed it to me when he told me the story. One night, this group was firing mortars at defensive targets, and Ron, who was in charge, gave the wrong coordinates. They'd been high that night on beer and weed, and their actions killed an American soldier and wounded three others. It never was clear if Ron was given the wrong coordinates, or if he'd mixed up the numbers himself. But regardless, he took responsibility for it. He was horrified. How could he live with himself? They called a hearing, and he could see his life going down in flames. But the army, dealing with an already unpopular war, buried the information, along with other lies they told about the war. He was exonerated in a court-martial by the army, but not by his conscience."

When he paused, I put my hand to my mouth, which was open and shocked. "I can't imagine the judge doing something like that."

He smiled. "You were twenty-two or -three once, weren't you?"

"Yes, and Angie and I did a few things we'd rather not remember, but nothing like that."

"Of course not. It's hard to know how you'd react in his situation, death all around you."

I stood and walked over to the counter. I needed a moment to take it all in. Unbelievable. Once I sat, I asked, "What happened then?"

"Liam Axel had been killed in a friendly fire incident—and the other three came back from the war and for a time stayed in touch. But you know how that goes. Days, months, years flew by, and they all went their separate ways. Perhaps they didn't stay in touch because they didn't want to remember."

"Wow. I had no idea. How did the judge get himself straightened out and become a lawyer?"

"As he told me, he came home a changed man. His experience had sobered him up, and he spent a year trying to get his life back on track. His parents worried about him, sending him to a psychiatrist. Deep depression followed him home, and he considered trying to find the families of the man they'd killed or the three others they'd wounded. When he first stayed in touch with the other two soldiers from their group, it seemed like they had gotten on with their lives. Only Ron was teetering. By the time of his death, he hadn't heard from any of them in twenty years."

I thought about that. "I wonder if either is still alive."

He shook his head. "Don't know."

"Found a sticky note with Ted Bender's name on it. I think the judge planned to find him after he'd gotten these threatening cards. Perhaps he wanted to check and see if Bender had too."

"That could be."

"This whole story is a much more detailed account of vague rumors Chad, my janitor at the art center, heard while he was in Vietnam. But I never connected his memories to the judge."

We were both silent.

"It was a terrible thing to carry around on his conscience. Sometimes, I believe he became a lawyer and judge to try to make the world work more fairly. As you know, he volunteered his time to causes he believed in and left money—from what I hear—to philanthropic foundations. Despite all these actions, he still carried that night around with him like a lead weight." Abe shook his head slowly.

"I think you should talk to Tom and tell him about this. It could be another possible lead. Peter Angelini is still in the running for the judge's death, as is Reggie Patterson, but maybe there's a thread to his Vietnam past too. Patterson was in Vietnam. Could be there's a tie-in with him and whatever else happened."

"He never mentioned Patterson to me. All right, I will talk to Tom. Say, I heard by the grapevine you'd had his paintings appraised."

"Yes. I should have the appraisals back before too long. His estate is huge." I stood, pushed my chair in, and said, "You know, I always wondered about that single Vietnam painting. It's the only realistic one he had. Even though it turned out to be a forgery, it shows a battery of three soldiers and another guy who's obviously in charge, and they're firing mortars off into the distance. Do you suppose it's a coincidence?"

He stood, too, smiling. "I thought you didn't believe in coincidences. Perhaps he bought it to remind him he'd been given a second chance to make up for what he'd done."

"Thanks, Abe. You know, Chad was in Vietnam too. Do you think he might have a connection to all this?"

"Lots of guys in Vietnam. Thousands. Now that *would* be a coincidence."

Chapter Thirty-Four

After visiting Abe Calipher and going back home to a dinner of chicken and noodles I had frozen a couple of weeks earlier, I drove to Priscilla's. Chad's car was in the lot. He'd told me he was meeting friends for a drink or two after work. He came in early and put in hours so he could leave. It made sense to give him flexible hours. I was getting used to having Chad around—he was good company, and I'd practically forgotten his name was Charles McKenna. He was handy too. He'd fixed several things that needed basic skills, like working with an electric screwdriver or a wrench. In the back of my mind, I thought about my conversation with Abe. I genuinely liked Chad, but could he have taken this job at the art center for a different reason than boredom?

I was glad he'd taken a class in fused glass. It helped him understand better what we were about, and he'd enjoyed it thoroughly. I loved to talk with him—often to the detriment of getting jobs of my own done—and as we got to know each other, I learned more about his wife and kids. He knew every little thing going on in Apple Grove, from the minister who left under a cloud because of an affair with a hot, red-headed parishioner to the owners of a new Mexican restaurant going into an old building on South Main Street. Between Chad and Louise—whose family extended into all kinds of helpful areas—I didn't need an old-fashioned Rolodex or a list of contacts. All I needed was to mention a problem, and either Chad or Louise had options.

As I walked into Priscilla's, Wiley came toward me from the far end of the bar. I stopped and sat on a stool.

"What's up?" he asked.

"Does something have to be for me to come see my best bud?"

He smiled. "She'll be back in a while. Things have been quiet, too quiet. It makes me wonder what you're up to."

"*Moi?* I've been good." I didn't mention the DNA conversation or the pending tests that would help me figure out my parentage. Angie's the only one I told. We had enough dirt on each other to ensure closed mouths forever. Most of that dirt involved both of us, like the time we'd had too much to drink at the lake one summer in high school, and we'd used each other's houses to tell our parents where we'd be. They bought it until Andy blabbed. But we got him back. Don't ask me how. That secret will go to our graves.

"Angie's mom called, and she went to help her with a problem. I didn't hear the whole story."

"Thanks, Wiley. I'll hang around a bit. Honest, I've been so busy with the art center I haven't had time to do much else." I walked over to the far end of the bar and stared out at the main floor filled with tables and evening imbibers. Seeing Chad and Chance, I went over to their table.

"Mind if I join you?"

"Have a chair. We were just laying bets on the winner of the football game this weekend," Chad said.

Chance was watching a television screen behind me with rows of football statistics on it. "Here, take a seat." He pulled out a chair. "What'll you have?"

I told him a Bent River Uncommon Stout, and he left to catch Wiley's attention. Meanwhile, I sat next to Chad and said, "You know, we may make an artist out of you yet."

He laughed. "Never thought I could do anything like that. I must admit it was fun, and when I took home the leaf I made, Sandy set it right out on the coffee table. I may try another class. We'll see. Keeps me out of her hair."

"Good. And I think your suggestion for a senior group is fantastic. I've had twenty-five RSVPs. Wednesday morning. We'll see if they all show up."

Chad's face beamed. "Wow."

Chance was back. He handed me the beer and sat across from Chad and me.

"Thanks. You didn't have to buy me a beer."

"Nonsense. My pleasure."

He held up his beer bottle, and we all clinked. Then he said, "I guess you have a little more time to relax now the art show's installed. I don't think I've ever been to an art gallery before. You have amazing paintings on the walls. I might have to come back over and study it all a little more closely."

"Absolutely. That's what it's all about. I'm glad you came, especially if it's your first time."

"Tom back yet?" Chad asked.

"Now, how do you know Tom's gone?"

"Little escapes me in Apple Grove. Actually, I was driving past the airport and saw him getting out of his car with an overnight bag."

"Oh. I think he's on a trip for his job. He's often in and out."

"When will he be back?" Chad asked.

"Why?"

"Just curious," Chad said.

"I don't know. Whenever he's done, I guess."

Someone put money in the jukebox, and Jason Aldean's "Whiskey Me Away" came on.

"I hope you come back and check out the rest of the artwork in the exhibit," I said to Chance. "Chad has no choice. He has to come every night. Were there any pieces you especially liked?"

He leaned back in his chair, the front legs coming off the floor, and rubbed his chin. "I'd have to think about it a bit. Hmm. There was a painting I think you call an abstract. Lots of splashes of orange, yellow, and black. Very striking."

I smiled. "Oh, yes. That's by Julie Quan, who lives in the UP of Michigan. And yes, it is an abstract. It's one of my favorites too."

Chad stirred. "Chance here is starting to think about going back to classes to become a paramedic."

I raised an eyebrow. "I guess I'm not sure what the difference is between an EMT and a paramedic."

"A paramedic is kind of a glorified EMT," Chance said. "He's an EMT with more training hours so he gets paid better. You'll see him more often in charge."

"I see. What made you want to go into this line of work? I hope I'm not being nosey, but I don't know much about what EMTs do."

Cleary yawned. "Sorry. Late night last night. I spent time in the Iraqi War. Desert Storm in the early nineties. I was in Special Forces. We went in ahead of everyone else and scoped out the landscape. Helped liberate Kuwait in record time." He paused and took a gulp of beer. "Guess it was the adrenaline rush. Once I got back to the States, I found life dull. Talking to buddies who knew far more than I did, I learned about EMTs. Now that's an adrenaline rush. Emergencies, having to think fast, be organized and logical, but all while keeping control of situations…it's what I'd been missing. I'm not the most patient guy in the world, but this job has taught me self-discipline. I'm still working on patience."

Chad laughed. "You have a way to go on that one."

"And you get to help people?" I asked.

"Sure. Helping people's part of it too. This afternoon we had a cardiac arrest, and he's alive and well at the hospital. There's that."

Chad pointed his thumb at Cleary. "Chance here is kinda a rolling stone. He's lived in lots of places."

"Is that so? What brought you here?"

"I heard about the job at the hospital from a buddy who works in Chicago. He mentioned the hospital here was hunting for an EMT for their ambulance service. I like smaller towns like this. It's been perfect. If I pick up more hours, I'll make more money, and the prices here are so much lower than in places like Chicago."

"Makes sense to me," I said. "And we've appreciated your help at the art center. It's mostly volunteer work." I felt someone approaching and turned to look. Sam. He walked over, and I stood and gave him a hug. "Hi."

He took a deep breath. "Chad, Cleary. Keeping my girl company?"

"Just trying to fight off the other guys who might get ideas," said Chad, laughing.

"Thanks." We sat, and Sam set a beer on the table. "Long day. You got out of the hospital in time, Chance. Had a bit of a lineup by the time you left."

Chance sat back. "Sorry to leave you in the lurch. Andrews came at the end of my shift, so I figured he could handle it."

Sam took a swig of his beer and turned to me. "I heard the Angelini guy you were talking about was arrested. Think he's the one?"

"The one?" Chad said.

"The one who killed Judge Spivey, I'd guess," said Sam.

I set down my beer. "He's definitely on my list of possibilities. Tom is running a lot of loose ends down right now."

Chance added, "I figured for sure the Spiveys might be involved. There was no love lost between them and their old man. You should have heard the things they said."

"They aren't off my list yet, and I imagine Tom is still checking them out," I said. "They keep popping up in town on weekends. Makes me nervous."

Sam leaned over and grabbed a handful of peanuts sitting in a dish on the table. "If not them, then who? This Angelini guy?"

I shook my head. "I have no clue." I couldn't say anything about what Tom and I had discussed. 'Loose lips sink ships,' my dad had always said. I had no idea what he'd meant by that, but it sounded appropriate.

Chad looked at Cleary, then at me. "I think Jezbhel Gushman said she planned to research the judge's past in the Vietnam War. I have no clue why. She didn't explain. Seemed kinda crazy to me."

His words startled me. Tom was checking into the judge's past too. I glanced over at Sam and noted his beer bottle was empty, and both Chad and Chance were looking at me expectantly as if I had a reply to his thought. "So, Dr. Finch. I'm exhausted and figure it's time to go home. I hope you don't mind if I leave."

"No," he said and smiled. "I won't be here long either. I'll walk you out to your car."

"Thanks. 'Night, Chad and Chance. Thanks for the conversation and the beer."

We walked to my car, and I unlocked the door. "You know, that Chance is really a smart guy," I said. "And he seems very disciplined."

"Probably comes from being in the service. He's a great EMT—knows his stuff and is smart and quick-thinking."

I nodded. "That's been my take too. He doesn't talk much about himself, where he's been and all."

"Well,"—Sam reached over and straightened the collar on my blouse—"some guys are like that. I know he served in the Middle East. That's about it."

Sam left me after an amazingly tender kiss or two, and I got in my car and drove back to the house. Before I went to bed, I set up my coffeemaker for the morning, put out some papers I needed to take in to work, and checked my phone. Just before I turned out the light, I told myself I hadn't taken Erika Spivey or Peter Angelini off my list of possible suspects, but this constant mention of Vietnam on the part of several of my friends was intriguing. A new rabbit hole to explore.

Chapter Thirty-Five

After work on Tuesday, Angie stopped by my house. We opened a bottle of Savvy B, our current favorite, sat on the deck, and stared out at the tree leaves of Naples yellow, saffron, and scarlet. Gorgeous.

"I love autumn in the Midwest," Angie said. "It's as if you're on another planet. All the greens suddenly explode into vibrant color. A strange planet. I never get tired of it."

I smiled. "This is hardly a conversation we would have had as teenagers. Trees. Sounds like my parents. We must be getting old." I filled each of our glasses a little higher. That might take the senior citizen conversation off in a younger direction.

"Tom still out in New York?"

"Yup. I keep thinking it would be cool to have this case of his about the judge's death wrapped in a bow by the time he comes home. But it's been three, almost four weeks since the judge died. I feel like I'm disappointing him."

"Tom or the judge?"

"The judge."

"He's dead. How can you disappoint him?"

"Oh, you know what I mean. It's like the guilt parents put on you. I'm feeling it. I thought it would be so easy to figure this all out, but no. I guess it's why Tom's the detective, and I'm a mere art curator."

"Don't sell yourself short. As an art curator, you should be running up the steps like Rocky out in Philadelphia, considering all the success you've had."

Angie took another sip of her wine. "We figured out who killed Carolyn. We can do it again. And I brought my iPad as you requested, but I'm not sure why."

I watched a cardinal fly from the bushes beside my art studio to a tree at the back of the property. "I don't think Patterson killed the judge. He's too stupid. Couldn't even kill a target as large as Editor Gushman."

"You know, Tom always says good detective work takes lots of time and concentration on putting together the details. He may be a plodder, but in the long run, Tom usually gets his man."

"Or woman."

"True. What's on your mind? I figure you didn't call this meeting to sink into the slough of despondency about our useless investigation so far."

"I came up with a thought...or two."

"Anything I can help you with?"

I set my glass on the small table between us. "Yes. I've been mulling over the connection to the past with this whole story. Even Patterson had a connection between his anger over his dishonorable discharge from the army."

"You think someone from Vietnam came back here to kill him?"

"I don't know, but it's worth investigating. We know one of the guys in the photo is dead, killed by what they called 'friendly fire.'"

"How do we find out anything else?"

"Good question. I'll run in and get my laptop. You open your iPad and connect to my internet. We have detail-digging to do."

I watched Angie take her iPad out of the bag next to her chair and power up as I walked into the house. Then I returned with my laptop. "I started thinking about who might have this information or be able to get it."

"Oh. I didn't realize you knew anyone in the State Department."

I chuckled. "I don't. But I know someone in the FBI, and she can find out anything. I called Agent Powers, who left me her card when she was here talking to Tom. I asked her about the three names of the Vietnam guys in the photo with the judge, and she faxed me information to the art center this afternoon. I played loose and said the info was for Tom. Here."

I handed Angie the fax sheets and watched her scan them quickly.

"Wow. They're from all over the place."

"True. I'll start with Sid Graham, and you see what you can find on Liam Axel, the guy who died."

We both started clicking keyboards, concentrating on following one link after another.

"I've got it," Angie said after about ten minutes. "Liam Axel from Georgetown, Kentucky. Evidently, they breed horses and make bourbon there. Thirty-seven thousand people. Near Lexington. The *Lexington Chronicle* had an obituary and a photo. He died December 3, 1968."

"That isn't November 17, is it?"

"Nope," Angie said. "Gosh, he was only twenty years old. Really handsome. Check him out." She turned the screen toward me. "There's an article a few days earlier naming the province where he died, and he was killed by friendly fire." She clicked a few more keys. "The obituary says he was one of those kids who found themselves in Vietnam because of the draft. He couldn't have killed the judge recently because he was dead and, according to this obit, he was an only child. What a terrible thing for his parents. I can see why the other guys might have wanted to remember him, but a tattoo seems kind of weird."

"It shows the closeness of the group. A tattoo can be removed, but it would be a constant reminder long after Vietnam."

Angie still clicked an occasional key. "What did you find about Graham?"

I was still scanning the screen. "He was from a small town in Ohio. Cambridge. He's dead too. He went back home, married, had three children, and was politically involved in the town. Thirteen thousand population. He was on the city council and involved in a lot of philanthropic organizations, like Judge Spivey."

"What did he die of?"

I scanned the end of the obituary. "Might have been cancer. One of the memorial organizations is the American Cancer Society. Left behind the three kids and seven grandchildren." Still scanning the article, I gasped.

"What?"

217

"There's a short story—just a small column—after his death. It says someone left a half dozen black roses on his grave at Northwood Cemetery. And there's a plea from the editor for people to stop playing practical jokes."

"OMG. That's morbid."

"It was last winter. Don't you see, Angie? Someone is out there doing this black rose thing. Does it say anything about Axel or black roses?"

"Nothing. But it was a long time ago. He died in 1968."

I switched screens. "I'll check on Ted Bender. The judge had his name written on a sticky note. Perhaps he planned to call him or did call him after receiving those black petal cards. He could have some valuable information."

"I'm going in to use your bathroom. See what you can find."

I pecked away at the laptop keys, checking out Huntsville, Texas, which was the town Ted Bender was from. It was a town of 47,000 on the east side of the state. As it turned out, all was a dead end. Ted Bender had died in a car accident several weeks earlier. I kept nosing around, looking through the *Huntsville Ledger.* A day before Bender's death, someone cleared out his bank account. Some unknown person walked into the First National Bank and took out all his savings. None of it turned up after his death.

"Well?" Angie said, walking back through the sliding deck doors.

I explained to her what I'd found. "Weird stuff here." After clicking on a connected link, I happened onto another gasper. "Listen to this about Bender, Angie. 'According to the state police who worked the scene of his death, a black rose was found on the back seat of his car.'" I stared into the yard, the bushes beginning to darken as dusk came on. Then I said, "By the time the judge read this, he'd bought the gun he kept in his desk."

"What? Do you suppose this unknown person has killed everyone in that group, and the judge was the last one for him to target? Except for Axel and the guy who had cancer. He didn't get to the cancer guy fast enough."

I glanced down at the keys on my laptop and shook my head back and forth. "It sure sounds that way. Angie, who could it be? There was no one else in the group."

Angie lifted the wine bottle and poured a few last drops in her glass. "I don't know."

I gazed at my studio in the yard. "Maybe Liam Axel wasn't killed by such friendly fire. Chad said events were often crazy in the chaos of battle."

"So, except for the cancer guy who got the black roses, you figure someone is killing this rose tattoo group, and the judge was the last victim?"

"It sure looks that way."

We both sat in silence, digesting this idea. Angie finally stirred.

"You were right. The Vietnam connection is real. Their past caught up with them."

I looked at her. "But who?"

Chapter Thirty-Six

After a night of tossing and turning, I got up on Wednesday morning, showered, and ate an English muffin before leaving for work. I was so tired. My brain was exhausted too. Black roses. They floated through my dreams all night. Fatigues. Army boots. Rifles. The judge must have known who was after them because he'd bought a gun. But who did he suspect? I threw my hands in the air. I hadn't a clue.

I walked to work, enjoyed the gorgeous trees, and smelled the leaves and an occasional smoky scent indicating people were burning them. The sights and smells of fall in my town. It brought back so many memories. Over on the corner near the Wendovers' house was where we had piled a huge tower of leaves and had ridden our bikes through them. When we played "monster" at night, it was a dead giveaway the person who was "it" was walking through leaves and gave her location away. And then there was "kick the can," a game we played for hours, night after night. We shouted and ran around till after dark before our moms called us in for a shower and bedtime. To be so young again with no other responsibilities. I didn't realize then how much harder life would be once I grew up, or how lucky I was to have had that childhood.

I watched the clock in my office, and at nine-thirty, I went out to the gallery and began arranging chairs with Louise's help. The new senior group was meeting at ten, and it would be exciting to see what they thought about this idea. As the digital numbers on the clock moved toward the hour, people came in the front door, the bell chiming each time. A few stragglers wandered in late, and I waited until people had had time to have conversations. Chad was there, along with several folks who already volunteered or were on our board. We didn't have an age bracket. I guess anyone who thought of themselves as seniors could come.

Once they had all settled in, we talked about the purpose of the group. Lots of people had opinions.

"To learn about artists and their techniques."

"It doesn't only have to be about artists of paintings or drawings, does it?"

"No, we could include local writers. They're artists too."

"And how about people who teach our classes at the art center? Might they have other artistic endeavors to talk about?"

"Could we tap a few art professors at the college to talk?"

"And the weavers. Couldn't they talk about how they make material and turn it into lovely things?"

We had an outstanding conversation, and I thought about my mom, whose name graced our building, and how wonderful she would have felt if she'd known how our little art center was encouraging people to learn about all forms of creativity. This was the whole point of the art center in her name: to educate people in the region about art, and to enable them to create art themselves. My mother had often said of the surrounding Midwest area, "People can't live on corn and beans alone. The arts give them a reason to live." As I considered their enthusiasm and ideas, I had to turn away for a few seconds, wiping the tears from my eyes with a tissue. I was such an emotional putz when it came to art, my mother, or a combination of the two.

They agreed to meet once a month, on Wednesdays at ten in the morning. A committee would provide refreshments and devise a list of programs at the next meeting. This would give them time to think about all that.

Chad stuck around a few minutes after the bell jangled on the door with the group's leaving.

"You appear a little tired," he said. "Having sleep problems?"

I sighed. "Oh, I'm trying to work out a problem about the judge's murder. Wish I could figure it out before Tom comes back from New York."

He tilted his head slightly. "Thought that was his problem."

"It is, but I feel a responsibility. The judge was my mentor and friend, and I owe him my job when things were going south here a few months ago. I'd like to find who killed him and see them brought to justice."

He paused a minute, thinking about what I'd said. "You know, second chances ain't given to make things right. They let us prove we can do better. Obviously, you did. I think you've already paid him back."

"Hmm. Interesting thought, Chad. You could be right."

An hour later, I was sitting in my office studying the photographs on my wall. It made me think of the judge's photo. Four men. All soldiers in an unpopular war. It seemed useless. My mind kept going in circles. I'd never find the judge's killer. I took a sip of coffee. I knew what the four had in common. It meant more information. I'd call Special Agent Powers again and hope I hadn't outworn my welcome.

Around two, Sam dropped in and took me out for ice cream again at Angela's Ice Cream. He talked to Louise in the gallery while I was finishing the last page of a report. I could hear them from my office. He was sweet-talking her, and she was eating it up. She already thought he was the perfect man for me.

"OK, let's go," I said as I closed my office door.

"Want us to bring you back ice cream, Louise?" Sam said.

She thought for a moment. "Nah. I'm fine. Have a good time, you two."

We walked hand-in-hand to the ice cream shop, listening to the leaves rustle as a gentle breeze blew them around on the sidewalk. I felt as if my whole body smiled.

"Thanks for saving me from the mundane world of board reports."

He smiled and stopped. "All work and no play, you know." Then he turned and kissed me lightly on the mouth. He tasted like peppermint.

We turned and stopped in at the shop where Cam and Minh were busy taking care of a group of five teenagers. Cam stood behind the freezer full of ice cream and smiled at us. Most people like to see the start of a lovely relationship. Once we'd gotten our ice cream, we sat at a table, licking ice cream from the sides of the cones, me, blackberry crunch, and Sam, strawberry cheesecake. "Have a good morning?" I asked.

"Quiet. Kinda boring, but that's fine. Cleary had a busy day, but mostly trips out and not serious problems. I'm working till ten tonight, so this is a treat to be able to see the two things I like a lot: ice cream—"

"—and?"

"Louise."

We both laughed.

"Nah. You. Big plans for the rest of the day?"

"Not sure." I licked some ice cream rolling over the cone. "Angie and I plan to get together. She's going to help me with some odds and ends at work since the opening is over. I have some organizing to do. We'll see. I've been checking out details about Judge Spivey's past."

"You seem a bit obsessed with that. Maybe you should leave it to Tom."

"I would because he's a great, but slow-moving detective. This is grunt work."

"Sounds like the tedious paperwork I have to do at the hospital. Much of my life is exactly that, reports and paperwork. My dad was a doctor—"

Now this was news. "He was?"

"Yeah, you know, the kind who actually made house calls. A simpler time. And his father before him, who drove around in a horse and buggy to make calls. Sounds like nostalgia, but sometimes I think it would be much better if my work concentrated more on my patients and less on all the paperwork."

"I hear you." I licked more dribbles from my cone, almost done.

And then, scampering in a new direction, he said, "Someday, you must tell me what happened with your friend who was killed, you know, the one you mentioned who was buried in the basement of the art center."

I paused. "Yes. Buried in the basement. Horrifying. Someday if we have some time, and I'm not sure about breaking the romantic ambiance with a horror story, I will."

"Of course, I know how it ended because you came to my ER."

I closed my eyes tightly. "I don't want to think about that. In fact, it's amazing, after seeing me, covered in sweat and vomit, that you even wanted to talk to me again."

"Well, Ms. Madison, I've seen far worse. Glad you're still alive."

"Yes, Tom gave me a good dressing down after that one."

"Really? Does this mean you're staying on the sidelines now, just doing the research, and staying away from killers?"

"Absolutely. Strictly cerebral work."

Back at the art center, I almost jumped when the fax machine came on in the corner of my office. Information from Agent Powers or possibly answers to questions I'd asked earlier of an art center in San Francisco. I walked over, waited for it to stop magically whirring, and pulled out the papers. Agent Powers.

I read the first few lines. "The court-martial you asked me about involving Second Lieutenant Ron Spivey and Privates Graham, Axel, and Bender is included. Also, information on the incident involving the death of Private Liam Axel not quite a month later. Tell Tom I said good luck."

It was only a small fib making her think Tom was working on this. I'd told her he was out of town but had left jobs for me to do to tie up loose ends. It didn't hurt anything.

I began reading the information. The first thing it told me was that I was on the right path because of the date of the court-martial: November 17, 1968. Wow. My hunch was right. This did have something to do with the black rose tattoo group. I read through the details of the court-martial that exonerated them and noted the name of the soldier who was killed: Private James Manwaring. He died by a mortar round fired with the wrong coordinates. It led to the load of guilt the judge carried. Could be they had been too high to get things right that night. As I knew from Abe, the court-martial exonerated the four soldiers. I glanced through the rest of her notes. Manwaring was twenty-five years old, from Lincoln, Nebraska.

Back to my computer. I began searching for an obituary in the archives of the biggest Lincoln newspaper. This would take a while. Finally, I located it. The photograph was old, and I could hardly see his face well. There was a photograph of his wife holding the flag given to her at his funeral. She had dark glasses on and a scarf over what might be blond hair. Could she still be alive? If he was twenty-five in 1968 and she was even close to his age, she'd be seventy-three this year. Hardly someone running around puncturing peoples' arms with hypodermic needles. Then I remembered the elderly Miss Marple. Well, maybe. I sat back in my seat and thought about that. She could still be alive, have a different name, and be here in Apple Grove looking to avenge his death. But why wait all these years? It didn't make any sense. Stupid theory.

I began typing again and did another search for any Manwaring in the obituaries. It must have been a common family name because there were at least five in the archives. After skimming through each one, I found an obituary for Anna Mae Manwaring. She must not have remarried or left the area, and she was preceded in death by her husband, James Manwaring.

Well, this was a dead end. I'd have to let everything simmer for a while, like the best meals. I'd do some thinking about this rose tattoo group. Plenty of time before Tom returns.

Chapter Thirty-Seven

I t was Thursday evening, and I was sitting at my desk in the art center. When we talked yesterday, Angie volunteered to help me organize some things at the center. I had to laugh because she'd texted me our secret code from high school, which was a classic. CODE RED was our signal, meaning either "danger" or "hot guy in the vicinity." We always knew which. Yesterday it was a hot guy who delivered beer to the bar. It was silly and innocent, but little traditions like this were part of our shared happiness. Angie-Jill talk, just between the two of us.

Angie was down in the first-floor classroom where the weavers met. There were several corners of the room where things had been thrown into piles after the opening. It all needed organizing. Several long tables sat in the middle of the room, and Angie could spread piles of fabric or paper piles on the table and sort through them. Besides objects left over from the opening that needed to go up in the storage area, stacks of art project items were spread out all over the room. They needed organizing too. She could line up sides in a bar argument, award the winner, and send the loser home smiling without breaking a sweat, so I knew this would be no problem for my girl, Angie.

I glanced at my sports watch. Seven thirty. I'd been working on the accounts for an hour. I'd already texted Angie about mundane things like who was helping Wiley at the bar tonight. She texted me back he'd hired a temp. I could hear country music and occasional scraping noises on the floor upstairs, which meant Chad was moving chairs around as he cleaned. Otherwise, it was quiet and calm, the perfect atmosphere to get work done.

Pulling out a promotional piece I'd been working on, I checked for errors before it went to the printer. I began humming a song I'd heard yesterday as I realized that the promotional piece was in great shape. Very little to do there. Then I heard a knock on the alley door. I rose from my chair, walked to the alley door, and looked out. Andy. I let him in.

"I saw all the lights on and wondered what was going on so late."

"I have a stack of work for the board meeting coming up and am very, very busy. It's OK. Chad is here upstairs. I'm not alone."

He glanced around suspiciously. "Where's Angie?"

"If you must know, Angie's here too. She's helping me with some organizing. Sometimes I'm so busy during the day I can't get everything done. So, I put in some evening work."

He looked around. "Evening work. That's what I worry about with you. Tom isn't here, and you've had a few warnings lately. Tom mentioned a written threat. Remember the car accident? Maybe I should stick around and make sure you get home all right."

Once again, I was the youngest in the family. If Tom weren't here, I guess Andy sprang into action. There was nothing to fear tonight in the building. Three of us were here, and the doors were locked. I figured I'd change the subject rather than argue with him. "Thanks for helping me with the DNA test for Tom's gift."

"Sounded like a great idea." He looked around once again. "I'm headed home. It's good Chad is here, and don't stay too late. You have my number—if you worry about anything, call me."

"I won't stay much longer, Andy. It's fine." I was thirty years old, and my brothers still treated me like I was a kid.

He looked around again over my shoulder. "If you're sure you'll be safe, I'll go. Oh, and lock the door again." He went out the alley door, and I locked the door behind him.

I rest my case. They all worried too much.

Back to my desk. I could hear the music from upstairs, but Chad must have finished moving the classroom chairs around. I checked my phone. Seven fifty. I thought I heard a noise on the first floor, but then nothing. I was hearing things. Darn, Andy. He had me spooked. Back to work.

Then, I heard pounding on the alley door. I walked down the hallway, figuring Andy elected himself to be my bodyguard. This time it was Chance Cleary. Geez. The whole world was coming to my art center tonight.

"Hi, Jill. Saw the lights on. Is Chad here? I need to check with him on something."

"Sure," I said. "Upstairs. Follow the music."

I shut the door, locked it, and went back to my office with all the paperwork piled on my desk. I was humming a country tune I'd heard from Chad's radio. Four files later, I began thinking about the rose tattoo group. Suddenly, it hit me. By *not* thinking about my research, my mind had sorted through the online obituaries I'd read. That was it! I glanced at my watch. Almost eight-fifteen. I needed to tell Angie my amazing discovery that would lead us straight to the judge's killer. She was probably done organizing colored paper and watching a video on her phone.

Then I did hear something. Footsteps. Quiet, stealthy. I could hear my heartbeat surge. I held my breath. Nothing. I crooked my neck, listening intently. Hmm. I texted Angie, but she didn't answer. Maybe I should go see if the footsteps I heard were hers. Or maybe it was Chad. I left my office, stopping at the top of the steps that went down to the weaver's room. That was strange. The lights were off. Staring hard at the corner of the room where she'd been sitting quietly on the floor organizing various colors of papers, I made out her shape. There was just enough light from the streetlamp outside the back door. Oh, my God. I flipped on the light switch. She had tape over her mouth and around her ankles, and her hands were behind her back. Her eyes got huge, and she began making muffled sounds. She was staring past me.

"Mmm. Mmm," she said in muffled tones. Her eyes were huge, her taped-up mouth impossible to understand.

I turned, searched the hallway, and my heart practically stopped. A man was standing there, a ski mask over his head. My pulse raced, and my breath became ragged, like I was hyperventilating. Then I realized I was holding my breath. I felt in my pants pocket for my phone. "Is this what you're looking for?" He held up my phone, dropped it on the floor, and smashed it. Even so, I heard a ping and knew exactly whose text it was. Even with my phone smashed, Ivan could get through. I'm a little tied up here, Ivan. I stared at my smashed phone. Tom told me I should have paid for insurance. And that's when I realized there were a few safety contingencies I hadn't thought about when it came to working at night.

Before I could even think, the black wraith came forward, grabbed my arm, and marched me back to my office. I could see he had plastic gloves on, the better to get away with whatever he planned to do. He dropped me in my desk chair, reached in a bag that had been over his shoulder, and brought out a huge roll of duct tape. I didn't know who this was, a nameless, faceless specter.

He swiftly unrolled a long piece of tape and taped my arm to the chair arm. I always heard duct tape had so many uses but taping someone to a chair wasn't one I'd had at the top of my list.

"Why? Why are you doing this?" I tried to protest and slap him with my free hand as he kept ducking my arm.

"Because you can't leave well enough alone. And"—he paused, grabbing my other arm— "once you started stirring up the past, that would not stand."

My other arm was bound, too, I watched as he pulled out more tape. I tried to kick him, but he was agile and managed to tape both legs to the chair.

"This'll keep you still at least."

I thought about Chad cleaning upstairs. The masked guy saw me looking up.

"Don't figure on anyone helping you."

"You didn't hurt him, did you?"

"Nothing a little time won't heal." He stood back from the desk, examined his handiwork, and set his bag next to him on the floor.

By now, I recognized his voice. "You aren't Chance Cleary," I spit out.

"You're correct about that."

I knew who he was simply by seeing his eyes through the holes in the mask. And it now made sense after researching the death of James Manwaring and his wife. Then he pulled the mask off. Startled, I sagged in my chair. "When I read your parents' obituaries, something didn't quite click. Blond hair like your mother, and an only child, a boy."

"It's too bad. I genuinely liked you, and I decided to stick around because I grew fond of this small town. But now I'll have to go once your funeral's over, and no one notices my departure. Too bad. When your detective brother gets back, it'll be too late."

"It was about the court-martial in Vietnam, and you sent the black rose petals and the note to me sounding like Erika Spivey." I felt triumphant despite my present inability to even move.

He let out a long breath. "My mother died last year. She wasn't an imaginative woman except about my father. I was only four when he died. A hero, she said. Someone who'd earned a lot of medals and died saving the lives of men in his unit. I could be proud, she said." He stopped a moment as if listening for a sound in the art center. "Do you know what it's like growing up without a father?"

I should keep him talking. Taped to this chair, I couldn't figure a way out of this. Angie was stuck in the classroom, but perhaps Chad would come down. That was my only hope. We were locked in, and Andy was gone. Why, oh why, had I pushed him out the door? I considered Chance Manwaring. Maybe a sympathetic reaction would work, or at least keep him talking. "I imagine it must have been awful. Not having a father."

"Awful doesn't cut it. I never had a dad like other kids. It left an indelible mark on my life, my emotions. But at least I could slug the other kid and tell him my dad died a hero serving his country. My mom had his medals in a case in his study to prove it."

"How did you find out?"

"About the true story? After she died. I was cleaning out her house, and among her papers I found this letter from the army about my dad. James Manwaring, killed by friendly fire. How could this be? Why would my mother lie?"

This was it. The reason he was sitting here talking to me with little emotion. He needed an audience. Someone to hear why he had killed two men and attempted to kill the newspaper editor. I hadn't been able to figure out why a person would wait decades to seek revenge, but because he only learned the truth when his mother died, that was the answer.

"I hacked into the army archives and discovered the hearing and the four men who'd killed him. It was all buried. But the notes of one of the judges said they were drunk and had smoked marijuana while they were on duty. No wonder they got the coordinates wrong. Spivey. I saved him for last." His voice took on a pleading note. "All I wanted to do was find them and make them admit their guilt. But when I realized how well they were living when my father never had a chance to have a life because of them, I couldn't stop myself. They didn't deserve to live."

I stared into his eyes. They seemed almost blank, emotionless.

"The judge and I had a nice chat before he died. I'd called him the night before, said I was Ted Bender's son, and I wanted to give him a message from my dad. He fell for it. Once I told him who I was that morning, he was confused at first. He got it—a life for a life. Because of him, I didn't have a father. Oh, he pleaded a bit at first. But this was the end of my mission and the end of the story. Now I can go live my life without this hanging over my head. He had a peaceful death, at least. You'll have the same."

My mind sputtered, trying to think logically. Stall for time. "Why did you try to kill Gushman?"

"Stupid woman. She was going to research the judge's war history. She'd be sure to find out about the trial and my father. Then she'd stumble on the deaths of the tattoo group."

"But why me, Chance? I didn't have anything to do with it."

"You're collateral damage. Because he said you were like the daughter he'd never had. His two other kids were worthless. We sat in his office having coffee and talking about the life he'd had since he'd murdered my father. I figured it was the right thing to do—to cut the branches from the tree. You could join them. Besides, you never stopped. All you could talk about was figuring this out. I ran you off the road, thinking it would warn you to stop. But no. You had to keep digging."

Never, ever, would I tell Tom that my stupid digging had put me in this position. Who was I kidding? I wouldn't have a chance to tell him. And then I thought, *his two other kids? Was I the third?* But I said, "Join them?"

"Yeah. I went to the Ohio town where Graham lived. He'd died of cancer a month before, so he escaped me. Bender lived in Texas. He was a retired cop. Told him I was the son of an old army buddy. Got drunk together, and he talked about this rose tattoo group in Vietnam. Guess they drank and smoked weed a lot and were hell-raisers. I'd show him. I cleaned out his retirement savings after confronting him. Then I set up a one-car accident. He was so out of it, I didn't have any problem. Word around town was he was a drunk, and they couldn't get him off of the force fast enough. I wonder if his life in the bottom of a bottle had gone in that direction because of his guilt over my father's murder?"

"I can understand your pain. Seeing these lives of the men who were involved in that terrible night. It would be hard to carry those facts around. But with Ted Bender, it sounds like you didn't need to punish him. He'd punished himself for decades."

His voice took on a more belligerent tone. "God didn't punish *any* of them. Especially Spivey. Look at the life he had after killing my father. Where's the justice in that? Well, now he's had his sentence. All of them are gone."

"And none of them deserved a second chance?"

"Why? After what they did to my family? To me? No. Killing was too good for them."

Now anxiety crawled up my arms and into my brain. Knowing what he'd done to the judge, I began to sweat, feeling the beads trickle down my neck. I couldn't think of a single way to stop him. How could I get help? Angie and Chad were out. All the doors were locked. Andy and Tom were gone. More sweat trickled down my back. I tried to pull my arms up. It was no use. Reason didn't seem to work, but I'd try one last time. "This is ridiculous. Everyone deserves a second chance, especially if they understand what they did wrong and vow to do better."

"You bleeding hearts amaze me. No one gave my dad a second chance. Now it's time to make sure I leave here and clean up the details, nice and tidy."

I watched as he searched on the floor beside him where he'd dropped his bag. Reaching down, he pulled out a syringe and a small bottle. Oh, God, no. Whatever was in that bottle would kill me quickly. How could I stop him? I thought about Andy and wished he'd come back again. Or Tom, who wouldn't know what happened to me. Sam was at work. I took several deep breaths as I watched him with the tiny bottle, turning it upside down, filling the syringe, flicking it. Slowly, carefully, methodically. I began screaming, "Help!"

"That won't do any good. No one's around to hear you."

He stood and began to move toward my desk, the syringe in his right hand. My lips trembled, and I bit my lower lip till it hurt. My heart was pounding, my breathing was so hard, and I could feel my legs shake despite the tape. There was nothing I could think of to do. I tried to move my arms again, but they were pinned tight by the tape.

Just then, there was a movement at the door of my office. Angie. She had tape over her mouth, her hands behind her back, and tape around her ankles. How did she get up here? I tried not to look at her so he wouldn't follow my eyes. Concentrate on him. I had to keep myself from looking at Angie. She'd see Manwaring with his mask off, and he'd kill her too.

As Chance moved toward my desk, Angie—her blond ponytail flying around her face like an avenging angel—gave a muffled scream and came hopping across the room like a kangaroo, jumping and jumping until she leaned over and head-butted Chance. He'd turned to see where the noise was coming from, but too late. He fell toward my desk, hitting his head on the corner, and dropped to the floor. Angie was right on top of him. Angie, my best bud who always had my back.

Now what? Taped to a chair, I was unable to move, and I could scream, but no one was around to hear me. Angie was like a turtle upside down in its shell, making muffled noises. What if Chance regained consciousness? What a fine mess this was! Angie could move slightly, and I could scream at the walls but couldn't move. Something was very wrong with this picture.

That's when I heard steps plodding down the stairs. Chad came around the corner, his hand holding the back of his head.

He looked up at me. "Jill? What the heck? Am I hallucinating after this bump on the head?"

"Hurry, Chad. Find the syringe on the floor and break it. Check and see if he's alive. Angie's muffled voice urged him to help her. No, help Angie up first. No! First, use my desk phone and call 9-1-1. Then unlock the alley door for the police."

Chad grabbed my desk phone, dialed 9-1-1, reported us, left momentarily, and then returned. He verified Chance was alive, pulled Angie away from the still body beneath her, and put masking tape around Manwaring's wrists.

And that's the way Jake Singleton and Ned Fisher found us after they'd turned their sirens off and come into the art center. Me, taped to a chair, Angie on the floor with duct tape everywhere, Chance Manwaring with his wrists taped and out cold, and Chad holding his head. Ohhh, so glad no one had a camera. If they had, think of the social media hit we'd have been, going viral after catching a killer. This was a CODE RED if I ever saw one.

Chapter Thirty-Eight

"How could you do such a stupid thing?" Tom yelled at Angie and me in his office at the police station. Lack of sleep hadn't helped his disposition. It was the next morning. Mary had called him, and he'd flown back home during the night, and now he was berating us for our foolishness. I had to admit he had a point. The whole reason Chance Manwaring came after me was because I wouldn't stop. Yes, he had a point. After nearly being killed months earlier, I should have learned my lesson. I'm a slow learner.

"But we found the judge's killer and Gushman's almost-killer, and you have him in your jail. Wasn't that what you wanted?" I asked. I felt like I had to justify myself yet again.

He shook his head, moved around to his desk, and sat. He'd been standing over us, yelling at us for a good ten minutes. Not sure I'd ever seen him so angry. Not only had we caught Chance Manwaring, but the newspaper headlines this morning screamed. "Detective's Sister Catches Killer." I winced. I could see why he might be angry.

"Manwaring's in jail for Jezbhel Gushman's attempted murder, your attempted murder, and the judge's actual murder. Gushman boasted about researching Judge Spivey's war background, and Cleary—uh, Manwaring—figured he'd rake up the facts on his father's death. Gushman's muckraking ways finally brought about a serious attempt on her life. You might as well be related to stupid Patterson after pulling such a foolish stunt. Don't you ever let me catch you doing that again. Leave the detecting to me."

Angie glanced at me, then at Tom, and said, "You must admit we're a little faster at this."

"It's because you pay no attention to the legalities. The next time—and there won't be a next time—you'll end up getting some idiot off because you ignored the law. Read my lips. No more investigating."

"Might I remind you that you kept me filled in on this investigation? And—" My phone went off with a text. I'd bought a new phone this morning as soon as the store opened and hadn't changed my number. How stupid of me. I could have had a few days with no Ivan interruptions if I'd changed it.

Ms. Madison. CONGRATULATIONS on catching the art center killer. GOOD publicity for a change. I'll add up the damage and take it out of your celery next month.
     Ivan F. Truelove III

"Even Ivan agrees with me, Tom, although he's evidently paying me in celery now. That should appeal to his misery nature, but I haven't checked out the price of celery lately."

Tom sputtered, his face turned red, and I became a bit concerned.

"Get out of here, both of you."

We both stood and scurried out of his office as fast as we could. He'd forget he was angry in a few days. We'd just have to lie low.

Sam got someone to cover his shift, and we met at Priscilla's that evening for a celebration—that Angie and I were still alive. I'll never get the picture out of my mind: Angie hopping like a kangaroo right into Chance Manwaring. She hopped through my dreams, and I'd wake up laughing. Not sure I'd ever get that picture out of my head. Wiley was not as amused. Angie—my loyal friend forever who always had my back.

When I arrived, Sam came over from the back, put his arms around me, and I melted into them. It was a perfect fit.

"After being the heroine of the day, do you feel like celebrating?"

"Bring it on!"

We settled down with beers, Angie came over, and because it was Friday night, Lance and Andy's band was playing at the bar. Sam, Angie, and I sat at a table, and Chad joined us. Then Andy and Lance surprised me.

"This song is for my little sister, who had quite a day yesterday. And, man, I think she'll understand." With that, they played Jason Aldean's "Good to Go." Angie and I laughed, but Sam wasn't quite so sure he saw the humor. I suppose Tom did have a point. I should have been more cautious. But I'd been thinking for a long time about the judge and all he'd meant to me. As I listened to the lyrics, it reminded me of a conversation I'd had with my mentor on one of those Saturdays not very long ago.

Usually, when we had lunch at his house, we'd have lively discussions about his art collection or artists we didn't agree on, but on this particular day, he'd been a bit nostalgic. I have no idea what caused his state of mind. But I remember, clear as a bell, what he'd said to me about his life. The "Good to Go" song reminded me. The memory was in the context of celebrating the judge's birthday.

"You know, I've been lucky, and I'm humble and grateful for the amazing chances I've had in life. My parents gave me a secure home and foundation, law school honed my mind and created a passion in me, my wife was the love of my life, and I won't regret leaving this life and seeing her once again. But all of this might have come to naught because of a mistake I made, an error in judgment that's haunted me forever. Regret is a useless emotion, and it gnaws away at you. I finally managed to forgive myself, but it took years. I moved on and felt I'd been given a second chance to help people. I considered myself fortunate for that chance. I'm glad you came home and into my life. You've been a reminder second chances are rare, and we must use them well."

Now I knew what he'd meant by that, although at the time I was confused because I didn't know about his past. He believed his work with the law enabled him to right wrongs and atone for his terrible moment in Vietnam. But I hoped his words about our relationship didn't hide something deeper I knew about when it came to my mother. I was of two minds about that. If he were my father, I'd be disappointed in my mother, even though I realized people couldn't always help who they loved. If he weren't my father, I'd feel grateful the knowledge I had of my parents' characters and marriage was true, and the judge was simply grateful for our friendship.

"Penny for your thoughts?" Sam said as he stared at the band and listened to the last chorus.

I laughed. "Andy knows how to pick songs. It reminded me of something the judge said to me about being grateful for the lives we have."

His arm hugged me a little closer, and he agreed.

"Do you mind, Sam, if Angie and I go outside for a few minutes? I need to discuss a problem with her."

"As long as it doesn't involve investigating anyone. I may not always be around to patch you up!"

"No. No more investigations." I nodded to Angie and we both walked past the bar and out the front door with newly opened beers.

"Did you really mean that about no more investigations?" Angie asked.

"I can't imagine Apple Grove is going to have another murder anytime soon. We didn't have much to lose with that promise."

Sitting on a bench overlooking the parking lot, I pulled an envelope out of my jeans pocket.

"What's that?" she asked.

"DNA test is back."

"Oh, my gosh, Jill! What's it say?"

"Don't know. Too scared to open it."

"Hand it to me, sister. I'll find out the truth."

I gave her the letter, my fingers trembling a bit on the envelope. It had been in my pocket all day like a scarlet letter—guilt about my mother? Shame? Concern for my dad? Did I really want to know? Might it not be better to leave it and go about my life with two parents who loved me? I'd be so disappointed in Judge Spivey. He took second chances seriously after the war. If he slept with my mom, it would deeply hurt my belief in my ability to judge character.

Angie tore open the envelope and began scanning the report. Her eyes flew over the contents, saying phrases aloud. "Sibship test. Biological siblings.

We make a genetic profile with a 'sibship index.' Hmm. It's a word I've never heard of before. If your sibship index is less than 1.00, you are not full siblings. The higher the index, the more likely true biological siblings. Test result accuracy is greater than 99.9999 percent."

"Good to know. This means we have the general railings in place. What's our score?" I closed my eyes, squeezed my hands together, and waited. Angie could be so dramatic. It seemed like minutes.

"Uh, scanning, scanning. Ah, here's your sibship number. It was 5.78. You and Andy are full-fledged siblings, which means you share the same two parents. Whew!"

I opened my eyes, smiled, and knew even though I had a little, teeny, tiny, bitty worry it might not be the case. I had faith in my parents. They came through. Howard and Adele. Thank you, Mom and Dad. Why had I ever doubted it? I threw my arms around Angie, and we both watched the paper go kiting to the ground. "Love you like a sister, even though we aren't."

"We don't need a DNA test to tell us we're closer than sisters."

I paused. "Someday, you must tell me how you got up a flight of stairs and down a hallway with your arms and legs taped up."

She laughed. "Let's just say I managed to push my shoes off, and the bruise on your face is about one-tenth the size of the bruises on my butt. Those stairs with metal strips on the edges are so hard. Thank God I'm mostly on my feet at work. I hope the green color goes away soon. Tough to hide from Wiley. Tougher to explain."

We both laughed. A guy we'd never seen before got out of a car a few yards away. He walked past us, and we both noticed his hunky bod, gorgeous hair, and stubbled face. Smiling, he walked by us and winked, saying, "Ladies." He tipped his Stetson hat. Then the door to Priscilla's closed behind him.

Angie and I turned to each other, clinked our beers, and shouted, "Code Red!"

Acknowledgements

When I first began writing the Art Center mysteries with *Death in a Pale Hue,* I was inspired by our own local art center, the Buchanan Center for the Arts in Monmouth, Illinois. Its executive director, Kristyne Gilbert, gave me a tour of all the nooks and crannies of their building. When we reached the basement, I knew I had my idea for my first Art Center mystery. Kristyne is equally—if not more—as passionate about art education and appreciation as my character, Jill Madison. I thank her for her help, knowledge, and encouragement. Because of her dedication, the BCA is a gem in the downstate Illinois region.

Writing a mystery series about a small town takes the help and expertise of others in my own small town and beyond. These are some of the people who have helped me get it right when it comes to the details of law and investigation. A grateful thank you goes out to Judge Andrew Doyle of the Ninth Circuit of Illinois; Micki Browning, an author who worked in municipal law enforcement for twenty-two years; Marcum Spears, generous and knowledgeable attorney; and Aloysius J. McGuire, Warren County coroner.

Before a book ever joins bookstore shelves or internet outlets, many people make sure it's ready. I'm grateful to my agent, Dawn Dowdle, of the Blue Ridge Literary Agency for steering my projects. My editor, Lourdes Venard of Comma Sense Editing, has stayed with me for eleven years, and she never fails to root out every missing comma or plot hole. I'm thankful she makes my books better. Shawn Reilly Simmons of Level Best Books is my final pair of eyes, who makes sure I didn't leave out a word, a chapter, or a deliciously sneaky suspect. And a huge thank you to all the people at Level Best Books for believing in my series.

My beta readers add three more sets of eyes before my book ever goes off to the publisher. Thank you to Jan DeYoung, Hallie Lemon, and Eileen Owens. They're not only friends, but also master readers and experts at sleuthing out dangling modifiers.

Sarah Henderson, the library director at Monmouth College's Hewes Library, did some digging for me, and I am grateful she came up with the information I needed. Sarah Twomey Walters, owner of Market Alley Wines, had all the right answers when it came to brewing in the Midwest. Thanks to both these ladies who helped me make sure that my book was accurate.

And finally, thanks to my readers who have encouraged me with their kind words. The inhabitants of my small town of Monmouth provide so much material for small-town mysteries that they're never far from my thoughts. Thanks to all.

About the Author

Susan Van Kirk is the President of the Guppy Chapter of Sisters in Crime and a writer of cozy mysteries. She lives at the center of the universe—the Midwest—and writes during the ridiculously cold and icy winters. Why leave the house and break something? Van Kirk taught forty-four years in high school and college and raised three children. Miraculously, she has low blood pressure. She's a member of Sisters in Crime and Mystery Writers of America.

SOCIAL MEDIA HANDLES:
   Facebook: http://www.facebook.com/SusanVanKirkAuthor/
   Pinterest: http://www.pinterest.com/sivankirk/_saved/
   Goodreads: https://www.goodreads.com/author/show/586.Susan_Van kirk
   Instagram https://www.instagram.com/susanivankirk/

AUTHOR WEBSITE:
   https://susanvankirk.com

Also by Susan Van Kirk

The Education of a Teacher (Including Dirty Books and Pointed Looks)

Three May Keep a Secret

The Locket: From the Casebook of TJ Sweeney

Marry in Haste

Death Takes No Bribes

The Witch's Child

A Death at Tippitt Pond

Death in a Pale Hue